Other Books & Stories
by Lynn Bohart
<u>NOVELS</u>

Mass Murder

Murder In The Past Tense

Grave Doubts

Inn Keeping With Murder

<u>SHORT STORY BOOKS</u>

Your Worst Nightmare

Something Wicked

A CANDIDATE

FOR MURDER

An Old Maids of Mercer Island Mystery

By
Lynn Bohart

Cover Art:
Mia Yoshihara-Bradshaw

Published by Little Dog Press

ACKNOWLEDGEMENTS

I owe so much, to so many. First and foremost would be my writing group: Lori Church-Pursley, Tim McDaniel, Michael Manzer, Gary Larson, Timera Drake, Jenae Cartwright and Irma Fritz. These guys read the manuscript chapter by chapter over a period of eight months, helping to clear up ambiguities, character flaws, and plot points. Thank you to beta readers Karen Gilb, Bill Dolan, Valerie O'Halloran and Chris Spahn, who read it from cover-to-cover and helped with flow, clarification and consistencies. As always, thanks to my friend and editor Liz Stewart, who is so generous with her time and talent. My deepest thanks go to Chief Kevin Milosevich, Renton Police Department, Judge Bob McBeth, and Northwest Gourmet Foods, who gave me advice on the barbeque sauce. Lastly, I want to thank Barb Nilson for allowing me to use the "gnome home" concept. Barb actually created and lived in the gnome home, which I was completely enthralled with and just had to use.

I am deeply indebted to my friend, Mia Bradshaw, who designed the cover. Mia is a wonderful artist and craftsperson in the Seattle area and shows/sells her work locally. Please check out her website at www.miayoshihara.com.

Disclaimer: This book is a work of fiction and while many of the businesses, locations, and organizations referenced in the book are real, they are used in a way that is purely fictional. And I took some liberty with locations on Mercer Island to fit the storyline.

Dedicated to my friends and colleagues
in Renton, Washington
for their ongoing
encouragement and support.

CHAPTER ONE

It was a good night for a murder. A storm raged around him as he waited patiently in the shadows. The wind wrestled with the trees, and a punishing rain flooded the parking lot. With the temperature dipping precariously close to freezing, he anticipated sleet soon, if not snow. There were only a few cars on the road and fewer individuals foolish enough to wander outside on foot.

Yes, it was a good night for a murder.

His father would have disagreed. Not that his father would have cared about the murder. He'd been an ornery bastard. But his father would have never considered leaving the house in such awful weather. But then, his father had been an overly cautious man who never traveled anywhere without matches, a Swiss Army knife and potable water – just in case.

"*Son,*" he would say. "*It's better to be prepared than dead.*"

And yet his father had died at the age of 43, killed while crossing the street in a small town in Oregon. In his pocket were the box of matches and the Swiss Army knife; the potable water was stowed in the car. So what good had those things been to him in his moment of need, when on a sunny summer afternoon a distracted soccer mom with three screaming kids in the car mowed him down in the middle of the crosswalk?

None.

Well, he wasn't his father, and he had none of those things with him tonight; he didn't even own a Swiss Army knife. Resting heavy in his pocket was the one thing that mattered right now – the planishing hammer he'd bought at the hardware store the day before. He wouldn't be doing any metal work with it like he used to do in high school, but it was designed perfectly to do the job tonight.

Afterwards, he had the assurance that enough money would follow this job to set him up for life. Because unlike his father, the woman he expected to see in a few minutes craved attention enough to brave this storm, and she *would* come.

He finished the last of his brew and set the bottle aside. A gust of cold air found its way inside his coat, forcing a shiver down his back. The rain had turned to sleet, and the puddles were freezing over into tiny ice rinks.

It was time to get this done before he froze to death.

He stood on the far side of the small building, away from the prying eyes of the occasional passing car. He had already sent the incriminating message that would lure his victim to the library this late at night; the message that would also throw suspicion on the person this woman would never refuse.

As he watched for the bright red BMW that would bring her to him, a black and white police car glided slowly down the street in the other direction.

His pulse quickened.

This wasn't good. Why would the police be patrolling the library? Then he remembered.

Someone had breached the front door of the library just two weeks before, spray-painting obscenities on the walls and trashed the place. The library had closed for a week of repairs and clean – up, and then the library board had approved a new alarm system. That brought a smile to his lips. Part of the plan tonight was to use that very same alarm system to make his escape. But he hadn't counted on extra police patrols.

Fortunately, the squad car didn't stop. It disappeared almost as quickly as it had appeared.

He let out a sigh of relief, but knew that now he had a finite amount of time before the patrol car returned.

A glance at his watch told him that in another minute, she would be late. He held his breath, wondering if his source had been right and if she would show at all. Perhaps she would display more sense than his accomplice gave her credit for.

But then the BMW pulled into the far end of the parking lot. It was almost exactly 10:30 p.m.

The expensive car approached him straight on, forcing him to duck down so the headlights didn't reveal him. The car slid into the handicapped spot next to the front door, a few feet from where he crouched in the darkness. His muscles flexed. His fingers wrapped around the handle of the hammer in his pocket.

He made ready to move, but the car's engine continued to purr, shooting a faint, white exhaust into the nighttime cold. What was she waiting for? Did she suspect something?

He'd purposely parked on a side street so there were no cars in the parking lot. Maybe that had been a mistake. She might wait for the woman she'd come to meet.

As the sleet slapped the hood of the expensive vehicle, he feared the weather might also work to his disadvantage. He'd hoped the security light inside the library would draw her out, but maybe she wouldn't get out of the car unless she absolutely had to.

And then the BMW's engine died. The headlights flicked off, and the car door opened. A hooded figure emerged and ran for the protection of the overhang.

÷

Trudy Bascom left the warmth and comfort of the million-dollar home on Placer Drive cursing Dana Finkle, who had stayed behind to extract a fat campaign check from Christine Newall. Christine was married to the President of Puget Sound Bank and had made a last minute request for the meeting. Since Trudy was Dana's campaign assistant, Dana had asked Trudy to join her. All through the evening, Dana had practically salivated at the prospect of not just getting the couple's endorsement, but a sizable donation to her mayoral campaign.

Just as the discussion turned to the campaign, however, Dana received a message from Julia Applegate, owner of the St. Claire Inn. The message read:

"Meet me at the library tonight at 10:30. We have to talk. Trust me; I'll make it worth your time."

Julia was a minor celebrity on the island. She and her friends had recently helped solve a major murder case and saved the life of a young pregnant woman in the process. As a result, the mayor awarded each of them with the first-ever "Hero of Mercer Island Award" – something Dana hated. But not something Dana hated more than Julia. Nothing could beat that.

"You know damn well that Julia just wants to gloat more about that stupid award the mayor bestowed on her," Dana said when Christine left the room to grab another bottle of wine. "I don't know how he ever came up with such a ridiculous idea. 'Hero of Mercer Island.'" She said this with a derisive snort, nearly blowing snot out her nose.

"But maybe she wants to help on the campaign," Trudy countered.

Trudy knew full well that it would be a cold day in hell before Julia would offer to help on Dana's campaign. Julia hated Dana almost as much as Dana hated her.

"No," Dana spat. "I have it on good authority that Julia and that group of misfit old hags she hangs around with filed for her campaign yesterday. Julia is going to run against me. *Me!*" she said, as if the very thought that Julia would have the gall to run against her was as ridiculous as the moon being made of cheese.

"What do you think she wants, then?" Trudy asked.

"I don't know," Dana replied, tapping her fingers thoughtfully on Christine Newall's expensive Riverstone cocktail table. It was made to look like a rounded stone plucked right out of a river, and as Dana tapped her fingers, she left sticky fingerprints all over it. "Maybe she's going to try and get me to drop out of the race," Dana murmured, sitting back.

"But you wouldn't do that, would you?" Trudy asked, rubbing out the fingerprints with a cocktail napkin.

Dana flashed an incredulous look at Trudy. "Of course not. I'm going to be Mercer Island's next mayor. You can bet on it. And then I'll be making some big decisions around here."

And then Dana made her biggest decision yet – she sent Trudy out in the storm to meet with Julia in her place.

So here Trudy was, winding her way around corners on side streets, heading towards the top of the island and the library instead of Dana. She hadn't played *that* very well. She could have said, "No, Dana, I think you should go." But then, Trudy was what her mother had always referred to as a doormat with a bad perm. She was an extreme introvert by nature. In fact, she was so meek and mild she had a tendency to blend in with the furniture. At last year's New Year's Eve party, Fred Stiller had actually sat on her as if she were part of the lumpy sofa. It wasn't until she'd squealed that he'd jumped up and apologized.

Now, here she was running an errand in the middle of a winter storm, just so Dana could bask in the glow of a big donor.

It was so like Dana.

Trudy often questioned her decision to become Dana's campaign assistant. She worked for Dana's husband at his collection agency in downtown Mercer Island. Dana owned a small antique shop not far from the collection agency, which competed with Julia Applegate's sale of antiques at the St. Claire Inn. It was one of the things that twisted Dana into knots. Dana sat on the City Council and had tried for almost two years to cancel-out the exception to the zoning laws that allowed Julia to have three businesses on the same property. If successful, it would force Julia to move the antique business, and maybe her bakery, downtown. It would force her out of business. That was just like Dana, too – if you didn't like someone or felt they might outdo you in some way, make their life hell.

If asked, Trudy would have to admit that she didn't actually care much for Dana. Dana would always just blow past the front desk at the collection agency as if no one behind the counter mattered in her world. But when Dana had stopped one day and asked Trudy if she would like to help on the campaign, Trudy thought it would be a chance for her to step out of the shadows. And she had some good skills, which of course, Dana took advantage of. In the end, Trudy had agreed, thinking she had to stop being the wallflower and blossom a little.

She chuckled at that little pun.

"Oh well," she murmured to herself.

This would only take her a few minutes, and she'd get to talk to the great Julia Applegate. Julia wasn't just a hero on Mercer Island; she was the ex-wife of the Governor of Washington State.

Trudy had never met Julia, so this was one of those big opportunities she was looking forward to. And it was important she didn't blow it. She would have to graciously find out what Julia wanted and then head back to Christine's, where Dana was sure to throw a fit. It seemed just the mention of Julia Applegate's name caused Dana's blood pressure to rise.

But at least Trudy would leave Julia with a good impression. Maybe someday Julia would even ask Trudy to join her book club.

That would be sublime, she thought.

As Trudy navigated the nearly empty streets of Mercer Island and passed Ellis Park, the rain turned to sleet, making it all but impossible to see. Dana had picked Trudy up for the meeting with Christine and so was forced to allow Trudy to drive her new BMW, but not without a lecture on taking care she didn't put it into a ditch.

"I'll go over every inch of that car tomorrow in the daylight," Dana had warned. "So be extra careful. Don't get yourself killed, or I'll kill you myself."

It was 10:29 when Trudy pulled into the far end of the library's parking lot on 88th Ave. SE. The building's front entrance faced away from the street, and so she pulled up to the two handicapped parking spaces right next to the front door.

She paused before pulling in. After all, she wasn't handicapped, and her sense of right and wrong made her consider whether to break the law. But there was no one around, and it was the closest parking spot to the front door; that meant a lot in this weather.

She pulled all the way in, but kept the engine running and the heat flowing. A glance around her told her Julia wasn't there yet. The parking lot was empty. She checked her watch. It was now 10:30 on the dot. So, where the heck was Julia?

A sliver of light peeked out from the back of the library's main room. Was it a security light? Or was Julia waiting inside? Julia was a member of the library board and probably had a key. But if she was inside, where was her car?

Trudy peered through the BMW's windshield, wondering if she should get out and try the door. Then something caught her attention. There was a white piece of paper taped to one of the glass front doors, and it was flapping in the wind. Trudy peered more closely at it. It looked like a small envelope. Maybe it was a note from Julia.

"Damn!" she cursed.

With her luck, she'd have to get wet, only to find out that Julia had cancelled. *Well*, she thought, *better to get this over with so I can go back and report to Dana.*

Trudy turned off the engine, pulled up the hood of her coat and threw open her door. She stepped out of the car right into a puddle.

"Damn!" she cursed again. *This better be worth it.*

She slammed the car door and ran for the overhang. Two large pillars stood in the way, and she had to step around them. Once on the other side, she was in the entrance portico and safe from the rain. But it was still icy cold, and a shiver snaked its way down her spine, sending chills to every extremity.

She was about to grab the note, when a sound made her stop short. She turned and peered into the parking lot.

The pole lamps illuminated Dana's car while it sat quietly in the parking lot, little piles of ice crystals forming around the tires. The portico was lit by a small light above the double glass doors, casting much of the area right around her in darkness. She felt suddenly vulnerable.

Time to get this over with.

She turned and stepped up to the door. A small envelope was taped to one of the glass panels. It had Dana's name printed in small, careful lettering. With a gloved hand, Trudy removed the envelope and opened it. A small, folded piece of paper was tucked inside. It read:

Ain't karma a bitch?

"What?" Trudy said out loud.

The answer came in the form of a soft, but distinct rustle. She spun around to find the hulking shadow of a man behind her, his hand raised above her head.

"No!" she screamed.

With a downward swing, something slammed into her forehead, sending a searing pain through to her brain. She crumpled to the pavement, and the note slipped from her fingers and fluttered away. She landed with her cheek resting on the cold concrete. Her eyes were open and warm blood pooled around her face. She tried to take a deep breath, but it got caught in her throat.

As darkness began to close in around her, two scruffy feet appeared. Then an ugly face swam into view, as a hand reached out and pulled back the hood of her coat.

"Shit!" the face said.

"Why?" she whimpered.

The man sat back on his heels and allowed a chuckle to emanate from that evil face. "Because mistakes happen, I guess. Too bad," he said with a shake of his head. "Too bad for you, anyway."

Then the hand holding the hammer rose and fell a second time, and the lights went out for Trudy Bascom.

CHAPTER TWO

The weather was miserable. Christmas had come and gone, and New Year's Eve was just a loud but fading memory. A cold front had moved into Seattle, and the wind and rain had threatened all day to derail my first date with Detective David Franks. The heavy winter storm that had gripped the Seattle area for two days had brought intermittent bouts of sleet, ice and even snow; but it failed to keep us home. We were tucked inside the warmth of the Mercerwood Shore Club, enjoying dessert after a movie, and I loved every minute.

I had waited several weeks for this date, while I healed from a car crash that happened just before Christmas. One of my book club members, Blair Wentworth, and I had been fleeing a couple of killers late one night on the Enumclaw Bridge. The crash had sent both of us to the hospital. Me with two broken fingers, a twisted ankle, and a face that looked like it had been used as a punching bag. And Blair with a broken leg. But that's a story for another time.

Despite the weather, the club's dining room was packed, and the air was filled with enthusiastic chatter and the smell of fajitas and grilled seafood. Outside the big bank of windows, the rain had turned to sleet, hitting the windows like little bits of splintering glass.

I glanced toward my date, thinking he looked handsome in dark slacks, a dark turtleneck and camel-colored blazer. The color combination set off his deep brown eyes and thick silver hair. We'd chatted briefly at the theater before the movie started, and I'd learned that his wife of twenty-two years, Jolene, had died of ovarian cancer.

Instead of immediately falling into the arms of another woman as many men do, he'd moved from their home in Sammamish and taken the job with the Mercer Island Police Department. For the past eight years, he'd been married to the job. That's how we'd met. He'd been one of the detectives that investigated the murder of my good friend, Martha Denton. The thought that I was the one to take him out of his self-imposed social retirement made my heart flutter.

We were both rusty at dating, so while the wind rattled the awning outside the window, the two of us sat awkwardly toying with our desserts.

"So, Julia, did you enjoy the movie?" David finally asked, sneaking a glance my way.

I shrugged at his question. "I did enjoy it. Although there were so many near misses in that car chase, I thought I was back up on the Enumclaw bridge."

He winced. "Sorry. I knew it was an adventure flick, but I didn't know about the car chase. You've barely healed from the accident."

I flexed the fingers on my right hand. "Well, my fingers have healed pretty well. And at least my face isn't all black and blue anymore."

His luscious lips pulled into a smile. "I'd say that pretty face has healed very nicely."

I felt my face grow warm.

I wasn't sure of David's exact age, but he appeared to be in his early sixties, like me. He wore his gray hair a little long, which I liked. But it appeared he'd had it trimmed. I wondered if that was on my account. I felt my face grow warm again at the prospect. Of course, I'd been to the beauty parlor myself that afternoon, having my hair newly colored and coiffed. While I loved the look of his thick silver mane, nary a gray hair would show through *my* auburn curls tonight.

"Who'd have thought I'd be having dinner with the detective from a murder investigation?" I said with a smile. Then I took a big sigh. "Too bad I had to lose one of my best friends in the process."

The mention of Martha's death momentarily dragged down my spirits. David had given me the last few weeks to heal before suggesting tonight's movie and dessert. But I wasn't sure I'd ever get over Martha's death.

"So, how is Rosa doing?" he asked, changing the subject.

I perked up and lifted my fork. "As far as I know, she's fine," I said, cutting off a piece of chocolate lava cake. "Her mother came from Brazil last week and took her home."

David's eyebrows arched. "How do you feel about that?"

I sat back and paused in thought before taking a bite. "Sad. But good. We saved Rosa from the sex-trafficking ring, and she gave birth to a beautiful little girl. It's better that she's back with her family. She went through so much."

David was toying with the edge of his own dessert. "You were very brave, Julia. There aren't many women who would have done what you did. You gave her and her daughter a second chance."

I shrugged. "Actually, there are at least four other women I can think of who would have done the very same thing."

I placed the bite of cake in my mouth and thought about my four best friends – April, Blair, Rudy and Doe – who had helped during the investigation.

He chuckled, forcing small dimples to appear at the corners of his mouth. "You're right," he said, putting up a hand in defeat. "The five of you are unstoppable."

"You got that right," I said, swallowing. "We don't like it when someone messes with us."

"That's putting it mildly. I'd hate to get on your bad side. You come with reinforcements," David said, putting down his fork. "I thought using the garbage truck as a battering ram was a nice touch, though."

The memory of my friend, Doe Kovinsky, driving one of the garbage trucks from her waste management company through the wall of the church where I was being held prisoner made me laugh.

"Yes, Doe had a lot of 'splaining to do the next day."

"So, what did your husband think of all that?"

David threw the question out carelessly; but the fact that he dropped his gaze to his plate told me he was worried that my past marriage had the potential of spoiling our budding relationship.

"Ex-husband," I reminded him.

"Sorry. Ex-husband," he said.

"He chastised me for taking chances," I said, stirring cream in my coffee. "But we were married for long enough that he's learned not to try and control me."

I raised my eyes to glance at my date, wondering what he thought of that. He looked up and smiled.

"I learned that in less than a few days," he said with a smirk.

"Very funny," I replied with mock annoyance.

My ex-husband, Graham, was currently serving as Washington State Governor. Even though Graham and I had been divorced for several years, and I had moved on with my life, everyone tiptoed around the fact that I had once been married to him. Whether he was the most powerful man in the state or not, to me he was just the guy I'd been married to who occasionally farted, scratched his nether parts, and had bad breath in the morning.

"Trust me," I said with a seductive smile. "You have nothing to worry about from Graham. We're friendly, but the relationship was over long before the divorce. We stayed together for my daughter's sake."

"When did you adopt Angela?" he asked. "Was she just a baby?"

"Yes," I replied. "We traveled to China to get her. Well, *I* went to China, along with a group of adoptive parents. Graham was busy with a major trial here in Seattle and couldn't get away."

David glanced at me. "Did that bother you? I mean, that he couldn't go to China with you? I often felt my wife was jealous of *my* work."

I pondered that question for a moment. "No. Not really. I had come to expect it. I knew Graham was ambitious, and I was ambitious for him. I *wanted* him to succeed. But somewhere along the line, we drifted apart. I started my antique business and became more involved in charitable work, and he got very serious about politics. Before long, we were like two different moons orbiting the same planet."

"And the same planet was the Inn?"

"No. I think the Inn was a consolation prize. He bought it for me just before he asked for a divorce," I said with a sneer. "I meant that the same planet was Angela. He was a good father, even if he wasn't around too much. And look, she's turned out just like him. She works in the prosecuting attorney's office, and I wouldn't be surprised if she runs for office one day herself."

"How do you feel about her dating Sean?" he asked.

Now it was me who had to be cautious. Sean Abrams was the lead detective in the Mercer Island Police Department. He'd been there about a year, having come over from the Seattle PD and was now David's boss. I used the moment to take a sip of coffee and consider my answer.

"Daughters don't listen to their mothers when it comes to men, no matter what I might think. I want whatever will make her happy."

David laughed. "Now *that* was a politically correct reply."

I smiled in return. "What did you expect? I was married to a politician. Now, if you'll excuse me, I need to use the ladies' room."

"I'll get the check," he said, starting to get up as a courtesy.

I waved him back down. "I'll just be a minute."

I stood up and pushed my chair back without looking behind me. Just then, the waitress crossed between tables with a tray of desserts. Her foot caught in the leg of my chair, and…well…the chair flew out from under me. I turned in time to see her go airborne, arms extended in front of her. Three plates filled with dessert flew off the tray, heading straight for a neighboring table.

I watched in horror as the waitress landed face down on the carpet. One dessert plate slammed down in front of a surprised Mabel Worth, splattering a glob of coconut crème pie into the center of her ample cleavage. The second one flipped over and landed on top of Marley Randeau's remaining lobster, burying it in chocolate pudding. The third one hit her husband's coffee cup, tipping it over and flooding the table with hot liquid.

Marley jumped up to avoid the scalding coffee. Her chair tipped backwards hitting a young boy in the back of the head. He began to wail as she stumbled and fell against the boy's mother, practically slamming the poor woman's head into her salad plate. As Marley regained her balance, the room went quiet – well, except for the seven-year old sounding like an air-raid siren.

I glanced around me. Mouths hung open. I have to admit that it was a little like watching a pileup on Interstate 5. The only thing missing was the steam escaping from the cars' engines.

David appeared at my side just as his phone rang. He pulled it from his pocket, still staring in disbelief at the scene in front of him.

"Franks," he said into the phone.

I leaned over to help the waitress pick herself up off the floor, but she yanked her elbow from my grasp. Meanwhile, Marley tried to console the little boy, while her husband stared at the glob of dessert wedged between Mabel Worth's breasts with the expression of someone in need of a long drink of water.

I stepped forward and stuttered an apology to everyone concerned, but it was accepted with all the warmth of an arctic blast.

"We need to go," David said, taking my elbow and turning me toward the door.

"But," I stammered, turning back to the field of destruction.

"They'll take care of things here," he said, nodding to a waiter. "I need to take you home."

Two men at a neighboring table had gotten up to help the waitress, while additional wait staff arrived to restore order. I pulled away from David to grab my purse off the back of my overturned chair.

"But why do we have to go? I really should stay to help these people."

David leaned in to me just as the mother picked up her inconsolable young son. "Because there's a body," he whispered in my ear.

"A what?" I said above the din behind me.

"A dead body!"

Silence.

We turned to the crowd.

The screaming kid had chosen that exact moment to suck it up and stop screaming. Everyone in the room gawked at us a second time.

"Um…not to worry," I said with a dismissive wave of my hand. "He's a police officer. So, it's good. We're all good."

More silence.

David grabbed my elbow this time and pulled me to the entrance. He helped me slip into my coat and then opened the door to greet the biting cold outside.

"What's going on?" I said, throwing my muffler around my neck. "What dead body?"

"I've been called to a case," he said, helping me out the door.

We were moving through the parking lot. The pavement was slick with ice, so he kept a hand on my elbow to steady me.

"I'm fine, David. I'm not the one who went flying in there. Now where are we going?"

He stopped at the passenger side door to his Jeep Cherokee. "I'm taking you home. They found a body at the library."

"The library?" I said in alarm. "Someone was murdered?"

He unlocked the car door and attempted to help me inside. But I wasn't budging. He sighed in defeat. "I don't know. That's why I have to get up there. I'll drop you off at the Inn."

"No you won't," I said, climbing into the car. "I'm going with you. I'm a member of the library board."

"No, Julia," he said firmly. "I'll call you first thing tomorrow morning. But right now, I'm taking you home."

CHAPTER THREE

Every guest room at the St. Claire Inn was full – unusual for this time of year, especially with the bad weather. If you had asked me two months ago if I thought murder would be good for business, I would have said no. I would have been wrong.

Since Martha had been poisoned in my dining room back in December, we'd barely had time to turn rooms before the next guests arrived. The Inn was booked solid six months out. Of course, it wasn't so much because Martha had died, but because my friends and I had helped to solve her murder, thus bringing lots of positive attention to the Inn.

Of course, the ghosts didn't hurt, either. Not only had we been featured on Jason Spear's paranormal investigation show the year before, we had also been listed in the latest version of his book, *The Most Haunted Hotels in the Northwest.* In fact, he had a book signing scheduled at the Inn the next weekend.

The second Monday of the month was my scheduled meeting with our accountant, Mr. Mulford. And while I waited anxiously for David to call as promised, I had to take care of business.

Mr. Mulford was a mousy little man who wore suits a size too large and shirts that had yellowed at the collar. He often smelled like the Italian restaurant next door to his office, and sometimes arrived with a box of cannoli, which of course, I couldn't refuse. But he was a whiz with numbers and never failed to produce a good financial statement.

My job at these meetings was to hand over receipts for all purchases during the month coded by expense sub-account, along with deposit slips and copies of checks. This could get complicated since both the bakery and the sale of antiques were considered part of the same business.

Mr. Mulford had arrived at 8:30 that morning and was spread out on one of the tables in the breakfast room, his handy little calculator by his side.

"There seems to be a variance in the food budget in January," he said in his nasal voice. "Specifically, you purchased larger than usual quantities of sugar and cocoa."

He looked at me over the top of his glasses, his bushy brows clenched together like dueling caterpillars. I circled around the table to look over his shoulder. Mickey and Minnie, my two miniature Dachshunds, followed me and stopped to sniff his ankles – no doubt wondering where he'd hidden the spaghetti and meatballs.

"Oh, that," I said. I pulled out a receipt. "As you'll see, we not only bought a bunch of sugar and cocoa, we also bought a case of butter. We had to throw out our entire inventory of fudge in December and replace it," I said matter-of-factly.

His face betrayed his confusion.

"Martha's murder?" I prompted him. "You heard all about that, didn't you?"

"I'm afraid not, Mrs. Applegate. Martha who?"

"Denton. She was a close friend. She died after eating some of the fudge we sell." His eyes popped open, forcing his glasses to slip down his nose. "No, no. It wasn't our fudge that killed her. Well…technically it was, but someone else had poisoned it." If I thought my clarification would make things better, it didn't. His eyes grew bigger. "Like I said, she was murdered. We found the killer, but we had to get rid of all the fudge. No one would buy it. We don't even sell that flavor anymore. April developed a new recipe – raspberry mint chocolate chip. Would you like a sample?" I asked brightly, hoping to elevate the declining mood.

"No…no thank you. I'll just move on," he said, turning back to the spreadsheet.

"Speaking of Martha's murder, we'll also have a variance in our equipment budget," I said. "We installed a new alarm system last month. But it's on the fritz. So we may have a repair bill next month."

He gave me a curious look. "If it's brand new, shouldn't it be under warranty?"

"Yes. But they had to order a new keypad, and it won't be fixed until tomorrow."

I smiled sweetly and led the dogs across the hallway to the living room, leaving Mr. Mulford to his figures.

Since selling antiques was part of the business, I spent much of my time arranging and rearranging the antique furniture and collectibles at the Inn. Almost everything visible was for sale, and we often sold several pieces a day. This required me to bring over new items from our warehouse on a regular basis.

My maintenance man, Jose´, had placed a polished oak library table under the living room window. A collection of old clocks sat in boxes on the floor in front of it. I began unwrapping the clocks and arranging them on the table, but kept checking my watch because the girls in my book club were due to arrive at 10:00 a.m. I hoped to give them a full report on the dead body from the night before. But I was beginning to doubt I would hear from David in time.

I adjusted one of the steeple clocks, angling it toward the light, and then moved a lovely porcelain chiming clock onto a small wooden crate to give it more prominence. Then I stood back to admire my handiwork.

A noise made me glance out the paned living room window toward Ellen Fairchild's home across the street. Ellen had died ten months earlier when she drove her Lexus off a road at the top of the island. Her husband, Ray, put the house up for sale just before Christmas. The home had sold quickly, and now there was a moving van parked in the driveway. I watched two burly men carry a high-end leather sofa through the front door.

I had new neighbors.

A wave of sadness washed over me as I was reminded of the loss of my friend, Ellen. As I stared off into space, a big black Mercedes pulled down my driveway, catching my attention.

It was Doe, the first of my book club to arrive.

Today, the girls weren't coming to discuss books, but rather my campaign for Mayor of Mercer Island. I heaved a deep sigh at the thought. I didn't relish the idea of campaigning for political office. But the girls had talked me into it, since the only other viable candidate was Dana Finkle, a woman we all despised. However, now I had another potential murder on my mind, which was far more enticing than a political campaign.

I met Doe at the front door. The rain from the night before had stopped, but it was still bitterly cold and icicles spiraled down from the gingerbread cutouts that lined the porch overhang. Doe swept in, prompting the dogs to scamper around her feet, asking for attention.

"Why couldn't I be a few inches taller?" I said, eying her tall, slender figure. "You always look so elegant."

At 5' 2" and fifteen pounds overweight, I could hardly be described as elegant – pretty, perhaps, but not elegant.

Doe bent down to pet the dogs. "Being tall has its downsides. My first boyfriend was about your height. Believe me, it was awkward when…well, you know."

I exploded in laughter. "Thanks for that."

She straightened up and flashed me a smile. "You know, even though I'm pushing sixty-five, the first thing I do when I get home at night is to shed these work clothes and climb into my sweat pants."

I arched an eyebrow. "Yes, but I've seen you in sweat pants. I think you iron them." I drew her into the entryway and closed the door, shivering. "What meeting are you missing today by being here?"

"I only went in this morning for a couple of personnel reviews. I have to see my investment advisor this afternoon."

"Aren't you ever going to retire?" I chided, watching her strip off her wool coat to reveal her signature black pant suit and a robin's egg blue silk blouse, which perfectly accented her salt and pepper hair. "It seems to me that you've earned a rest by now."

I took her coat and hung it on a nearby coat tree and then led her down the hallway and into the dining room. Since we were only a bed and breakfast, the guests had their one meal of the day in the breakfast room. This left the dining room available for meetings.

The dining room was large, with a table that seated twelve overlooking the lake. We'd gone for elegance when decorating the dining room in rich red and gold drapes. A dark oak wainscoting and paneling ran the lower perimeter of the room, while a deep green floral wall paper flecked with gold stretched to the ceiling. Antique sideboards filled with vintage china sat at each end of the room. The pocket door gave us complete privacy.

"No retirement for me just yet," Doe was saying as she followed me into the room. "I'm not like you, Julia. I don't have a hobby or another skill I could turn into a business. I'm committed to garbage," she said, flashing her dark eyes at me with a broad smile.

Doe ran her deceased husband's waste management company, the company they had built together right out of college. She always carried an enormous black leather satchel, which she dropped with a thud next to one of the high-backed wooden chairs.

"What do you carry in that thing, anyway?" I asked her. "I've always thought you could anchor a small ship with it."

She laughed. "I take a lot of work home, so I carry my laptop and files. Plus this," she said, reaching into the bag and pulling out a revolver.

"Whoa!" I said, stepping back. "When did you decide to carry a gun?"

"When both Ellen and Martha were murdered," she said. "I live alone, Julia. I thought maybe I needed protection. I just bought it. It's not loaded, and I don't know how to use it, yet. But I've thought about this a lot. I've signed up for classes that start next week." She gave me serious look. "You should join me."

"No way," I said, shaking my head. "I'll stick to dogs, friends, and dating a cop."

She sighed and put the gun back. "I can't say I feel good about it. But who knows? Maybe my new hobby will be target practice. Anyway, if it makes me feel safer and more confident, it will be worth it."

"Actually, I was going to suggest that you travel," I said.

She smiled. "Rudy and I are talking about a trip to Mexico this summer," she said, pulling out a chair and sitting down. "Wanna go?"

"I have to take my mother home to Illinois, remember?" I said.

"Ah, yes," she smiled.

My mother had died the year before, and I kept her ashes in the garage, along with those of several of my past canine companions. It was a constant source of amusement for my friends.

Just then, the front door bell jingled and Rudy's voice call out, "I hope there's banana bread or something. I need comfort food."

I poked my head into the hallway.

"Maybe we should meet over in the bakery," I said to her.

She threw her deep green wool coat and plaid muffler onto the coat tree and marched down the hallway, rubbing her hands together to warm up. She stuck her nose in the air.

"Wait a minute, are you making your famous spaghetti sauce?" she said as she passed the breakfast room.

Rudy was a compact 5' 6", with an intense personality that was a little bit like a low-grade explosive ready to go off. I grabbed her wrist and pulled her into the dining room.

"No. That's Mr. Mulford," I said with a smile, but low enough that he couldn't hear. "He always smells like Juno's Italian Restaurant."

"Darn. I thought you'd made spaghetti for lunch. By the way, Blair said she'd be a few minutes late. She's having a new sofa delivered this morning."

"Speaking of sofas," I said. "I have new neighbors." I pointed across the hallway and through the living room window to Ellen's old house. "I saw the movers carrying in a sofa a little while ago."

Doe got up and both women craned their necks to look.

"I passed the moving truck on the way in," Rudy said. "Any idea who they are?"

"No," I replied, shaking my head. "I'll probably walk over there this weekend though and introduce myself."

"Well, let's hope they're as nice as Ellen was," Doe said wistfully. "God, I still miss her."

"Martha, too," I said.

The mention of our two friends who had died within months of each other brought the conversation to a halt, and we all stood in silence for a moment.

"Okay, let's get this meeting going," Doe erupted. "We have a campaign to plan!"

"Wait," I said, stopping them. "I have something to tell you first."

Before I could say another word, the sound of tires on gravel interrupted me. We turned and glanced out the front window again. A black SUV parked by the front door, provoking a collective intake of breath from each one of us.

"Uh–oh," Doe murmured.

The car doors opened. David and Detective Abrams emerged, and I felt a slight flutter in my chest. *Why hadn't David just called?* This looked like an official visit.

The three of us returned to the entryway. The bell above the door jingled again as they walked in. David came in first, his badge hanging on a lanyard underneath his coat. Detective Abrams stepped in behind him, filling the doorway with his action-figure height and broad shoulders. As an ex-Army Ranger, he carried an air of unyielding confidence that most people found intimidating. They both nodded to me with grim expressions, as Detective Abrams closed the door.

These two men had been regular fixtures at the Inn after Martha died. The thought of having them both standing in my entryway could only mean one thing – something was wrong.

"Good morning, Julia," David said. "Sorry to bother you so early."

His greeting lacked all the warmth of our date just twelve hours before.

"Go ahead, make my day!" a voice called out from the breakfast room.

Everyone turned to where Captain Ahab, our African gray parrot, was dancing around in his cage. I had purchased Ahab from an estate sale on a whim, not knowing that he came with an extensive vocabulary and a propensity to quote lines from old movies. The detectives ignored his remark.

"Julia, something's come up," David said, glancing at the front desk. Crystal, my manager, was working there. He glanced over at Mr. Mulford, who was bent over his work in the breakfast room. "Perhaps we could speak with you alone."

"By alone, you mean with Doe and Rudy?" I said, gesturing to my friends.

David glanced at the two women and turned to Detective Abrams, who nodded.

"Let's go into the dining room," I said, pointing down the hallway.

Mr. Mulford glanced up as we passed by, but went right back to work.

Most of our guests were out for the day. Only a young couple was in residence, and they were camped out in the library looking through some of my old books. I slid the door closed and the five of us huddled up next to the dining room table.

"You guys are making me nervous," I said. "Whose body did you find at the library last night?"

"Body?" Doe exclaimed, her dark eyes flaring.

Detective Abrams' hooded blue eyes shifted in David's direction. I wondered if David had told him about our date the night before.

"Do you know Trudy Bascom?" Detective Abrams asked me.

"Not really. I know who she is. She's Dana Finkle's campaign assistant. Why?"

"She was found dead last night outside the library," he said.

"Oh, my God," I said with a gasp. "How awful. What happened?"

"She was struck in the head, Julia," David said quietly. "A patrol officer found her when he was checking on the library. He noticed a car in the parking lot."

"Dear God," I muttered. "And no one saw anything?"

"No. But we think the patrol officer got there only moments after the killer fled."

"That parking lot is pretty open," Rudy said. "He didn't see anyone running away?"

David shook his head. "No. Remember there was a storm last night. But the blood…well, everything looked fresh. And her body was still warm."

David glanced at Detective Abrams and then pulled a piece of paper from his inside pocket. His guilty expression had my ears buzzing.

"What?" I said, glancing at the paper.

He handed it to me. "It's a search warrant. We need to confiscate any computers or electronic devices you have."

"Why?" Rudy demanded. "What would Julia have to do with Trudy Bascom's death?"

David leveled his gaze on Rudy. "We just spoke to Dana Finkle, and she said that she and Trudy were at someone's home last night collecting a campaign contribution." He turned toward me. "Just before 10:00, Dana received a message from you on her cell phone, asking her to meet you at the library at 10:30. Mrs. Finkle was busy, and so she sent Trudy instead."

I'm sure my eyes were as round as billiard balls by this time. "But I didn't send Dana a message. Why would I? I hate the woman."

David flinched. "Julia, be careful what you say."

"But I was with *you*," I declared.

David shifted his weight again. "I know, Julia. We've already discussed that," he said, indicating Detective Abrams. "But we have to follow the lead about the message."

"Are you here to arrest her?" Doe said. "Because I doubt an email or text message is much evidence."

"No. Of course not. But it appears that if Julia didn't send the message, someone is trying to make it look like she did. That's why we need to take a look at your computers," he said, turning an apologetic gaze my way. "Along with your cell phone."

The normally dominant Detective Abrams was unusually quiet. I glanced at him. "So, whoever sent that email meant to kill Dana? Not Trudy."

"We believe so," he replied. "And, of course, given the nature of your relationship, Mrs. Finkle is blaming you."

The fact that someone wanted Dana Finkle dead wasn't a surprise. Most everyone on the island hated her. Neither was it news that I might now be suspected of murder. Been there – done that.

But I had spent the last several years silently wishing someone would get rid of her. Not necessarily kill her. But having her disappear would have been nice. Now I wasn't so sure. This didn't have the feel of good news.

I took a deep breath and twisted my neck to look into Detective Franks' very handsome, but right now, very serious face. "I'm happy to have you take whatever you want," I said with a stiff lip. "But I didn't send her an email, a text message, or any other type of communication. Let's just get this over with. You guys can stay here," I said to Doe and Rudy. "I'll be back in a minute."

I turned on my heel and led them into the breakfast room again. Mr. Mulford looked up.

"I'm afraid we'll have to finish up later, Mr. Mulford," I said with a slight toss of my head. "These gentlemen will be taking my computers. I'll give you a call tomorrow to schedule another time. Meanwhile," I said, pointing to the paperwork already lying on the table. "Why don't you take everything else with you?"

"Yes, of course," he murmured. His eyes darted back and forth between the two detectives. "I'll talk to you tomorrow."

I nodded and left him to finish up, while I took the two men to the reception desk. Crystal kept her head down, but glanced up with her eyes as we approached. I use a small office tucked behind the desk and under the staircase and gestured towards it.

"You can take my laptop in there. But please be careful. We take all of our registrations on it, and I have several new guests checking in this weekend."

"Mrs. Applegate," Detective Abrams started to say. He glanced at Crystal. "We're just doing our job, you know."

For all of his youthful machismo, Detective Abrams often seemed timid in my presence. I wondered if it was because he and my daughter, Angela, were dating, and he felt he had to tread lightly. It couldn't be my size. After all, I only came up to his chest.

"I understand that, Detective," I replied. "Remember that I've been through all of this before. I just want it over so that I can get back to work. Crystal, can you help Detective Franks unplug everything? You can come with me," I said to Detective Abrams.

Crystal sidestepped past us into the office, her eyes veiled with apprehension. I turned and started towards my apartment at the far end of the Inn. A familiar voice rang out again behind us.

"Norman, what do you think you're doing? Don't touch me! Don't!" Ahab squawked.

I stopped and turned. Ahab was bobbing back and forth on his perch. I glanced up at Detective Abrams, who was a few steps behind me.

"You make him nervous," I said. "He thinks you're Norman Bates. Stop channeling your inner Alfred Hitchcock and don't look so intimidating."

The detective rolled his eyes before following me down the hallway. I used my key to open the door and led him to my personal office. I pointed to my desktop computer.

"While you get that one, I'll get my other laptop," I said. "It's on the table."

"Wait," he said. "Technically, I can't let you do that alone. If you'll just wait right there, I'll get this one and then go with you."

"You don't trust me? After all we've been through?"

"It's not that. It's protocol. Please. Just stay there."

He disappeared into my study, while I remained in the hallway humming to myself. A moment later, he flew back into the hallway, his blue eyes ablaze with alarm.

"Who did that?" he demanded, glaring at me.

I stood still and stared at him. "Did what?"

Detective Franks appeared at the apartment door with the office laptop in his hands. "What's up?" he asked.

"Someone pinched me," Detective Abrams said, glancing around as if he thought I had hidden someone in the apartment.

I sighed. "You know the Inn is haunted, don't you?" They both looked at me with blank stares. "Seriously, it's haunted," I said. "That was probably Chloe. She likes to follow me around and play games." They continued to stare. "Oh, for heaven's sake," I said, turning for the kitchen table. "We have ghosts. Get over it. Now, here's my laptop," I said, grabbing it and coming back to hand it to Detective Abrams. "And here's my cell phone." I reached into my pocket and pulled out my phone. "Now, I'm going back to the dining room to work on my campaign. Close the door behind you when you leave."

CHAPTER FOUR

I rejoined Doe and Rudy in the dining room and slumped into a chair. But it wasn't until I heard the front door bell jingle and the big SUV's engine start that I relaxed.

"God help me, Dana Finkle will be the death of me one way or the other," I said with a frustrated exhale.

"Why? What's going on now?"

I turned to find the fourth member of our book club, Blair Wentworth, standing in the doorway. She was married to an import car dealer and usually drove up in one of her husband's sports cars, so I was surprised I hadn't heard her roar into the parking lot.

"What were Mutt and Jeff doing here?" she asked, referring to the detectives. "Sorry, Julia," she quickly added, acknowledging my feelings for Detective Franks.

I sighed and stood up. "I need either caffeine or alcohol first. Anyone care to join me?"

I strode past Blair, whose inquisitive, sky blue eyes glanced at Doe and Rudy. The three of them followed me towards the kitchen.

As Blair passed Mr. Mulford, she murmured, "Good morning, Mr. Mulford. You're looking quite festive with that plaid scarf around your neck."

Mr. Mulford had just put on his coat and almost tripped over the table leg as he turned to acknowledge Blair. His face flushed, and he nodded three times, like a hen pecking for food.

"Th…thank you, Mrs.…Mrs. Wentworth," he stuttered. "You're looking…quite…quite…"

Blair flashed him a brilliant smile and stripped off her coat, exposing a deep blue cashmere sweater, stretched tightly over her breasts. "Oh, Mr. Mulford, I know what you mean," she said shyly. "Thank you ever so much."

The poor man's eyes practically teared-up because he was staring so hard at her chest. At sixty-two, Blair was the youngest of our group. While we all tried to keep fit, Blair worked at it. And what she couldn't accomplish on her own, she paid someone else to accomplish for her. The result was a body that looked like it belonged to an eighteen-year old, or close to it. She knew it and flaunted it whenever possible.

Once she had Mr. Mulford's undivided attention, she whirled around and waltzed through the kitchen door, which I was holding open for her.

"Perfect example of why I nicknamed you 'Catnip,'" I said, letting the door swing shut behind her. "You do that on purpose. He might have a weak heart, you know."

She smiled demurely. "Ah, men will be men at *any* age," she said with pride, throwing her coat and purse over a hook on the wall. "Now, c'mon, you guys. Don't keep me in the dark. What's going on?"

"You may wish you didn't know," Rudy said.

"Someone tried to kill Dana Finkle," I said, going to the refrigerator.

I pulled out a bottle of Diet Pepsi, my caffeine of choice, and then grabbed a large glass out of a cupboard.

"So?" Blair quipped, going for a glass of her own. "Too bad they didn't succeed."

I stopped and gave Blair a warning look. "No, Blair. Whoever it was succeeded in killing Trudy Bascom instead."

Blair stopped with her glass halfway out of the cupboard. "You've got to be kidding. Wasn't that her campaign assistant?" She threw a fearful glance in the direction of Rudy and Doe, who merely nodded to confirm the information. Blair put her glass back, went to the cupboard in the corner and grabbed a wine glass. "Alcohol it is."

"And what's more," Doe said. "They think Julia had something to do with it."

"What? Why?" Blair asked, turning to me.

I took my glass of Pepsi to the table. Blair crossed to the refrigerator and found an open bottle of white wine. She brought it to the table and poured herself a glass.

"Anyone else?" she said.

"Too early for me," Rudy said.

The main kitchen at the Inn, though large and functional, often made me feel as if someone had just hugged me, it was that cozy. Distressed white cabinetry framed the room, while a marble-topped center island provided a gathering place in the middle. A butcher-block farmhouse table sat in front of a bank of cottage windows that overlooked the back deck and lake beyond. At the far end of the kitchen was the original arched fireplace we'd filled with artificial flowers. Above that were wooden letters that read, "Let's Eat."

Rudy sat down at the table with her back to the window, while Doe went to a cupboard and pulled out a mug. She proceeded to make herself tea. The girls knew the kitchen almost as well as I did, and knew they were welcome to anything I had.

"Someone tried to lure Dana to the library last night by sending her a message from Julia's email account," Rudy said.

"Really? Can they do that?" Blair asked.

"Hacking people's emails is very common," Rudy replied. "By the way, I suspect they'll figure that out pretty quickly, Julia."

"I know," I said.

I sat with my Pepsi gazing out at the lake. There were puffy gray clouds hanging over the water, with patches of blue sky peeking through. A light breeze flapped the green awning that extended out past the back door. No one was on the lake. It was too cold. But I was thinking of Martha and Ellen, and now Trudy.

"You know, everyone expects to start losing people they know as they get older, but not like this. What happened to cancer, heart disease, or just old age?"

As I stared out the window, a familiar figure crossed in front of it. My business partner, April, came through the back door, dressed in a heavy sweater, turtleneck and loose-fitting jeans. She took one look at me and said, "You're looking pensive."

She was carrying a bakery box and still wore her apron. While I handled the antique side of the business, April was our cook and first-class baker. She had her braided hair pulled back in a clip, and wore a little flour on her chin for good measure, which stood out in stark contrast to her ebony skin. She crossed to the counter and pushed the bakery box up against the backsplash.

"Bad news?" she asked, turning toward me. "You're all looking pretty grim."

"Did you know Trudy Bascom? The woman who agreed to be Dana's campaign assistant?" I asked her.

"No. Why?"

"She's dead. Murdered."

April glanced from me, to Rudy, to Doe and then to Blair. Blair just held up her glass of wine in a fake toast.

"What happened?" she asked.

I explained what little we knew about the case, while the big grandfather clock by the front door chimed the half hour.

"So, here we go again," April said, leaning back against the marble-topped island.

"Yep," Rudy chirped. "The boys just left with every computer Julia has."

"That had to be awkward," April said.

"To say the least," I replied. "So much for dating a police officer." I took a long drink of Pepsi.

"That's right. We never even got to hear how it went last night," Doe said. "How was the date?"

I swallowed, shrugged and sat back in the chair. "Fine, if you consider going from a 007-type, action-packed movie, to a pile-up in the main dining room at the Mercerwood Shore Club, to a dead body at the library as fodder for a romantic date."

"Pile-up at the Mercerwood Shore Club?" Rudy asked, creasing her brows. "You didn't trip while you were dancing down the yellow brick road, I hope."

I glanced at her. Rudy didn't like it when I found ways to interject my favorite movie into otherwise boring situations, so I was surprised that she had done it herself.

"No. Nothing like that. There was just a little accident at the restaurant as I got up to go to the ladies' room."

Everyone relaxed with a collective, "Ahhh."

Before I could take umbrage with their reactions, Rudy said. "I take it the date was cut short?"

"You could say that," I replied. "David got called to the crime scene. And now I'm back under suspicion. I can't catch a break. Somehow I don't think it's going to look good on his personnel record if David is dating someone who keeps getting implicated in murder investigations."

Doe chuckled. "He's a big boy."

"Yeah, but Julia hasn't had a chance yet to find out *how* big," Blair said wistfully.

"Blair!" Rudy snapped.

"What I *meant*," Doe said, shooting Blair a severe look, "was that I think he can handle himself." She pointed an accusing finger at Blair. "And don't even think about making a joke out of that."

Blair's eyes glimmered, but she merely took a sip of wine.

"Besides," Doe continued, "they'll clear you very quickly, Julia."

"Well, I refuse to be intimidated this time. It wasn't me. I didn't do it…even though God knows I've thought of killing Dana many times myself."

April pushed off the counter and turned for the sink. "Don't let them hear *you* say that."

"Are you kidding me? Everyone knows I hate her. And don't forget the little *moment* we had at the Christmas Eve party. Don't you remember when Dana and I were standing in front of Ahab's cage, and he shouted out, '*I'd like to kill Dana Finkle?*'"

Dana had come uninvited to our annual Christmas Eve party, saying that she was there at the request of Mayor Frum, whom she thought would endorse her campaign. When Ahab squawked the threat, she had openly accused me of teaching him how to say it. I hadn't. But Dana never let facts get in the way of what she believed.

"Let's face it," I said. "If the police try to find motive when they're solving a murder related to Dana Finkle, I'm looking good for it. I just wish I knew who was trying to set me up."

I glanced over at April, who was putting chocolate chip cookies into an airtight container. She was my best friend and one of the most beautiful women I knew. She had rich, dark skin, big expressive eyes, and hair she liked to wear in corn rows, accented with colorful beads.

She also happened to have a finely tuned sixth sense. She often answered the phone before it rang, told me there was someone at the door before anyone knocked, and sensed the moment someone passed over.

I eyed her now, wondering what she might know. She seemed to recognize the pause floating in the air and turned. We were all staring at her.

"No," she said, with a wave of her hand. "I don't know anything, but maybe you've heard from your mother, Julia."

She turned back to the counter, but her comment about my mother got everyone's attention. That would be because my mother was also dead. Since the St. Claire Inn was haunted, and my mother had died there, I had always thought I might see her ghost at some point. But I have to admit that even I was shocked when she contacted me back in December by calling me on her cell phone. It was unnerving to say the least.

"No. I haven't heard from my mother," I said. "Maybe she's finally made it all the way to the other side."

"I wouldn't count on it," April said. "By the way, how's the campaign coming?" she asked, closing up the Tupperware canister.

I shrugged. "We haven't even started yet."

"It doesn't matter," Blair said. "No one wants Dana to be mayor, anyway."

"Yes, but now Dana will look sympathetic," Doe said, bobbing her tea bag in the hot water. "After all, someone just tried to kill her."

"Maybe she'll drop out," Rudy said with a conspiratorial roll of her eyes.

"Maybe someone's trying to get *me* to drop out, and that's why they tried to frame me," I said.

"Oh my!" Blair exclaimed. "Maybe Dana set this whole thing up."

"Oh, pshaw," April said with a swish of her hand. "This isn't a campaign for President of the United States. It's only mayor of a little town in Washington State. No one could actually believe that Julia *or* Dana would commit murder in order to win."

"Maybe not, although I'm not sure I'd put it past Dana. And now, she'll find a way to milk this for everything she can," I said.

"Who in the world would care enough to *kill* Dana Finkle anyway?" April said, coming back to the table with a plate of cookies.

"Everyone!" the four of us said together.

We all looked at each other in surprise and then burst into laughter.

"Okay, it's not really funny," I said, trying to straighten out my smile. "Seriously," I said with a cough. "Trudy was killed by mistake. That's not a laughing matter."

That short-circuited the mirth, and the room grew silent.

"Well, I have zucchini bread in the oven, so let me know if you need me for anything," April said. She put a hand on my shoulder. "And don't worry, this will all calm down shortly."

A moment later, she left for the converted old horse barn out back, which we'd turned into a retail bakery and warehouse for our antiques. Rudy reached out and grabbed a cookie, just as we heard the sound of a bell tingling. It was the front door to the Inn opening and closing.

"I wonder who that could be," I said.

"I'll get you, my pretty! And your little dog, too!" Ahab squawked from the other room.

And just as if we had been watching a rerun of the *Wizard of Oz*, the Wicked Witch of the West blew into my kitchen.

CHAPTER FIVE

"Julia, I want an explanation!"

The dogs streaked across the room, barking and yapping at a pair of stubby feet encased in heavy boots. It was Dana Finkle in all her amphibian splendor. I say that because she's not much taller than me, is built like a box, has thick folds at her neck and large, fleshy lips. To me, she looks like a toad. And right now the dogs had her backed up against the wall, her eyes bulging.

"Call them off!" she screamed.

The girls and I looked at each other in surprise. Miniature Dachshunds only weigh about nine to ten pounds.

"Mickey! Minnie!" I commanded. I clapped my hands, and they stopped and turned to me. "Go lie down," I said, snapping my fingers. I pointed to their dog bed.

Mickey threw a final bark over his shoulder at Dana, and then the two scuttled over to the corner, their little nails clicking on the hardwood floor.

"Sorry about that," I said.

Dana slid off the wall, her muscles relaxing, but her eyes never left the dogs, who were watching her with interest from the dog bed.

"Now, what do you mean?" I said, taking in her outfit with a quick sweep of my eyes.

She was dressed in bright red wool slacks and a purple and white checked sweater, with a yellow scarf tied around her thick neck. Over all of that, she was wearing a peacock blue wool coat. I had no idea where she got her fashion sense, but the entire image made me a little nauseous.

"It's your fault, isn't it?" she said, turning her attention away from the dogs. "I mean, Trudy has been murdered, and it was your note that drew her to the library."

"No, Dana," I said, glaring at her. "*You* sent her to the library. The note was meant for *you*!" I said, realizing too late that it sounded as if I really had sent the email.

"So you admit that you sent the message?" she spat, pointing a short, dark lacquered fingernail at me.

Good God! She painted her fingernails black.

"No, of course not," I said, bringing my attention back to the conversation.

Just then, Crystal came in from the front desk. "Julia, there's a phone call for you."

I reached for my cell phone, and then remembered that David had taken it. So I followed Crystal to the front desk. I picked up the land line. It was David. "Hello, David," I said tentatively.

"You're off the hook," he said. "Our tech guys said your email was hacked."

"Thank God," I said with a deep sigh. "Can they tell who did it?"

"Not yet. They're backtracking through the system now. But we've been assured that it wasn't you. I'll let you know when I have more information, and I'll get everything back to you this afternoon."

"Thanks. I know you were just doing your job. Sorry if I was short with you this morning."

"Hey, no problem," he said. "I'll talk to you soon."

I hung up. I returned to the kitchen where four sets of eyes were staring at me.

"Well?" Dana croaked.

"They've cleared me," I said with relief. "Someone hacked my email account."

"I knew it!" Rudy said, slapping the table.

"That's great," Doe said.

"But too bad for you," Blair said to Dana as she took a sip of wine.

"Why do you say that?" Dana asked, glaring at Blair.

"Because now you don't know *who's* trying to kill you," she replied, allowing a hint of triumph to seep into her voice.

Dana turned back to me. "Then you need to help me. Someone is still out there. And they want me dead."

"Needle in a haystack," Rudy murmured, studying her fingernails.

I shot Rudy an exasperated glance. "Dana, it's in the hands of the police. They'll find out who did it."

"No," she said, stomping her foot and jiggling the flab around her neck. "You owe me."

"Why does Julia owe you anything?" Rudy said, as she stood and came around the table with her fists clenched. "Why should any of us help you?"

Rudy had been an athlete in college and still played on the senior fast pitch team. Even with a titanium knee, she was fit as a fiddle. And her brusque manner could be intimidating. Dana backed up a step.

"Because everyone knows you all hate me," she said, dialing back the previous demand in her voice. "You have tremendous influence on this island. Especially you, Julia," she said, turning to me. "Clearly someone is following *your* lead."

"What?" Doe and Blair said, both rising from their chairs.

Dana backed up another step.

"Wait," I said with a raised hand. "Maybe she's right."

"Oh, c'mon, Julia," Doe exclaimed. "You don't owe her anything."

But I was staring at Dana, my mind racing. "I'll make you a deal," I said.

Those double-lidded eyes blinked warily. "What deal?"

"If we help you, you'll agree to drop out of the mayor's race."

"I knew it!" she exclaimed again. "This is all about the race. You just want to win."

"No," I said, raising a hand to stop her. "If you drop out of the race…then so will I."

She paused. I heard a few intakes of breath around the room.

"But Julia…" Doe said from behind me.

I put up my hand again to shush everyone.

"And then what?" Dana asked with suspicion. "Who will run for mayor?"

"Tony Morales," I replied.

"What? He can't be mayor! He's a…he's a…"

"A what? An amputee?" I said.

Tony Morales was our City Administrator and an Afghanistan vet who had lost his left leg and left forearm to an IED. He wore prosthetics and got around in life just fine. But to someone with Dana's underdeveloped sense of compassion, his injuries seemed to always make her uncomfortable. I'd seen her on more than one occasion just ignore him, even though he was right in front of her.

"Why can't he be mayor?" Doe said, taking the lead. "He has more experience than you do."

"Right," Rudy said, moving in close. "He has a degree in business and has already been in his position for three years."

"Besides," Blair said with a flip of her head. "People *like* him."

Dana looked from Blair, to Rudy, to Doe and then to me. "So, that's the deal?"

"Take it or leave it," I said.

"But he hasn't even filed for the race," she replied stubbornly.

"The deadline isn't for another two weeks," I said.

"The clock is ticking," Doe said in a threatening tone.

"And someone is out to kill you," Blair hissed in the background.

"But how do you know he even wants to run?" Dana whined.

I could tell she knew she was between a rock and a hard place and didn't like it. "I wouldn't worry about it," I told her. "You have more important things to worry about."

"Yeah, like saving your life," Blair said mean-spiritedly.

"Okay," she said with a disappointed sigh. "I suppose it's the risk that comes with being a public figure. I owe it to my supporters to stay safe, so I suppose dropping out of the race makes sense. After all, who could blame me? Someone *is* trying to kill me."

God, I knew it! I thought. She was going to milk this for all she could. Oh well, let her. At least she wouldn't be mayor, and I wouldn't have to run against her. You have to grab life's little rewards when you can. Just then, the front door jingled again.

"By the way, why isn't Clay helping you?" I asked. "He's your husband. Why didn't you turn to him instead of us?"

"He offered to hire a private detective," she said. "But…I didn't want…"

The kitchen door opened, and a voice rang out, "Mom, I heard about…"

Angela came in along with her large Harlequin Great Dane, Lucy. She stopped short when she saw all of us staring at her.

"Aaaargh!" Dana screamed again. She was back up against the wall, this time with the nose of a dog the size of a small horse pressed to her crotch.

"Lucy!" I yelled.

Lucy was mild-mannered and sweet by nature, but Dana didn't know that. I reached out and grabbed the dog's thick, leather collar, pulling her back as she looked up at Dana, drool spilling out the side of her mouth.

"Please…please, get it away from me," Dana blubbered, barely able to breathe.

"Not much of a dog person, are you?" Rudy said with a sarcastic twist to her mouth.

I handed Lucy off to Angela. Mickey and Minnie had run over, and Minnie started bouncing up and down at Lucy's feet as if her short little legs were equipped with tightly wound springs. For a small dog, Minnie could gain some real altitude. Dana's chin moved up and down as she watched the Doxie get higher and higher, looking all the while as if she might pee in her pants. I nodded to Angela.

"Let's take them out of here."

Angela and I ushered all three dogs into the breakfast room and then let them go. They wandered into the entryway, with Mickey and Minnie running back and forth under Lucy's belly and around her feet, while she tried in vain to catch them.

"Why aren't you at work?" I asked my daughter.

Angela was a workaholic, just like her dad, and rarely took vacations. So I knew there was an ulterior motive for her unscheduled visit.

"I took a vacation day," she said. "And don't try to change the subject."

I raised an eyebrow. "I wasn't aware there *was* a subject."

"Really? What's *she* doing here?" she said with a yank of her head in the direction of the kitchen. "You shouldn't be talking to her."

My back stiffened. "Why not? I just got a call from the detectives, and I've been cleared. Someone hacked my email."

"I know," she said crisply.

I crossed my arms over my chest. "Since you seem to have a direct line to the Mercer Island Police Department and know everything before I do, why are *you* here?"

She slumped back against the long counter we used to set up the breakfast buffet. "I just wanted to check on you to make sure you were okay. I know how you get when you think you're accused of something."

"Defensive would be the word you're looking for, don't you think? After all, I haven't done anything wrong."

"Then why is Dana here? You two aren't exactly friends."

Angela was two inches taller than me, had beautiful high cheekbones and dimples, and lustrous long black hair. And then I noticed it.

"When did you cut your hair?"

Her eyes narrowed, and she stared at me suspiciously. "You're doing it again. Changing the subject."

"Sorry," I replied without conviction. "It just dawned on me that you cut your hair."

She had, in fact, cut her hair to chin length with bangs down to the graceful arch of her brows. It was a stunning look.

"I like it," I said.

"Mother!" she said in her most admonishing tone.

"Okay, okay," I said. "Dana is just here to do what she does best…harass me. She came to accuse me of sending the message that got Trudy killed. But now that I've been cleared, she'll be leaving. Happy?"

I wasn't about to tell my nosy daughter the truth, so a long pause stretched between us as she studied me.

"Really, honey," I said, breaking the silence. "Thanks for checking up on me." I put a hand on her shoulder and began to move her in the direction of the front door. "Say hi to Detective Abrams for me."

"Look, Mom," she said, pulling away. "I know you. You make bad decisions when you get all riled up. Don't get involved in anything. Let the police do this."

"I'm sure that Detective Franks and Abrams have it all covered. Now you have a nice day off." I pushed her toward the door where Lucy had settled down to allow the smaller dogs to crawl all over her.

"Mickey! Minnie!" I called them. The dogs scrambled off Lucy and over to me, while Lucy hefted herself to her feet. "I'll give you a call later, Honey," I said brightly.

Angela slipped past me. "Okay, but *do not* get involved."

"Got it. Thanks, Honey," I responded, waving goodbye.

I returned to the kitchen, where I found the air as frigid as it was outside. Doe, Rudy and Blair had returned to the table, while Dana had retreated to the center island.

"All right, then," I said to break the ice. "If we're going to find out who's trying to kill you, Dana, we're going to have to know everything we can about you – past *and* present. Are you ready for that?"

Dana's eyes grew wide, and she drew her bulbous lips together. "Uh…sure," she replied. "By everything, you mean…"

"Everything," Blair said. "Someone's trying to kill you."

Dana's eyes darted from Blair and back to me. Then her eyebrows furrowed. "Uh…well, I've already talked to the police."

"Do you want us to help you or not?" I said, my patience running thin.

"Uh…yes, of course. But first," she said, holding up a stubby finger. "I need to do something. Then we can talk tomorrow." She started to back toward the kitchen door.

"What?" Rudy exclaimed in disbelief. She stood up and came around the table again. "What could be more important than finding out who's trying to kill you?"

Dana turned to Rudy with her best indignant pose. "Not all of us have hired help to do everything we need, Rudy," she said with all the venom she could muster. "Some of us have to get our hands dirty."

"What the hell is that supposed to mean?" Rudy said.

Rudy had a strong right arm, as any batter on the fast pitch team she played against could tell you. And right now, I was afraid she was going to use it. I think Dana did too, because she backed right up to the door.

"What I mean is that, uh…I need to finish up something, a project, and then I have to call my campaign committee together and plan a press conference to drop out of the race." Her hand reached out for the door behind her. "Then tomorrow, we'll get together, and I'll tell you everything you want to know." She turned and was about to push her way through the swinging door.

I stopped her.

"Dana!" I snapped.

She turned back to me.

"You *do* realize that every minute that goes by, someone out there is probably still planning to kill you?"

Her fingers clenched her purse straps. "Yes, of course. I'll be done tonight and will call you tomorrow. I promise."

And as quickly as she'd appeared, the Wicked Witch was gone.

CHAPTER SIX

"I don't trust her," Blair said.

"Yeah, that was pretty weird," Rudy agreed. "One minute she's demanding that we help her solve the crime, and the next minute she has more important things to do."

"You didn't really want to run for mayor did you, Julia?" Doe said, changing the subject.

"Yeah, I thought you came up with that compromise a little too quickly," Blair said with a hint of reproach.

"Let's face it," Rudy chimed in. "We made you do it, didn't we? We wouldn't take no for an answer."

They all cast forlorn eyes my way, as if their favorite aunt had just died.

"Okay," I said in frustration. "No, I didn't want to run for mayor. I told you that from the beginning. But I didn't want Dana to be mayor, either. So now both problems have been solved."

"Except Trudy Bascom had to die in the process," Doe pointed out.

"Yes," I said with a sigh. "That's the tragedy."

"And now someone has to convince Tony Morales that he wanted to run for mayor all along," Blair said.

"I'll do that," I said. "I've gotten to know him pretty well since he joined the library board. He has aspirations – he just needs encouragement. His physical issues make him self-conscious, that's all."

For the second time that morning, the kitchen door flew open and a squat, little woman marched in.

"Julia, did you hear about the murder at the library?"

It was Goldie Singleton, my neighbor on the north side of the Inn. She and her husband Ben lived in a large, ramshackle home they'd built in the late Seventies. I sometimes thought they were both still living in that era. Goldie was usually draped in long skirts or baggy pants and sloppy t-shirts. She often wore a fanny pack strapped to her waist and Birkenstock sandals. Today, she was encased in cargo pants and a huge jacket made out of what looked like upholstery fabric.

"Yes, Goldie, the police were just here," I said, realizing that she'd come in through the back door off the breakfast room. We kept it unlocked during the day.

Her gray eyes popped open in surprise. "Really? Why were the police here? Did they want your help again? You and the other heroes?" She sent an appreciative gaze around the room at the rest of the girls.

"Uh...no," I replied, hoping to downplay the hero bit. I glanced around at Rudy, not wanting to reveal what we knew to Goldie, but Rudy just shrugged as if it didn't matter. "Actually, I uh…"

"Oh, that's right," Goldie interrupted me with a finger pointed at my chest. "You're dating that good–looking detective."

I sighed. Apparently I had no secrets in this world.

She moved to the table and lifted a cookie off the plate and proceeded to eat it like a squirrel, taking little bites around the edges at lightning speed. Even at the age of seventy-three, Goldie had enough energy to fuel a power plant.

"Um...that's right," I said, realizing she'd given me an out with the bit about dating. "David stopped by to let me know about the murder since I'm on the library board. But how did you find out about it?"

"Ben," she said, stopping to wipe cookie crumbs off her lips. "His short wave radio buddies let me know. They're tapped into the police radios. But I just saw that Dana Finkle leave. What the heck was she doing here?"

"That's what I was about to say. Dana was the real target. The woman that was killed, Trudy Bascom, was her campaign assistant and was killed by mistake."

Her eyes grew round again as she held the half-eaten cookie in her hand. "Wow, that's a bad piece of luck."

"Yes, it's tragic," I said.

To the absolute delight of the Dachshunds, Goldie began pointing at me with the cookie and dropping crumbs all over the floor.

"I wonder if it has anything to do with the guy who's been breaking into homes around here. You know — the guy I shot at a few weeks ago?" Goldie said. She accentuated her comment by gesturing with the cookie. A chocolate chip dropped to the floor and quickly disappeared.

I considered the rash of thefts we'd had in the surrounding neighborhoods. The thief had stolen small electronics like iPads and cell phones. But when the unfortunate criminal selected the Singleton's home to visit, Goldie had run him off with her shotgun. The police were not amused, but then, Ben was retired military and held firm to his Second Amendment rights. The couple owned an arsenal of guns, one of which was an old shotgun handed down from Goldie's father.

"Whatever happened with that?" Rudy asked her.

"Oh, he got away," she said, turning to Rudy with disappointment. "He ran into those trees over by the parking lot."

"But what did the police say about you shooting off your rifle?" Rudy asked this cautiously, knowing she was treading on uneven ground.

Goldie made a grimace. "First of all, it's a Browning automatic 12-gauge shotgun that my daddy bought in 1954. And I have a right to protect my property," she said obstinately. "So they didn't have much *to* say." She turned to me. "I wish I'd got that guy though," she said, her gray eyes fixed in an intense glare. "Maybe that woman would be alive."

"I wouldn't jump to conclusions. This wasn't some random break-in. It was very well planned."

"What do you mean, planned?" she said.

"Julia," Doe blurted, getting up and placing a hand on my shoulder. "We really need to get busy planning your campaign."

I looked up at her in confusion. "What? No, I..."

"Doe is right," Rudy jumped in. "We're pretty busy, Goldie. You understand."

I saw Blair's expression transition from confusion to one of recognition, which finally registered with me. I turned to Goldie. "Yes, you'll have to excuse us, Goldie."

"Oh, sure," she said, grabbing two more cookies off the plate. "Let me know if you need help putting up campaign signs. Ben walks all over this neighborhood anyway. See you girls later," she said, waving the cookies in the air. Mickey and Minnie followed her trail of cookie crumbs until she disappeared through the swinging door.

Doe gave a great sigh and dropped back into her chair, as the dogs finished cleaning up the floor. "Sorry, but I thought if I didn't come up with something, she'd be here all day," Doe said.

"And all the cookies would be gone," Rudy lamented, reaching out for one of the last cookies on the plate.

"I know. She's a bit of a busybody," I said.

"That's putting it mildly," Doe said.

"By the way, do you have some crackers?" Blair asked. "Or nuts?"

Blair was a diabetic, and I'd forgotten that she needed something to eat with her wine.

"Just a sec." I jumped up and grabbed a box of crackers from the cupboard and handed them to her.

"Thanks," she said, reaching in for one.

"So how are we going to solve Trudy's murder?" Doe asked, sipping her tea. "That is, without getting in the way of your new boyfriend?"

"Or, Angela," Rudy said.

"Let's not worry about Angela. I say we go back to basics," I said. "Whoever killed Trudy has to be someone who not only hates Dana, but doesn't care if they implicate me."

"Right," Rudy said. "And also understands your relationship with Dana. Whoever sent that message had to be pretty sure that Dana would jump at the chance to meet you at the library, even in the middle of a storm."

Doe sat back down at the table and said, "But what they didn't count on was the fact that Dana would be out collecting money for her campaign. If they had, they'd know even a meeting with Julia wouldn't drag her away from that."

"So, it had to be someone that isn't close enough to Dana to know that she wasn't home last night," I said.

"Right," Doe replied. "Probably not a neighbor because a neighbor might have seen her leave. Or her husband. He would have known where she was."

Rudy spoke up. "We should have asked Dana who knew she'd be out campaigning last night besides Trudy."

I turned to the drawer in the center island and pulled out a small pad of paper and a pencil and came back to the table and sat down.

"Okay, let's make a plan. I'll call Dana and ask her about that. What else have we got?"

"We need to find out why someone would want her dead," Doe said. "I mean, everybody hates her, but who would actually go to such lengths to kill her?"

"Especially hitting her in the head with something," Blair said with a distasteful twist to her full mouth. "That sounds personal."

"Does anyone know anything about her past?" Doe asked.

"Just that she used to live down in Vancouver," Rudy said.

"And that she was married before," I added, writing it down. "I heard her mention that at a meeting once."

"She's been married twice?" Blair said, almost spitting out a mouthful of wine. "I can understand one man being that lonely, but not two."

Blair was on her fourth husband, so if anyone knew about multiple marriages, it was her. Her ex-husbands all still adored her however, and would come to her aid at the drop of a hat. I always suspected it was because her libido was as strong as any man's, and they were all secretly hoping for a reconciliation, if just for one night.

"Am I the only one who is suspicious about why she ran out of here so quickly?" Doe said, letting her eyes connect with each one of us.

"What are you thinking?" Rudy asked.

"Just that Dana is one of the most aggressive people I've ever met. She's always on the offensive, not the defensive. And yet, as soon as you mentioned that we'd need to know everything about her life, she became way too elusive."

"I'd say more like nervous," Rudy nodded. "I've never seen her like that. She couldn't get out of here fast enough."

"She's obviously hiding something," Doe said.

"Then I say we figure out what that something is," Blair said.

"But how?" I asked.

"We could break into her house," Blair offered, her cool blue eyes dancing with enthusiasm.

We all frowned at her.

"No," I responded. "Somehow getting arrested for breaking and entering doesn't sound like such a good idea. But…" I looked over at Doe. "Dana lives over on North Marchand Drive. What day is her trash picked up?"

Doe shrugged. "I don't know, but I'll find out." She pulled out her cell phone.

While Doe checked in with her office, I looked at Rudy. "Any chance you can do some digging into her life down in Vancouver?"

"Sure, I'll just make some phone calls. I know a couple of people who used to work at *The Columbian* newspaper down there. If she was as much of a pain in the ass back then as she is now, they'll remember her."

Doe hung up and put her phone on the table. "Bingo," she said. "Her trash is picked up tomorrow morning. So what are you thinking, Julia?"

I looked around the table considering my response. "Look, I admit that I can't stand Dana. As a result, I've studied her over the years more than I care to admit. She is the most calculating…uh…individual I know," I said, tempering my remark. "She doesn't do anything that doesn't have a purpose, and that purpose is *always* in her best interests."

"So? We all know that," Blair said.

"Well, she wouldn't stall for time unless she had a reason. I think she needs to get rid of something."

I could see the light bulbs go off over everyone's head.

"So the project she mentioned is that she's going home to get rid of some incriminating evidence?" Doe said.

"It may not have anything to do with her attempted murder. But it's definitely something she doesn't want other people to know about. Remember that she referred to a deadline – tomorrow," I said.

"Trash pickup," Doe said with a nod.

"Can you get your guys to pick up her trash and separate it out for us?" I asked Doe.

Doe frowned. "Boy, I hate to bring any of them into this. Isn't there another way?"

"Wait!" Rudy said. "Isn't it true that the moment someone puts their trash out at the curb, it becomes public property, so-to-speak?"

"Yes," Doe replied.

"Then, I say *we* pick it up."

"Oh, good," Blair exclaimed with a childish clap of her hands. "A midnight trash run."

Doe and Rudy exchanged skeptical looks.

"We'll need rubber gloves," Doe said with a look of distaste. "After all, this is Dana Finkle's trash we're talking about."

CHAPTER SEVEN

I never thought I'd be picking up Dana Finkle's trash. For that matter, I never thought I'd be picking up anyone's trash. But we met back at the Inn just before midnight to do just that. It was bitterly cold and had started to rain again. I had dressed in jeans, long johns, an undershirt and sweater and wore tennis shoes in case we had to run. I was probably overthinking this since our plan was just to drive up to the curb, empty the cans into the back of the Inn's van and take off. But you never know what life will throw at you.

Dana's husband owned a collection agency, and they lived in an expensive neighborhood overlooking Bellevue on the other side of the island. We parked a couple of houses down on the same side of the street. I was driving. Doe sat in the seat next to me holding a pair of binoculars, and Rudy and Blair were in the back seat.

"So how was it when David returned your computers this afternoon?" Doe asked hopefully. "Any plans for a second date?"

"He had someone else bring them back," I replied with a distinct edge to my voice.

"I'm sorry, Julia," Doe said, glancing my way. "He could just be busy on the case."

"Did you call Dana?" Rudy asked.

"Yes. She said Christine Newall had called at the last minute and asked her to come over to discuss the campaign. So, she asked Trudy to go with her."

"Who else knew she'd be gone?" Doe asked.

"Apparently no one. Clay wasn't home, and she didn't talk to anyone else."

"And the storm was so bad, I doubt neighbors would have even seen her leave," Rudy speculated. "I mean if you look around here, most of the homes are angled away from hers," she said, glancing around.

"There's still one light on upstairs and one downstairs," Doe said, bringing our attention back to the task at hand. She was peering through the front window with the binoculars. "I wonder if that's just for security, or if someone's still awake."

"That upstairs light must be the bedroom," I said.

A minute later, the front door opened. Dana appeared carrying something in each hand.

"Wait! There she is," Doe said.

"What's she doing?" Blair whispered, leaning forward.

Rudy scowled at her. "We don't need to whisper, Blair. She can't hear us this far up the street."

"But what if she sees us?" Blair asked.

"She won't see us, either," Rudy hissed. "We're too far away, and the interior of the van is dark."

"Shhh! Let's see what she does," I said.

"She's carrying something," Doe said, watching her through the binoculars. "It looks like two trash bags."

We watched Dana as she scuttled down her front walkway to the curb with a hood pulled up over her head. She glanced up and down the street in a jerky fashion and then dumped what she was carrying in one hand next to the Waste Disposal Company trash can. She looked up and down the street again and then opened the recycling bin and dropped the other bag inside. Then she turned and ran back up the walkway and into the house. The front door closed and a moment later, the downstairs light went out. Half a minute later, a different light went on upstairs.

"That was weird," Blair said.

"Everything *about* Dana Finkle is weird," I said.

We waited another five minutes, listening to the rain drum on the windshield. Finally, the upstairs light went out.

"Okay, let's go!" Blair exclaimed.

"No, we have to wait," I replied. "We need to give her some time to get to sleep."

"And do what, exactly?" Blair complained.

Blair was leaning over my right shoulder, and I could smell the wine she'd had at dinner.

"Let's just give her ten minutes," I said. "Here, listen to some music."

I switched on the radio, turning the sound down low.

"Oh great!" Blair snarled. "Can't we at least have some country music?"

I happened to glance in the rear view mirror. "Wait! There's a car coming."

I flipped off the radio and everyone froze. As the headlights approached, I noticed that the car was moving toward us very slowly and had a row of lights on the top.

"Get down! It's a police car."

Doe and I ducked down, while Rudy and Blair actually bumped heads in the back seat as they scrambled to get out of sight. Blair let out a yowl.

"Shhh," Rudy said. "Now someone *could* hear you."

We huddled in fear as the squad car passed by. A strong flashlight beam lit up our windows, flashing squiggly rain shadows across the interior. That made Blair squeal. Rudy shushed her again, and then the flash was gone.

Count to five.

I peeked over the steering wheel. The police car had passed and continued its slow progress down the street.

"Damn," I said. "They're patrolling the neighborhood. Probably because of Dana. I never thought of that."

The squad car disappeared around a corner.

"We'll have to be careful," Doe said, sitting up. "Maybe we should just go now, before they come back."

"What do you think, Rudy?" I asked, glancing back at her.

She was adjusting a heavy, padded vest she'd worn under her coat. "Can we do it quietly?" she asked, throwing a skeptical glance at Blair.

"I can be quiet," Blair whined.

"Shhh!" we all shushed her.

"I thought you said no one could hear us," she said in exasperation.

"If we're talking in regular voices," Rudy chastised her. "Not yelling at the top of our lungs. Half the neighborhood could hear you."

"Fine," Blair said in a pout.

"Okay, how are we going to do this?" Doe said. "There's a compost bin, a trash can, the recycling can, and the bag she just brought out."

"No need to go through the compost bin," I said with disgust.

"I agree," Rudy said. "But everything else should come with us."

"Even the garbage?" I asked. "That's most likely just empty potato chip bags. She *likes* her potato chips."

"But we don't know that for sure," Rudy retorted. "We can't take a chance."

I sighed. "Okay. So who gets what?"

Both Blair and Rudy were leaning forward, looking out the front window. The way everything lined up at the curb, the recycling bin was on the left. The small trash can sat in the middle next to the compost can, and Dana's trash bag sat at the right end.

"It will take two of us to lift the recycling can to dump everything in the back. How about Doe and I do that?" Rudy said.

Doe nodded.

"I'll get the trash bag," Blair offered quickly.

That left the garbage can for me.

"Great! I'll take the garbage can. But I swear, she better have everything tied up nicely into individual bags because I am NOT reaching in there and pulling out Dana Finkle's snot rags by hand. Even *with* rubber gloves."

Chuckles from everyone but me.

"All right," Rudy began. "Pull up right next to the curb, Julia, but don't turn off the engine. Then on the count of three, we all jump out. Blair, you get the back doors open. Then we all grab our stuff, toss it in, close the doors, and we're gone."

Sounded simple enough.

"Okay, on with the rubber gloves!" Rudy ordered.

We all donned the gloves. I started the engine and released the emergency brake. The van rolled forward. We were two houses away and across an intersection, so it didn't take long to arrive at our destination.

I did as Rudy instructed. I put on the emergency brake and left the engine running. On the count of three, we threw open the doors.

I jumped out and rounded the front of the van, coming up to the passenger door. My goal was to cut in front of the recycling bin and go for the garbage can in the middle.

Bad choice.

Doe had just come out her door with her hood up and we collided. I rebounded back against the van, slamming the passenger door shut and falling to my right. I got wedged between the curb and the van. Doe lurched forward, falling against the recycling bin and knocking it over, which in turn knocked over the small compost bin. Rudy was just coming out of the van's sliding door as I fell. She tripped over me and flew forward, landing face down in some compost, taking the small garbage can with her.

Meanwhile, as the rain pelted us, Blair had come out the back of the van and just stood there with her hands on her hips. "Really?" she sniped. "And you were worried about *me* making too much noise. You guys are like the Keystone Cops."

Rudy got up stiffly and flicked something off her sleeve. "Let's get this done. I'm soaked."

Doe rolled off the recycling bin with a groan and got up, while I picked myself up off the street, wiping grit and dirt off the palms of my hands.

I struggled up onto the curb and righted the trash can and flipped open the lid. The pungent odor of rotting tuna from empty cat food cans wafted over me, making me gag.

Dana had a cat. Who knew?

Doe and Rudy righted the recycling bin and rolled it down the walkway and off the curb to the back of the van. I reached into the garbage can and grabbed two full plastic bags and turned for the van, leaving the cat food cans behind.

As Doe and Rudy tipped the recycling bin and unloaded it, a light went on in the house.

"Hurry up," Blair ordered.

I quickly tossed in the two big bags of garbage. Rudy and Doe finished emptying the contents of the recycling bin into the van. They dropped it back onto the pavement, while Blair daintily placed her one bag of trash on top of everything else and closed the doors.

And we were off.

CHAPTER EIGHT

I drove like a mad woman back to the Inn, and not just because the interior was quickly filling up with the gagging smell of rotting food. I imagined a boogey woman named Dana following us like a banshee.

I parked the van in the garage. Rudy's sleeve had filled the van with the aroma of beef and onions, so that by the time we got the doors open, we were all coughing and hacking.

"God," she said, climbing out of the van. "I'm throwing this coat away."

"Sorry, Rudy," I said, apologizing for the accident. "Let's leave everything until tomorrow."

"Copy that," Rudy said. "I think my arm's starting to putrefy anyway."

Rudy grabbed her purse and hurried out of the garage. Doe and Blair murmured their goodbyes and followed. I closed up, stealing glances around me, hoping no one was watching.

Back in my apartment, I took a shower to wash off make-believe Dana cooties and to warm up before getting ready for bed. When I stepped out of the shower, I was surprised by the smell of rose water trapped in the small confines of the bathroom, along with a cold blast of air that raised goose bumps on my skin.

I jerked my head from side to side.

It had to be Elizabeth, the wife of John St. Claire, the original owner of the house. Although she was long dead, her favorite fragrance still followed her around, and she seemed to like to make appearances in my bathroom.

Elizabeth had died in the fire that also killed her eldest son Fielding, her daughter, Chloe, and their dog, Max. While Elizabeth, Chloe and Max continued to haunt the house, no one had ever seen Fielding. I suspected he was still there, perhaps just shy.

All of us had seen Elizabeth at one time or another. She was often seen strolling through rooms on the ground floor, or coming down the stairs. Once, she'd passed right through Mayor Frum when he and I were talking in the living room. Mayor Frum hadn't seen her, but reacted as if someone had just poured ice water down his back. Since we were alone, I allowed the moment to pass without comment.

For whatever reason, Elizabeth had attached herself to me. I thought it was because, like her, I was the woman of the house. She would occasionally show herself to me in my apartment, even try to communicate with me. After Martha died, she had struggled mightily to inform me through a bizarre game of charades that Martha had been poisoned. She kept wrapping her ghostly hands around her throat and gagging.

A few times she had left cryptic messages scrawled in the steam left behind on my bathroom mirror after a shower. As I watched now, I was rewarded with the beginnings of another message, and my heart rate stepped up a notch as I wrapped a towel around me.

A line began to appear in the steam, tracing what looked like a picture. Once Elizabeth was done, I stared at the drawing with my brow furrowed. It appeared to be the picture of a bird.

And then she was gone. The fragrance. The steam on the mirror. The cold air. All gone, and I was alone again in my bathroom.

I got into my pajamas and climbed into bed a few minutes later, puzzled. What was Elizabeth trying to tell me? It could have been a game. But usually, she was trying to give me a message. I just had no idea what it was.

I had trouble falling asleep, partly because I was keyed up, and partly because I kept picturing poor Trudy Bascom being bludgeoned to death. No one deserved to die like that, not even Dana. But what kept Trudy's image scrolling through my head was the fact that someone hated Dana enough to want to inflict that kind of harm on her.

It was well after 1:30 by the time I fell into a troubled sleep. I was awakened a short time later by my phone. I reached out and grabbed my cell phone off the bedside table and mumbled a garbled hello.

"Julia! Are you okay?" April asked.

I sat up, dislodging Mickey, who liked to tuck himself under one arm. "Yes, I'm fine. What's wrong?"

"I don't know," she said with a deep sigh. "Something woke me up. I…had a dream…or something. I thought you were in trouble."

April lived in our guest house, but I hadn't told her about our sojourn to steal Dana's trash. I knew she wouldn't approve. I also didn't want her to talk me out of it. So I wondered if she was just receiving a belated sighting of the Keystone Cops routine.

"What did you see?" I asked, sitting up against the headboard and rubbing my eyes back to life.

She took a deep breath. "You…and the dogs, barking. I don't know what it meant."

"Was *I* in danger?"

"I'm not sure," she sighed. "But I thought you were in trouble of some kind."

"Hmmm," I murmured.

"What?" April asked.

"I had a visit from Elizabeth tonight after my shower. She drew the picture of a bird on the bathroom mirror."

"Nothing else?"

"No." I replied. "And the only bird we have is Ahab. Was Ahab in your dream?"

"No," she said. "Just the dogs."

"Well, I'm fine. You go back to sleep," I told her. "And I'll call you if I even hear an owl outside my window."

"*Speaking* of birds," she said with a chuckle. "Okay, but be careful and call me if you need me."

"Will do."

I hung up and tried to relax back into the bed, feeling uncomfortable at April's phone call. The fact that she had had a vision right after someone had been brutally murdered on the island wasn't good news.

As Mickey pushed his way back under my elbow, I stroked his head and contemplated April. We'd been friends since college. When Graham announced he wanted a divorce shortly after finishing renovations on the Inn, I'd asked April to join me in the business. Word of her baking skills quickly brought in customers, making her orange scones legendary. She was living in Bellevue with her husband at the time. He was retired from the surgery department at the University of Washington Medical Center. Shortly after, he was diagnosed with Alzheimer's disease. April had cared for him as long as she could, but eventually had to put him into an expensive care facility. He died just before Christmas, and it was then that I'd learned that he'd also left April deeply in debt.

Right around the same time Jose´ decided to move out of our guest house and in with his boyfriend. This gave April a chance to move in and save some money. But something changed after her husband died. She was quieter and more solitary. She and her husband had been together since high school. And although he'd been a very successful surgeon, the disease had impaired his judgment before he'd been diagnosed, forcing him to make a myriad of bad decisions. I suspected she was not only lonely, but embarrassed by her financial situation.

My eyelids began to droop, and I dozed off. I was jerked awake a few moments later by the musical tones of the song, *Rock Around the Clock*. It had been the ringtone on my mother's cell phone before she died, and I came suddenly awake.

No one would claim my life was normal. But one of the strangest parts about it was that during Martha's murder investigation, my deceased mother had begun calling me on her cell phone. At first, it had freaked me out. But in the end, she had helped to keep me safe during those dark days, although her cell phone had been destroyed in the process. So I was surprised to hear her ringtone on my phone.

I sat up and grabbed my phone, but this time my hand shook as I answered it. "Hello."

"Julia!" my mother snapped. "What's happening? Are you okay?"

My excitement at hearing from my mother again was cut short when I realized she was repeating April's question.

"What? You, too? What's the big deal? I'm fine."

"What d'you mean, you too?"

My mother had been a big smoker and had died from emphysema. For as long as I could remember, she spoke in a husky, Lauren Bacall voice, with a slight mid-western accent.

"April just called and asked me the same thing. What are you two seeing that I can't?"

"I don't know what April saw, but I just had an overpowering sense that you were in trouble again. There was lots of commotion. Barking. Squawking. Why would that be? What did you get yourself into this time?"

My mother and I had always sparred. It's what we did when she was alive, and apparently, things hadn't changed much just because she was dead. "Why do you always assume that *I'm* the one who gets me into trouble? Maybe it was someone else's fault."

"Are you kidding?" she snapped. "Don't forget that just a few weeks ago you were being held prisoner in the basement of a church because you'd gotten involved in a murder investigation."

I sighed. "No. I haven't forgotten. But this time someone tried to kill Dana Finkle."

"Oh, for heaven's sake. Who cares about that?"

"Mother!"

"You don't like her any better than I did. By 'tried to kill,' I assume you mean they failed."

"Yes," I replied.

I told her about Trudy and my email account. My mom had been pretty tech savvy before she died.

"Wow," she exhaled. "That's got to be a piece of bad luck."

"That's just what Goldie said," I commented. "But you mentioned squawking. Did you hear Ahab?"

"I don't know if it was Ahab," she said. "I just heard a bird squawking."

"I'm not a target, Mom. But I think someone was trying to set me up for the fall."

"Okay, Button," she said with relief, using my childhood nickname. "Good to know. Well, not good for Finkle's campaign assistant, but you know what I mean."

"Yes, I do. Thanks. I just haven't heard from you since Christmas. It's good to know you're still looking out for me."

"Always," she said. "Now, I have to go."

"Mom."

"Nope, gotta go. Take care of yourself."

And with that, she was gone. I was left to look at the cell phone as I had so many times before, befuddled at how she could contact me from the other side and frustrated that I never got enough time to talk to her.

I slammed the phone back down on the bedside table and flopped back onto my pillow, eyes wide open, my brain humming.

Two warnings in a matter of minutes, along with Elizabeth's pictograph in the bathroom mirror. How could I sleep after all of that?

I couldn't.
I needed chocolate.

CHAPTER NINE

Chocolate was my alcohol. It relaxed me and made me feel comforted. I glanced at my alarm clock. It was now 2:20 a.m. I sighed and threw my legs over the side of the bed. There were no sweets in my apartment because I was trying to lose a few pounds now that I had an admirer. But the thought of chocolate was too strong, and I had to have it. So, I slipped my feet into my slippers and donned my robe.

My destination was the Inn's main kitchen, where I knew April had stashed the chocolate chip cookies for the snack tray we put out for the guests every day. I usually get up a couple of times a night to go to the restroom, so Mickey and Minnie merely looked at me from the center of the bed as I headed for the bedroom door. As soon as I stepped into the hallway, however, their little internal alarms went off. They scurried out from under the blanket and flew off the bed, shaking and wiggling to wake themselves up.

"Okay, but you have to be quiet," I warned, looking down at them.

They watched me eagerly. They were both long-haired miniature Dachshunds, with short, stubby little legs. Mickey was black and tan, while Minnie was a copper red. Mickey plopped down into a prone position and let out a pathetic groan, as if he thought I was going to leave him behind.

"Oh, c'mon," I said.

The hallways in the Inn are floored in dark hardwood, softened with red and gold carpet runners. Small plug-in night lights lit my way. My slippers made little sound as I padded toward the kitchen, but the dogs' nails clickety-clacked as they wandered off the carpet.

My apartment sat down a curved corridor, with only a public restroom and the laundry past me. I wound my way around to the front entryway. No one was about. It was the middle of the night after all – or the early morning, however you chose to look at it.

As I passed the Inn's front door, I could hear my big grandfather clock ticking softly in the entryway. It was one of the few antique pieces *not* for sale at the Inn. I used the area to the right of the door and next to the clock to display small collections of other antiques that were for sale. Currently, I had crafted a shipboard themed display, including two steamer trunks, an old ship's wheel, a captain's cap and a solid brass ship bell. We always leave one small lamp lit on a table in the entry, and another one on the reception desk for anyone coming back late. The rest of the ground floor was left in shadow.

Ahab's cage sat next to a patio door on the far side of the breakfast room, but I always draped it at night. I glanced that way as I tip-toed into the room, hoping I wouldn't wake him. The breakfast room was shaped in the half of an octagon, which jutted out onto the back deck. Each of the four angled walls held paned windows. We always drew the lightweight drapes at night, so I was startled by the flash of a light from outside.

I stopped and stared a moment, wondering if I'd seen it at all.

The breakfast room looked out onto Lake Washington and the South Seattle shoreline. To the right was a grove of trees and a path that led to Goldie's home.

I couldn't imagine anyone out for a stroll at this time of morning, especially because it was so cold. The rain had stopped, so more likely it was a boat out for some early fishing.

I shrugged it off and turned for the kitchen, pushing through the swinging door. The dogs scooted in after me as the door swung closed. I headed straight for the big Tupperware container that sat on the counter next to the sink. I didn't have to turn on a light, because April always left a small hurricane lamp lit on the kitchen table.

My first task was to give the dogs each a dental stick. That would keep them busy, while I grabbed a couple of cookies and a glass of milk. They settled in on opposite sides of a big dog bed we kept in the corner, and I sat at the center island to enjoy my snack.

The cookies were divine. If I didn't know better, I would have sworn they were still warm, but I knew that was just my over-active imagination.

Thunck!

A soft noise made me glance outside. A flowering cherry tree hugged the window, and I looked past that to the stake lights, which dotted two small lawns on either side of the deck. The dock was lit by a string of lights along the railing so that boats didn't ram into it in the dark.

I surveyed the area, looking for moving shadows, but didn't see anything. No one was about.

The lights from the far shore glistened and a breeze rattled the branches of the cherry tree, scraping them against the window. Another storm was probably moving in. No doubt tomorrow would be wet and blustery again.

I relaxed and glanced over at the dogs, who were oblivious to all else but making mincemeat of the dental chews. Give them a bone, a chew toy, or something with a squeaker in it and they entered a state of complete nirvana. It was like drugging them.

That's why the second thud was only acknowledged by Minnie, who glanced at the kitchen door and then went right back to her dental stick.

It was time to investigate. Perhaps someone had, in fact, come in very late and was knocking at the front door.

I went to the kitchen door and listened first. A rattling sound raised the hair on the back of my neck. Then I heard a squawk.

I pushed the kitchen door open and stepped through, allowing it to swing closed behind me.

The shadow of a large man wearing a hoodie stood at Ahab's cage. The patio door was open behind him, letting in a draft of cold air. Ahab's drape was off, and the cage door was open. Ahab squawked again, and the intruder reached in and grabbed him and stuffed him into a bag.

"What are you doing?" I erupted, starting forward. "You can't do that!"

The intruder glanced at me, but his face was draped in shadow. He drew the bag closed, trapping the frantic bird inside. As I rushed across the room, he started to turn toward the open door. He was about to escape, but I snagged the back of his hoodie and yanked him backwards.

"Come back here," I yelled. "You can't take him."

The man whipped around and shoved me away, but I came at him again, grabbing his left arm. He dropped the bag and whipped *me* around and put me into a headlock. I kicked over a chair and managed a short cry, which was enough to set off the dogs.

"Shut up!" the man whispered, his forearm pressing against my windpipe. "Or I swear I'll kill you."

This man was a good six inches or more taller than me and had the strength of a bull moose. I made a feeble attempt to loosen his grip around my neck, all the while gagging from the chokehold and his cheap cologne, with the dogs barking frantically in the background.

I finally managed a strangled cry and the kitchen door swung open. Mickey rocketed into the breakfast room. Unfortunately, Mickey goes into a frantic spin when he gets excited. So my would-be hero stopped at my feet, turning like an egg beater and barking in circles.

Good dog, Mickey.

Minnie was still in the kitchen squealing like a stuck pig at being left behind. The man's leg shot out and kicked Mickey, eliciting a cry of pain, which sent Minnie into overdrive.

She must have finally taken a run at the closed door, slamming her tiny body against it. She shot through like a bullet and used the springs in those back legs to leap onto one of the chairs, launching herself at the man's face.

I saw her coming and pulled my head to the side just before she slammed into my attacker. There was a cry of pain, and a warm liquid ran down my neck.

Blood!

He let me go and began to howl louder than the dogs. I fell forward gasping for air, while he struggled with Minnie, who had attached herself to his face. Mickey continued to turn circles and bark.

Then a cannon went off.

"I have another barrel just for you!" a voice called out.

My ears rang as the intruder flung Minnie free and grabbed Ahab. He ran for the front door, followed by two very fast miniature Dachshunds who were mad as hell.

The dogs followed him out the front door and into the night, their very high-pitched barks ringing through the neighborhood.

I took a deep breath and stumbled to my feet, one hand to my throbbing throat, and the other to my ear. A light went on, and I glanced up to find a gaggle of guests staring at me from the entryway with a mixture of fear and alarm etched on their faces. I turned to find Goldie, standing behind me with her shotgun in her hand, a look of sublime satisfaction on her face.

"You okay, Julia?" she asked.

I looked from her and back to my guests and thought, *Damn! Here we go again.*

CHAPTER TEN

I left Goldie in the breakfast room and went to address the guests.

"It's okay," I lied, and massaging my throat. "Someone...uh...someone broke in and stole our parrot. But no one was hurt."

"But that woman shot off a gun," an older woman said in an accusing tone.

Her name was Mrs. Fenster, and she was in town for her granddaughter's christening.

"Yes, just to scare him away," I said, turning toward Goldie. "But no one is in any danger. We're fine."

"Well, I called the police," she stated, straightening up. "As soon as I heard the dogs bark."

"Very good," I replied. "That's good. Now maybe everyone should go back upstairs."

A new guest, Mr. Dalton, appeared at the open front door. "What's going on?" he said upon seeing the gathered crowd.

He wasn't much over twenty-five and was in town for a conference at Microsoft. The cold air made me step past him to close the door.

"There was a thief," an elderly man named Mr. Brewster said. "You missed all of the excitement." He and his wife were in town for a second honeymoon, and he looked pleased to have a story to tell.

Mr. Dalton's face was flushed, and he smelled of alcohol. He looked around. "Too bad. I was...uh, out with a friend."

"Did you see anyone running away from the Inn?" I asked him.

He paused and glanced around to the anxious faces. "No. Sorry. Is everyone okay?"

"Yes," I said. The sound of sirens made me look out the sidelight window. "Um…the police will take care of things. Maybe you all could just go back upstairs." I made a motion to usher them along.

"Won't they need to interview us?" Mrs. Fenster asked.

"I doubt it," I said, thinking she was just a busybody who wanted in on whatever gossip she could muster. "Unless you saw something, of course."

I stared at her for a moment, but she shrugged. "No. Of course I didn't."

She turned and retreated up the stairs, followed by the Brewsters. Mr. Dalton was last to go.

"Are you sure you didn't see anyone as you were coming in?" I asked him.

"Uh…no. I heard some dogs barking, but my friend dropped me off at the street. Sorry. Well, I'm going to bed," he said, and climbed the stairs.

I stood for a moment, listening to the sirens as they got closer and dreading the approaching encounter.

"Sorry about your ceiling," a voice rang out from the breakfast room.

"Goldie," I said, whipping around and putting a hand to my chest. "Sorry, I forgot you were here. But then how could I? You just blew a hole in my breakfast room."

Goldie was dressed in a baggy hooded sweatshirt thrown over a long nightgown, with a pair of hiking boots peeking out from beneath. She was a good two inches shorter than me, which made the enormous shotgun in her hand look like a bazooka.

"Psshaw," she waved the bazooka in the air. I flinched backwards as the barrel rounded towards me. "I didn't point it at anyone."

"Yes, but, my wall," I said, pushing past her to look for holes in my walls.

She followed me as I studied the walls, and then tapped me on the shoulder and pointed an index finger to the ceiling above Ahab's cage. I rolled my eyes upwards and groaned. My hammered copper ceiling looked like Swiss cheese.

"See? I was very careful, Julia," she said. "Besides, that fella looked like he was about to kill you."

My hand reached for my throat. "I know," I said, flinching at the tenderness. "I'll be black and blue tomorrow. I owe you my gratitude. You just scared the hell out of me. You do have a license to carry that thing, don't you?"

She puffed up her chest indignantly. "Don't need one."

The front door flew open and April rushed in, limping. "Julia! Are you okay?"

"Yes, yes, I'm fine, but what happened to you?"

"I twisted my ankle getting over here. I was in a hurry. I heard a gunshot."

"Yes, someone broke in and took Ahab."

"Ahab's gone?" Her eyes darted toward the cage and then the open patio door behind us.

"Yes," I said, wrapping my arms around me to ward off the cold.

April turned to me. "It's what I saw. Remember? My dream?" She glanced around her feet. "But where are the dogs?"

My head came up. "I don't know. They followed the guy out the front door." I turned and ran into the entryway and opened the front door again. "Mickey! Minnie!" I yelled.

Nothing.

A moment later, red and blue lights flashed across the pine trees as the police swung into the Inn's circular drive, their sirens dying. After Martha's death, having police at my front door had become a common occurrence, and I suspected my neighbors weren't amused.

April had followed me onto the front veranda and said, "The dogs just came back to the patio door. I put them in the kitchen."

"Okay, I'll take this."

April limped back to the kitchen, while I crossed my arms over my chest and shivered from the cold. Two young patrol officers emerged from the squad car with their hands ready to draw their weapons. I assured them all was well and led them into the breakfast room where Goldie had planted herself at a table, the bazooka lying in front of her. The taller, dark-haired officer introduced himself as Officer Graver. He introduced his blond counterpart as Officer Capshaw.

"What happened here?" Officer Graver asked.

"Someone broke in and stole my parrot."

"We had a report of a gunshot," he said, as if he hadn't heard me about the theft.

I turned toward Goldie. He followed my gaze and stepped forward. "Did you discharge the weapon?"

"Sure did," she said.

"And your name?" the officer asked.

"Goldie Singleton," she said with pride. "I live next door."

I saw his eyes flare, as if he'd heard that name before.

"Why did you fire the gun?" he asked.

"Because someone was stealing our parrot," I said again.

He turned to me with his lips parted, and I had the feeling he was about to say, "You're kidding?" He must have thought better of it, because he merely cleared his throat. Just then, April came in from the kitchen.

"Was the bird valuable?" Officer Capshaw asked. He had a notepad out, ready to write.

"Not to anyone but us," I replied. "He was just a parrot."

"What about the alarm system?" Officer Graver asked. "We saw a sign out front that you have one."

I groaned. "It malfunctioned over the weekend. We had the repair guy out yesterday, but he had to order a new keypad."

"Pretty convenient," he said. "What's the name of the company?"

"Island Security. It's owned by Roger Romero."

"Okay, we'll talk to him. You're the owner here, I take it?" Officer Capshaw asked.

"Yes. This is my business partner," I said, nodding toward April.

"I live in the guest house," April offered.

"The guy attacked Julia," Goldie said. "She left that part out. He had her in a choke hold when I got here."

"I don't understand. Did you see him break in?" Officer Graver asked her.

"No, of course not. Like I said, I live next door." She pointed in the direction of her house. "I saw someone through the trees. I was just going to bed. Our bedroom is in the back, on the second floor."

"You saw someone in the dark, through some trees?"

His skepticism was apparent.

"No, first I saw someone cut across the beach, heading towards Julia's. We've had a bunch of burglaries in this neighborhood, so I got out my binoculars and watched him. After all, it could have been one of Julia's guests, too. Anyway, he stopped in the trees in between our houses and waited. I saw the flare of a light through the trees. I figured it was someone lighting up a cigarette. I got curious because he was there so long. So I sat down and waited. I could just barely see the shadow of him standing there," Goldie continued. "It looked like he was facing the Inn while he smoked. He lit up at least twice. I thought it was weird."

"And how long did he stand there?" Officer Capshaw asked.

She shrugged again. "A good thirty minutes or more. I finally got my boots on."

"And you never thought to call us?"

"No. Why would I? I have old Betsy here. She takes care of things."

He sighed with annoyance. "Could you tell what this man looked like?"

"It was too dark. All I saw was his silhouette. Look, Julia's had some trouble here before. That plus the burglaries made me suspicious. So when he moved out, I grabbed my gun and snuck over here after him. When I got here, that door was open," she said, pointing to the patio door. "And he had Julia by the neck. As I got to the door, one of her dogs attacked him. Got him right in the face," she said with a smile. "Anyway, I came up behind him and shot into the ceiling to scare him off."

She sat back with satisfaction, her gray eyes glistening. I had the feeling she'd been waiting her entire life for this moment.

The two officers glanced at each other. "In the future, Mrs. Singleton, we'd prefer it if you'd call us first," Officer Graver said.

Goldie's eyes flared this time. "Look," she said, standing up. "I…"

She knocked the table off balance as she stood, and Old Betsy slid off the edge. The gun butt hit the floor and it discharged. Everyone ducked for cover as a spray of buckshot slammed into my breakfast room wall, shattering the framed picture of a garden scene and sending shards of glass across the room. The dogs went ballistic again in the kitchen, as the room filled with smoke.

I thought Officer Graver was going to throttle Goldie. He stood up from his crouched position, glared at her and then yanked the gun up off the floor. "I'll take that, if you don't mind."

"Wait a minute," Goldie said, stepping around the end of the table. "I do mind. That was an accident. That gun belongs to me. I have a right to carry it."

"Yes ma'am, but not to shoot it indoors. So I'll be taking it down to the Mercer Island PD to have it checked out for a faulty trigger mechanism. You have a problem with that?" he said, challenging her.

This guy wasn't kidding. His dark eyes were boring holes into Goldie's. She matched his stare for a moment and then relented. "Okay, maybe we should have it checked out."

Officer Graver handed the shotgun off to his partner. I looked up and realized the entryway had filled with guests again. I hurried over and waved them all back upstairs.

"Everything's okay. The gun just went off accidentally this time. The police are here. They have things under control." But I could tell Mrs. Fenster wasn't buying it.

"Well, this is really too much," she spat. "The threat of ghosts is one thing. But guns going off and people breaking in are quite another. I'll be checking out first thing in the morning."

With that, she spun around and marched up the stairs. The rest of the guests just stood awkwardly glancing back and forth between her retreating figure and me.

"I'll understand if anyone else feels the same way," I said.

There was a pause, and then Mr. Brewster smiled. "Are you kidding? We haven't had this much excitement in twenty-five years," he said with a grin. "Now if we could only see a ghost, we'd have our grandkids attention for months."

I smiled. "Well, let's keep our fingers crossed that when Jason Spears, the paranormal investigator, is here this weekend, you'll get your wish."

Everyone returned to their rooms, while I went back into the breakfast room. April had come out from the kitchen and was pulling out a broom and dustpan from a long cupboard in the corner. Officer Graver was inspecting the patio door jam, while Officer Capshaw was looking at Ahab's cage.

I sidled up to April. "That time it was an accident," I said.

She turned concerned eyes my way. "Are you kidding, Julia? She could've killed someone."

"I know. But the police are taking the gun this time," I said.

The officers asked me a few more questions, but I wasn't much help. I hadn't heard a car, seen anyone other than the man who attacked me, and couldn't give them a description. The door's lock had been jimmied, but it appeared that nothing else had been taken other than Ahab. Dusting for fingerprints seemed useless since so many different people stayed at the Inn, and we have so many special events.

Forty-five minutes after they'd arrived, the police were gone, telling me that these kinds of thefts were rarely solved. I was left with bruises on my neck, matching buckshot in my breakfast room ceiling and wall, and an empty bird cage. I turned to Goldie.

"Well, I don't know about you, but I'm exhausted," I said, hoping she'd leave.

She took the cue and began to move towards the patio door. "Glad I could help, Julia. Maybe I'll get one of those Hero of Mercer Island awards."

I smiled, despite the fear that Mayor Frum might actually bestow one on her. "Could happen," I said. "Thanks again, Goldie. Can I get the dogs and walk you home?"

She chortled. "No." She pulled out her cellphone. "I called Ben and he's waiting for me."

After I locked the patio door behind her, I went into the kitchen, where the dogs greeted me, tongues hanging out of the mouths.

"Are the police gone?" April asked. She was dumping the dustpan filled with glass into a trash can.

"Yes. And I just said goodbye to Goldie."

"Thank God! I was afraid we were going to lose the windows and maybe a guest or two."

We both chuckled. "She means well," I said. "But I'm kind of hoping they don't ever give her that gun back." I slumped into a chair. "How are you doing?"

"Okay," she said, sitting down. "I just twisted my ankle. It's not bad, but I'll have to ice it. How are *you*?"

Tears sprouted, and I grabbed a paper napkin. "Not so good. Why would someone steal Ahab? He's just a stupid bird."

"I don't know," she replied. "But it seems a little coincidental, don't you think?"

I looked over at her. Her dark eyes were glowing.

"You think it has something to do with Trudy's murder? Or, Dana's attempted murder, I should say?"

"All I know is that someone is working pretty hard to put you right in the middle of this whole thing."

"I need a cup of tea," I said, wiping my eyes and pulling myself out of the chair.

I made tea for both of us and grabbed the cookies, while April grabbed an ice pack from the freezer and held it to her ankle.

"Fill me in," she said.

"Here, wait," I said. I grabbed a short stool and brought it over. She carefully lifted her foot and placed it sideways on the stool and then draped the ice pack over her ankle. "There, how's that?"

"Better," she replied. "Now, what happened?"

I told her first about my mother's phone call. "I think she connects with me mostly when something is wrong," I said, after relating my mother's message. "Anyway, she couldn't tell me any more than you did, but I couldn't go back to sleep. So I came out to have a cookie. I heard someone in the other room and went to check."

I rubbed my throat, which was still sore. April watched me and then said, "And you tried to stop him?" I nodded. She shook her head. "You live a charmed life, Julia. You could have been seriously hurt."

"I know, but I couldn't just let him take Ahab. Unfortunately, he got him anyway."

A wave of despair washed over me. I glanced down at the two little wiener dogs at my feet. They were focused on me like lasers. Not because they were worried about me. They thought I had food.

"But you're good dogs, aren't you?" I said, reaching down to give them each a pet.

Both dogs climbed up on my leg. "That reminds me. Minnie may have taken a chunk out of the guy's face," I said.

"Really?" April said. "You should let the police know."

"Yeah, I will. I think you two deserve a treat for your valiant efforts," I said to the dogs.

I went to the cupboard and grabbed a bag of dog biscuits. Mickey began turning circles again, and Minnie sprang up and down like a broken Jack in the Box. I couldn't help but smile as I tossed them each a cookie. As I joined April at the table again, I glanced out the window. A light breeze rustled the leaves on the cherry tree, making the lights strung along the dock flicker.

"I don't like thinking that people are lurking out there," I said with a slight shiver.

April followed my gaze. "No. I agree. Will the police come back tomorrow to look for clues?"

"No. They made that quite clear. They said these types of crimes are usually random and are rarely solved. I suppose they don't have the budget to worry about finding a parrot."

April frowned. "That's too bad. But *we* should check it out tomorrow, anyway. See if we can find anything in the trees. Maybe Jose´ can help."

"Good idea. Listen," I began, stirring my tea. "I have a confession to make."

She turned her dark eyes in my direction. "Yes?"

"After you left this morning, Dana arrived and demanded that I help her find out who's trying to kill her."

"Really? And you said no, right?" I concentrated on adding sweetener to my tea. April watched me and then exhaled. "Julia, you didn't!"

I took a sip and then put my tea down. "It's not all bad. I got something worthwhile in return. She agreed to drop out of the race."

April's whole face lit up. "So, you'll be mayor?"

I shifted uncomfortably. "Well, no. I agreed to drop out, too. I never wanted to run a campaign, April. You know that. That was Graham's thing, not mine. Besides, I'm going to talk Tony Morales into filing."

April shrugged. "Well, I'm sorry you won't be the belle of the ball, but I like that idea," she said with relish. "Think he'll do it?"

"God, I hope so. I kind of made it sound like it was no big deal. But the truth is, he's very self-conscious, and I bet the idea of campaigning will turn him inside out."

"Hey," April grunted. "He's a war vet. He's had to do a lot worse. Have a little faith. By the way, where were you so late tonight? I heard the van come in well after midnight."

We shared a moment of silence, and then I said, "Uh…picking up some stuff."

She furrowed her brows. "Stuff? As in antiques?"

"Well…what we picked up is old," I said, sipping more tea.

"What is it? Something we can sell?"

I swallowed. "Um…probably not," I replied. "But what's that saying? One man's trash is another man's treasure?" She looked at me curiously. "Let's just say I hope you don't have to use the van tomorrow."

CHAPTER ELEVEN

The next morning I woke up to black and blue marks around my neck. I contemplated masking the bruises with makeup, but decided to wear a turtleneck instead. I was more concerned with a bruise on my right elbow that I'd obtained when I hit the curb the night before. It hurt like the dickens.

April had gotten in ahead of me and had finished cleaning up the breakfast room, so I pulled down the destroyed garden picture and put it outside by the kitchen door. Then I wandered over to Ahab's cage and glanced out the window, hoping against hope that I'd see him sitting on a branch a few feet away. No such luck.

I helped April whip up some eggs for breakfast burritos for the guests. She said her ankle didn't really hurt, but she had it wrapped with an Ace bandage. After breakfast, I called Roger Romero, who owned the alarm company.

"Oh, Julia, I'm so sorry," he said. "An officer already stopped by to talk to me. Ahab was quite a character. I'm sure he'll be missed."

I felt a lump in my throat. "Yes, he will. I can't believe our bad luck, though. The one day the alarm system was down."

"Well, the keypad is in," Roger said. "I'll have it installed first thing this morning. And again, I'm so sorry. But at least no one was hurt." He took a big sigh. "You know, Julia, I went into this business to prevent stuff like this."

"That's right. Your wife," I said, remembering that his wife had been attacked when they'd lived in Portland.

"Yes," he said, lowering his voice. "She still has nightmares. So, I swore – never again." He paused again as if to compose himself.

"Julia, I'm going to finish the repairs myself. I'll be there within the half hour. And I'm going to make this up to you somehow."

"Well, I have a hole in my ceiling you could fix," I said.

"What?"

"Never mind. Let's just get the alarm system fixed."

"That's the least I can do. I'll see you soon."

He hung up, and I tapped my finger on the desk, thinking. Who might have known the alarm system was down? I racked my brain, thinking back to the day Roger's son, Peter, had come over to evaluate the problem. Crystal wasn't there. She had weekends off. Jose´ was also off, but I'd mentioned it to both of them Monday morning. April had been gone most of the day, shopping. The weekend manager, Evian, and the weekend cleaning woman were there, however. The Brewsters and Mrs. Fenster had checked in that day, while two singles had checked out. In fact, when Peter came out to tell me a short in the keypad had fused it, and he'd have to order a new one, there had been a small army of people hovering around the front desk.

I sighed. *Damn!* Once again, half a dozen people had been aware of the fact the Inn's alarm system was down. It was going to be hard to run a business if I continued to treat my guests and employees as potential suspects.

I made a mental note to get more information on the two single guests who had checked in Monday morning: an older man named Mr. Tooley, who was in town to visit his daughter, and Mr. Dalton, the young man who had come in late the night before.

I didn't remember seeing Mr. Tooley in the group of concerned guests at the foot of the stairs the night before. And young Mr. Dalton had come in afterwards. He had time to run out with Ahab, stash him somewhere, and then turn around and come right back in. But why would he?

I spent an hour paying bills and then was just beginning to clean up the breakfast things when Mr. Tooley appeared. As he came into the breakfast room, I felt myself stiffen.

"Not much left, I'm afraid," I said, wiping down the counter. "Just a few scones."

He came up beside me to survey the remaining scones. I stood up straight and mentally calculated my height compared to his. I would fit right under his chin, just like the intruder. But this man had to be in his late fifties to early sixties, with stooped shoulders, gray hair and a slack jaw. He just didn't seem the intruding kind of guy.

"I'm good with just a scone and some coffee," he said without looking at me. "The family is going down to Pike Place Market for lunch." He smiled as he put the scone on a paper plate and poured himself a cup of coffee. "Are you okay?" he said turning to me. "I heard about last night."

My heart rate sped up, and I felt the adrenalin thrumming through my veins.

"Uh…yes, I'm fine. Sorry about the noise last night. It must have woken you up."

He chuckled. "No, I wear hearing aids," he said, gesturing to his ears. "I take them out at night, so I didn't hear anything."

"How did you know about what happened?"

"Mrs. Fenster," he said with a frown. "She knocked on my door at five o'clock this morning and asked me to tell you she'd left and you could just mail her the bill. I get up early. I like to Skype with my grandkids in Boston. She must have heard me."

"Why didn't she come tell me?"

"I think she was pretty upset. My guess is that this is her way of letting you know."

I sighed. "Yes, she *was* upset," I said. "No one was ever in danger, but I can understand that it could be unsettling."

He glanced up at the wall. The buckshot holes were plainly visible. "A bit," he said, laughing. "Sounds like I missed all the fun."

"Some of it wasn't so much fun," I said. "The guy who broke in stole our parrot," I said, turning to indicate Ahab's empty cage. He followed my gesture.

"Oh, I'm sorry. He was cute. I thought my grandson would enjoy meeting him." He shifted his gaze to me. "Was anyone hurt?"

"No," I said, unconsciously reaching for my neck.

"I'm glad. You have such a nice place here. I'd hate to see your reputation tarnished. Hopefully Mrs. Fenster will be the only one to leave because of it. Well, I've got to get going. Have any suggestions for lunch downtown?"

I had been thinking and snapped to attention. "Um…there's the Crab Pot, and Lowell's is always good. Nice view of the water."

"Thanks," he said. He returned to his room carrying his scone and coffee.

I decided that Mr. Tooley wasn't the guy. He was too relaxed to be lying; besides, he didn't have any bite marks on his face. I went about my business and was at the front desk a half hour later when Mr. Dalton came downstairs, carrying his bags. My antenna went up.

"You slept in," I said to him.

He was a husky kid and a good head taller than me. He was dressed in nice khakis, a shirt and sweater, with a heavy overcoat. He had a leather messenger bag slung over one shoulder, which probably carried his laptop.

"I slept in. I don't have a session until 11:00," he said, referring to the conference.

"I'm sorry but the breakfast is all put away."

"That's okay," he said with a shrug. "Microsoft has a cafeteria. I'll grab something there." He stepped up to the counter and pulled out his wallet. "Actually, I think I'll check out now. The conference ends at 3:00 this afternoon and my plane leaves at 5:00, so I'll just head to the airport from there."

As he reached out to hand me his room key, I was momentarily overpowered by his cologne. It was the same brand the intruder had worn. I stepped back in surprise.

"Um...of course," I said with my heart racing.

Did this young kid steal Ahab and attack me? It seemed unlikely, and the cologne would be circumstantial evidence. But I froze in place, unsure of what to do.

He looked at me questioningly. "Is something wrong?"

I snapped to attention. "No. Of course not. I'll run you a receipt." I stepped into my little office and pulled up his record. A moment later, I was handing him a receipt for the two-day stay.

"Thanks a lot," he said with a friendly smile. "By the way, did you get your parrot back?"

The question startled me. "No. No, we didn't."

"That's too bad. He was funny. I used to have a talking parrot when I was young." He put the receipt away and grabbed his bag. "His name was Jabberwocky. I loved that little guy." He moved to the door and opened it. "Too bad I killed him."

CHAPTER TWELVE

At 10:30, Rudy and Doe arrived ready to begin going through the trash. Like me, they'd both dressed in jeans, turtlenecks and sweatshirts.

"My hip is killing me," Doe complained as she came through the door, favoring her left side.

"Was that from the recycling bin?" I asked. I pictured the tumble she'd taken the night before.

She scowled. "Yes. I feel like an idiot. I knew you'd be coming around to get to the garbage can. I don't know why I didn't just wait. Thank God I don't have to go into the office today."

Rudy limped up the stairs behind her. "Yeah, well I'm not in any better shape," she said. "I twisted my knee."

"Your new knee?" I exclaimed, stepping forward to help her up the last step.

"No," she said with remorse. "The *good* knee."

"Sorry. It was my fault."

Rudy waved away my apology. "No. It was bad planning. We shouldn't have been moving all at once."

I closed the door and followed them as they hobbled into the kitchen. I offered to make tea. They both accepted as they hung up their coats and lowered themselves painfully into chairs.

"I guess this is where the old, as in old maids, comes in," I said.

The year before, we'd nicknamed our book club the Old Maids of Mercer Island in reference to something Ellen Fairchild had said just before she died. She'd warned us not to be old maids. We figured out that what she'd meant was to live life to the fullest, prompting us to begin a series of personal adventures, ending with mine – solving Martha's murder.

"I'm certainly feeling the old part, right now," Doe said, shifting her weight off her sore hip.

"Yeah, but I have to be in shape for my fast pitch team," Rudy said. "So old or not, my knee can't hurt. By the way, I smell orange scones," Rudy said, sniffing the air.

"April made them for breakfast," I said.

Rudy cast a pleading look my way. "I don't suppose there are any..."

"I'll get you one," I replied. "April always holds a couple back for me. You sit tight. Doe?"

Doe shook her head. "No thanks. I'm not sure I want anything in my stomach when we go through Dana's trash."

That brought smiles to their faces. Rudy even chuckled. I put a beaker of water into the microwave and then got Rudy a scone. I reached up to pull the box of assorted tea bags out of the cupboard and winced.

"What?" Doe said. "You too?"

I turned, rubbing my elbow. "I landed on my elbow last night. Now it's killing me."

Doe stood and shuffled over to the counter. "Here, let me do that." She reached up and grabbed the box of tea bags and then got out the mugs from the adjoining cupboard. She put the last mug down and bumped my elbow. I yelped.

"Oh, Julia, I'm so sorry."

"Sorry about what?" Blair said behind us.

We turned to find that Blair had come through the swinging door, looking radiant in black stretch pants, a tight crimson, V-necked sweater and a short wool jacket.

"I hit Julia's sore elbow," Doe said.

Doe limped back to the table, raising an eyebrow from Blair. "What's wrong with you?"

Doe lowered herself carefully into the chair. "I hurt my hip last night."

Blair's blue eyes shifted in Rudy's direction, where she was kneading the muscles around her sore knee, her face tensed in pain. "And what's your story?"

Rudy sighed. "I twisted my knee."

"Humph," Blair grunted, dropping her purse on the floor. "It looks like I walked into the rehab unit on the orthopedic wing."

"Funny," Rudy replied a snap. "And where have you been? You're not exactly dressed for going through trash."

"Oh!" Blair exclaimed. She twirled around, stripped off her jacket and hung it on the wall coat rack. "Didn't I tell you? I'm volunteering."

There was a long moment of confused silence, while everyone stared at her.

"Um…really? Where?" Doe asked.

"I read with the fifth graders at Lakeridge Elementary School," she said with beaming smile.

Count to three.

"Really?" Doe said again.

I shot a glance at Doe. Her interest seemed suspiciously disingenuous.

"Yes," Blair replied. "I have three girls and one boy," she said. "And I think little Denny Ruffolo might have a crush on me, along with Mr. Vance, the principal," she said with a giggle.

Blair's eyes glowed with pride, but *my* eyes shifted to her tight-fitting sweater, and I was pretty sure I knew what Mr. Vance was in love with, if not little Denny Ruffolo.

"By the way, where's Ahab?" Blair said, going to the cupboard to grab her own mug. "I expected a movie review when I came in."

"I was just waiting for the right moment to tell you all. Ahab was stolen last night!"

Everyone gasped. I grabbed my turtleneck and pulled it down to reveal the big bruise. They all gasped a second time.

"What the heck happened?" Blair said, rushing forward. She reached out and touched my neck, making me flinch.

"Don't poke," I said.

I related the events surrounding Ahab's abduction as I pulled the beaker of hot water out of the microwave.

"But how did you get the bruises?" Doe said with her face twisted in concern.

I rolled my eyes. "I tried to be the hero. But the guy put me in a headlock."

"Oh Julia," Doe said.

"Jeez, Julia, what were you thinking?" Blair added.

"Good for you," Rudy said, lifting her mug in salute.

Rudy's no nonsense attitude had always made me think she could have been a Mother Superior, or perhaps a platoon sergeant, in a past life. It's why I nicknamed her, "The Boss." She didn't take guff from anyone, and I inwardly smiled at her salute.

"Well, it didn't work," I said in defeat. "Ahab is gone, and if it wasn't for the dogs, I would have been toast."

"The dogs?" Blair said in surprise, making herself some tea.

"Yeah, Minnie took a flying leap into the guy's face. She drew blood, so the guy should be sporting a big bite mark today. But then Goldie showed up with her shotgun."

"Oh, dear God," Doe exclaimed. "She didn't kill anybody, did she?"

"No. Just my ceiling. And a framed print."

They looked at me curiously. I jerked my head in the direction of the breakfast room, asking them to follow me. We all went into the other room, and I pointed out the wounded ceiling and wall.

"Oh, my," Blair said. "I think you should feel very lucky you're not in the ER having buckshot removed from your backside."

"Trust me, I am," I said.

"All of this and you still lost Ahab," Rudy said.

"How did he get in?" Doe asked.

"That door," I said, pointing to the door right next to the cage. "Goldie saw him cut across her yard and into the woods," I said, gesturing toward the grove of trees in between our property and Goldie's. "And our alarm system was down, remember? But one of my guests, a young guy who just checked out, could be the culprit."

"You're kidding!?" Doe said.

"No. When the gun went off, all the guests came downstairs. He wasn't with them. Then, as they were all going back *up*stairs, he came in through the front door. I'm thinking he could've run out with Ahab, hid him somewhere, and then come back in as if he was just returning from a night out with friends."

Rudy shrugged. "What makes you think he's the guy?"

"He wears the same cologne as the guy who attacked me. I could smell my attacker's cologne underneath the smell of cigarettes."

"So, he smokes?" Rudy asked.

"I would assume so. But this guest also told me this morning that he killed his own parrot when he was a kid."

Rudy frowned. "That seems weak. What would his motivation be? He stole Ahab because he missed the parrot he had as a kid?"

"I don't know," I said with timidity. "It *could* be him."

"Did he have an open wound on his face?" she asked.

I slumped back against one of the breakfast tables. "No. He didn't."

Doe shook her head. "Well, don't get ahead of yourself. But it wouldn't hurt to tell the police anyway."

"I'd bet my signed copy of Moby Dick that this all has to do with Trudy's murder," Rudy said.

"You have a book signed by a whale?" Blair asked, with her blue eyes opened in innocent curiosity.

Rudy gave her an exasperated look. "No, Herman Melville. I got it at that library auction two years ago."

Blair merely smiled to herself. Even Rudy knew she was only jesting. Blair was smart as a whip, and we'd learned recently that she had a photographic memory. She just enjoyed playing the airhead, especially if it would annoy Rudy. On the other hand, Rudy had been a career journalist and loved to read about as much as she loved to breathe. She had an extensive library that included several first edition books. She sought out auctions that included collectible manuscripts. One year for Christmas, she gave me a copy of the film script from *The Wizard of Oz*, signed by Bert Lahr. It was one of my most prized possessions.

"My guess is that the person who stole Ahab was the same person who made the comment about wanting to kill Dana at the Christmas Eve party," she continued. "Have you thought anymore about who that might be, Julia?"

"Yes. I've gone through the party guest list in my head, and I don't remember anyone hanging out by his cage. Do you?"

"No," Doe murmured.

"I was confined to my chair, remember?" Blair said. "So I was in the living room the entire time."

Blair had broken her ankle in the same car crash in which I'd broken two fingers. She'd been in a cast that night.

"I'll ask April again. Maybe she noticed something," I said. "She was back and forth a lot because the dessert table was in there. But she suggested we go out and check the path through the trees today to see if we could find anything the guy left behind. Maybe he dropped something."

"You mean like incriminating evidence?" Blair asked with a glint in her eye.

"Right. In fact, since we're here, I think I'll go out now and take a quick look." I started moving towards the office. "I'll get my coat and meet you all in the garage in a few minutes."

"Wait a minute," Rudy said, "I'm going with you." She put down her tea and went to get her coat.

"We're all going," Doe said.

All three of them grabbed their outer wear from the kitchen. *God, it was good to have friends.*

"Get a couple of baggies, Julia, just in case we find something," Rudy said, slipping her arms into her wool coat.

I got the bags and the four of us tramped outside and off the back deck to the rocky beach that lined Lake Washington. The temperature was in the lower thirties and thick, dark clouds blanketed the sky. There was no rain, but a good breeze blew off the lake, bringing with it the faint smell of algae.

The beach curved north and was comprised mostly of rocks and pebbles mixed in with dirt and sand. It wasn't a beach used for sunbathing. It was just too rocky. That's why the Inn had an enormous deck built onto the back, with a long dock.

We spread out, stepping gingerly through the sand and rocks, our eyes peeled for anything suspicious. Within a hundred feet, the grove of trees began and stretched along the water's edge for a good thirty to fifty yards. A narrow path wound its way through the trees and underbrush, until it opened up onto the rocky beach at the back of Ben and Goldie Singleton's large home.

"Guests are out here all the time," Blair murmured, tip-toeing through the sand in her expensive boots. "There will be a million candy wrappers and cigarette butts out here."

"But not fresh ones," Rudy said. "We'll probably be able to tell if one was smoked as last night."

We fell into line as we entered the woods along the path. The undergrowth was thick with grass, ivy, bushes and moss. Every so often, an open area would offer a view of the lake. About half way in, there was a big flat boulder on the lake side with little around it. As we passed it, I wandered over and looked over to the other side.

"Hey wait. I wonder if this is where he stopped."

"Find something?" Rudy said, coming in to lean over my shoulder.

I was peering over the rock to the ivy on the other side. "That looks like a beer bottle down there," I said.

The bottle was dark in color and difficult to see in the underbrush. But the label was green, gold and white.

"Here, let me," Rudy offered.

She stuffed her hand into a large plastic baggie and pulled up the bottle. It was a Smithwick's Imported Irish Ale. I'd never heard of it, but Rudy put the open bottle to her nose and smiled.

"It hasn't been here very long," she said. "I can smell fresh beer."

She flipped the baggie around the bottle so that it dropped into the bag, sealed it and then turned toward the Inn. "And look at that," she said, pointing.

We all turned. The back windows of the Inn were visible through a break in the trees.

"I bet that guy sat here last night enjoying a beer until he thought you'd gone to bed," she said. "Remember, we were out late last night for the trash run, so depending on what time he got here, he might have had to wait a while."

"Good job, Sherlock," Blair said with a smile. "Pretty soon, you'll be working for CSI."

"Goldie said she saw him light up a couple of cigarettes, so let's check around and see if we can find any cigarette butts," I said.

"I'm not picking those up," Blair said with distaste.

Doe and I wandered away from the path a few feet, searching through the grass and plants.

"Hoo-ha!" Blair whooped.

We all turned and rushed over to where she was standing on the other side of the path. She was pointing a long red fingernail into a bush, to where a cigarette butt had caught on a branch.

Rudy grabbed another baggie and stepped in front of her. "Here, Princess, let me get that for you." She flipped the butt into the bag, taking a whiff before closing it up. "It's hard to tell if it's fresh," she said. "It's pretty damp around here. C'mon, let's keep going. There might be more."

We finished our trek through the trees, but found nothing else until we neared the Singleton's home. Everyone referred to Goldie's place as the "Gnome Home" because she had an affinity for the little pointy-hatted creatures. She had over a hundred of them scattered throughout her outdoor gardens. Some were hiding behind bushes, while she'd arranged others in little vignettes on stumps. The large, two-story home had at least that many or more inside, tucked into every nook and cranny.

The gnomes started showing up along the path within a hundred feet of the Singleton property. Their little red hats rose above leaves, and their wrinkled faces poked out from behind bushes. Some were sitting on top of rocks or inside hollowed out logs. If you let your imagination run wild, it was a little creepy.

When we finally came out onto the beach in front of Goldie's, a voice hailed us from their back porch.

"What are you girls doing?" Goldie called out.

Goldie and Ben had built their home back in the Seventies, so the wood was dark and weathered, and the gardens were all mature and/or overgrown. A large deck stretched across the entire upper floor, facing the lake, shading a set of sliding glass doors on the ground floor that led into their recreation room.

Goldie was standing at the railing on their second floor deck. We could barely see her gray head above the top railing. I crossed the lawn and walked up toward the building so that I didn't have to yell.

"We're looking for evidence from that guy who attacked me last night," I said, gazing up at her.

She was looking at me through the space between the railings, and her gray eyes lit up. "Stay there! I'll be right down."

She disappeared into the house, causing Doe to say, "Oh, dear Lord, we'll be here all day."

Ben appeared on the deck holding a big mug of coffee. "Morning, Julia," he said.

I looked up at him. "Morning, Ben."

Ben was as big as Goldie was small. He had high cheek bones and a rim of white hair around the lower half of his head. He and Goldie had been married since they were eighteen, something not so normal since they were a mixed couple. They were mixed not only in ethnicity – Goldie was white, Ben was black – but in religion. Goldie was Jewish and Ben was Catholic.

They were known in the neighborhood as a happy and friendly couple, if not slightly offbeat. Goldie dressed like she was still living in the hippie days, and Ben liked to walk the neighborhood streets with a gold-topped walking stick and pipe that made him look like he was straight out of Wallingford, England. As an ex-military man, he held himself erect and would often gesture to things with the walking stick, as if he were giving a college lecture. On the other hand, Goldie liked her firearms and had discharged that old shotgun more than once, eliciting complaints from some of the neighbors. Her affinity for gnomes was seen as just another eccentricity.

"Goldie told me what happened last night. You okay?" he asked.

"Yes, I'm fine. I just miss Ahab."

He nodded. "I expect I'll be getting my shot gun back soon," he said, taking a sip of coffee. Goldie emerged through the sliding glass doors at the ground floor patio. She hurried out, dressed in the same faded hoodie she'd worn the night before.

"Did you find anything in the trees?" she asked, bustling up to us. "Cuz you know, I saw him stop for a light. He could've dropped his cigarette butt." She saw me glance up to the deck and followed my gaze. "I'm going to help the girls," she said to her husband. "Go back inside." She waved her hand dismissively at him, and Ben turned and disappeared through the bedroom door.

Goldie had thick, gray hair worn just below her ears in a pageboy style. And although she'd had two knee replacements, she moved with the frenetic energy of a four-year old.

"We found a beer bottle and a cigarette butt," I told her, moving away from the building. "Do you mind if we keep looking."

"No. I'll help," she said with enthusiasm. Her gray eyes twinkled. "Ben didn't believe me when I first told him about everything that happened. He doesn't hear too good anymore, you know, so he didn't hear me leave last night. But I said the police had come out and everything."

"And took your gun," I said.

"Yes," she replied. "He wasn't happy about that. You know how he is with the Second Amendment and all. They better return it soon, or he'll probably get some of his old military buddies to march on the police station. By the way, how are the dogs?"

"They're fine."

"Oh, they're good dogs, you know. Dachshunds. Had two of them when I was growing up. They love to bark though. I sure wish they'd caught that son-of-a gun. Our Dachshunds caught a kid trying to steal my bicycle once and nearly ripped his ankles up."

I knew all about her Dachshunds growing up. It was a story she told often, so I cut her off. "Yes, but sometimes I wish I had a German shepherd."

She shifted her weight from one foot to the other. Goldie carried an extra twenty pounds in her hips. It made her look as if she'd strapped on a pair of saddle bags. Every time she shifted her weight, she raised a saddle bag an inch or two.

"Hey wait a second," she said. "Let me get my gloves."

She disappeared into the house again as we spread out along the route where the path cut across her beach. She re-emerged a moment later with a muffler and heavy gloves.

"You know, Julia," she said, bustling up to me as I searched along the water's edge. "I went to bed late last night because I like to read. I'm reading a good mystery about a guy who murders old men because they remind him of his abusive father," she said.

I heard Doe sigh behind me.

"Anyway, you know Ben goes right to sleep. It's so irritating. Sometimes, he'll fall asleep right in the middle of a sentence…not his, mine," she chortled.

She got to laughing, and I found myself sighing myself.

"Anyway, I just had to finish that book, so I stayed up late. I was just getting ready for bed when I saw the light bobbing around outside."

"You saw a light, like a flashlight?" I asked her.

"Yeah. I think that's what it was. It bounced around like someone was moving from the parking lot to the trees," she said, using her fingers to pick up a piece of plastic left along the beach.

"What time did you see the bobbing light?" Blair asked her.

The two were standing close to each other. Goldie had to lift her gaze to answer Blair, who was 5' 8" – taller in her heeled boots.

"Oh, let me think. It was late. Maybe 1:30 or quarter to two," she said, putting a gloved finger to her chin.

Blair looked at me. "What time did we get…did we finish our…trip last night?" she asked.

I thought a moment. "I think it was around 12:45."

"So he wasn't here when we came home," Blair said.

"Do you remember what time you went to bed?" Doe asked me.

"I turned off lights and went right to my apartment," I replied. "But I took a shower." I stopped, remembering the two phone calls. "I didn't get to sleep until close to 2:00 though. Goldie, where did you see the light?" I asked.

"Over there," she said, pointing to the right. "And then it moved that way into the trees."

She had pointed towards a small parking lot that sat on a knoll in between Goldie's property and the Bartlett's on the far side. The parking lot was blocked from view, but the path picked up again on the other side of Goldie's lawn, weaving between some trees and up a slope.

"So you think whoever you saw was coming from the parking lot?" Rudy asked her.

"Yes. We get kids who do that all the time. There's no beach over there. The parking lot drops right off into the lake. So, they'll park there and come looking in this direction for a beach," Goldie said. "I have to chase them off. But I thought it could have been that guy who's been breaking into people's homes. I chased *him* off a couple of weeks ago, you know."

"Had he come from that direction, too," Rudy asked.

"Yeah," she replied. "I shot at him, but he got away."

"You're not thinking it could be the same person, are you?" I asked Rudy.

She shrugged her narrow shoulders. "Who knows? It seems coincidental, but let's go take a look," she said, moving off in that direction.

"I'm coming, too," Goldie announced.

And we were off again.

The five of us hurried across the back of Goldie's property and hit the small path that led to the parking lot. We climbed the slope and emerged into the tree shrouded lot.

There was room for two cars, but the lot was empty. People could access it by a short, one-lane paved road that came in from E. Shoreline Drive. A wooden railing across the end of the lot prevented cars from rolling right into the water.

We spread out once again, searching the pavement and the area around the perimeter of the asphalt.

"Here," Doe called out a few minutes later.

We converged on the spot. "Another bottle," she announced.

And sure enough, there was another empty Smithwick's bottle lying in the grass on the far side of the lot.

"Bag it," Rudy said.

Blair produced a bag and we rolled the bottle into it with a stick.

"Do you think that means something?" Goldie asked, as she poked her head around Doe.

"It's the same kind of beer bottle we found earlier. I think it means this guy was prepared for a long wait," Rudy said.

Blair was looking back and forth from where we'd picked up the bottle to the spot where a car would have been parked, facing the lake. "But, if he parked here," she said, "don't you think that bottle would have come from the passenger side window?"

Everyone stood and stared at the empty parking space for a moment.

"Meaning there were two people in the car?" Doe asked her.

"That's a good one, Blair," Goldie said, shifting her weight from foot to foot again.

"But wait," Rudy interjected, studying the area. "He could have backed the car in."

She was standing right where a car would have parked, but she was facing the street. Doe followed her gaze. While the lot could hold two, maybe three cars, it was a narrow, single lane road that led into it. And each side of the road dropped off into small but deep gullies.

"It would make sense," Doe said. "Especially if he wanted to get away quickly. If he'd pulled straight in, he would have had to turn around to leave. Backing out of here in the dark would have been tricky."

"So now what?" Blair said, pulling her coat around her. "It's cold out here."

Rudy turned to me. "I say we call Julia's new boyfriend."

At the mention of David, Goldie eyed me.

"Ask him about my shotgun," she said. "You miss your Ahab, but I miss my Betsy."

CHAPTER THIRTEEN

I wasn't surprised that Goldie had given her shotgun a name. I'd known many people who named favorite inanimate objects – and some *not* so inanimate. Although Blair's last name was Wentworth, as long as she'd been married to her current husband she'd referred to him as Mr. Billings. It was only recently that she'd admitted to me that the name referred to his private parts, based on a long weekend of lovemaking in Billings, Montana. However, now I couldn't look at him without thinking about that.

We were able to extricate ourselves from Goldie and said goodbye to her back door and tramped through the trees again with what we thought might be two good pieces of evidence: the cigarette butt and the beer bottles. Although I agreed that we should call David, I wasn't feeling very confident about it. Somehow, having him come all the way out to the Inn while he was in the middle of a murder investigation just to pick up what we *thought* might be evidence in a parrot theft, created a nervous sensation in the middle of my stomach.

Good thing calling David wasn't necessary. He and Detective Abrams were waiting for us at the Inn when we returned.

We met them in the breakfast room. David looked handsome in a blue shirt and tie, and I felt my heart speed up.

"What are you doing here?" I asked, attempting to keep my voice neutral.

"We heard about last night," he said in a scolding voice.

"I was going to call you about it," I said. "In fact, that's just what we were coming in to do." I tried to sound convincing, but it sounded like a lie even to me. I whipped out my baggie holding the first beer bottle.

David just stared at it. "What's that?"

The tone of his voice made me pause. "It's uh…evidence." I looked around at the girls for confirmation.

"Evidence of what?" he asked.

Crystal appeared behind him. "Julia," she said. "The man is here to fix the alarm."

"That's right," David said, turning to look at Crystal and then back to me. "How did your intruder get past your alarm system last night?"

"We had some problems with it over the weekend, so they came out on Sunday to fix it, but had to wait for a new keypad."

"So it wasn't even on?" David asked with his brows furrowed.

I gave him a haunted look. "No. What are the odds?"

"Too great," he said. "By the way, how do guests get in late at night when it *is* working?"

"We have an intercom at the front door that's hooked up to my apartment. I'm on call at night, and so I let them in. But if I know someone will be coming in late, I sometimes give them the code."

"So who knew your security system would be off last night?" Detective Abrams asked.

"I've thought that through. And there's a whole bunch of people, including some guests. But Peter Romero was the one who was working on it. The company is owned by his father. Anyway, I'll write down all the names for you."

Detective Abrams nodded. "Okay, and then we're going to need to talk to Peter Romero."

I turned to Crystal. "Who's here to fix the alarm?"

"It's *Mr.* Romero," Crystal said. "He's in the utility room."

"Can you get him for us?" I asked her.

She turned and disappeared down the hallway. A moment later, she returned with a tall, gangly man with angular features and thinning light brown hair.

"Roger," I said.

"Julia," he replied, his eyes filled with pain. "Again, I'm so sorry. I have the keypad and should have the system up and running in about thirty minutes." He stepped forward and put a gentle hand on my shoulder. "Are you okay?"

"Yes," I said, looking at him. "I'm just sick about Ahab, though."

"Of course," he said, his voice tempered with empathy.

"Roger, this is Detective Abrams and Detective Franks," I said, gesturing to the two men on either side of me. "They wanted a chance to speak with you and maybe Peter."

He straightened up and extended a hand to Detective Abrams. "Happy to meet you," he said, shaking hands with Detective Abrams. "Well, not happy…I mean, under the circumstances, well, never mind."

"It's okay," Detective Abrams said. "We were just wondering why the alarm system was down last night."

"We had to pick up a new keypad. Peter was here working on the system until late on Sunday and the place that stocks them was closed by the time he finished. We had to wait to order a new one. It just came in this morning. I never thought…I mean, boy…" he ran his long fingers through the thinning strands of his hair.

"Mr. Romero," David said. "Did you or your son tell anyone that the system was off?"

His eyes grew wide. "No. Of course not. We would never do that. Peter had another job this morning, so I offered to come over and get it installed right away."

"How did you find out about the break-in?" Detective Abrams asked with a suspicious curl to his brows.

Roger paused and then glanced at me. "A police officer stopped by earlier this morning to talk to me. And then Julia called."

"We need to talk with your son," Detective Abrams said.

Roger nodded. "Um, okay," he said. "Sure. He's over at the Cranberrys' house, by Island Crest Park. Do you want me to call him?"

He reached into his pocket for his cell phone. Detective Abrams put up his hand to stop him.

"No. That's okay. We'll drive over. You finish here and get Ms. Applegate's system up and running."

"Of course," he said. "Yes, I'll do that."

He glanced at me, glanced at Detective Abrams and then turned to return down the hallway.

"Why don't we go into the dining room?" I said, spying the Brewsters hovering in the background. I led the men into the dining room.

"So what's going on, Julia?" David asked.

"Why don't we all sit down," I offered.

I sat at the head of the long dining room table, and David sat to my left.

"We think that Ahab might have been stolen by whoever killed Trudy," I said.

The men exchanged curious glances.

"What makes you think that?" Detective Abrams asked with his sharp blue eyes narrowed with skepticism.

"I don't know if you remember, but at the Christmas Eve party, he squawked, '*I want to kill Dana Finkle.*' Dana accused me of teaching that to him, but I didn't. Not that I'd never thought of locking her in a tower with a big red hourglass, just like Dorothy," I said.

"Julia!" Rudy said.

"Sorry," I said, snapping out of my *Wizard of Oz* reverie.

"So you think Ahab overheard someone say that they wanted to kill Mrs. Finkle?" Detective Abrams said, hiding a smile.

He sat back, his broad shoulders stretching the confines of his shirt. I snuck a glance at Blair, who was openly staring.

"You've said often enough that you don't believe in coincidences," Rudy said.

"True," he agreed.

"I mean, c'mon," Doe began. "Otherwise, why would someone break into the Inn just to steal a bird?"

"We wondered the same thing," David said. He turned to me. "So what about the beer bottle?"

"I saw a light outside last night…out there," I said, pointing out the window toward the trees. "And Goldie – she's the one who had the shotgun – she says she saw someone light up a cigarette while waiting in the trees. Anyway, we went out to see if we could find anything he might have left behind."

"And look what we found!" Blair exclaimed, producing the baggie with the cigarette butt.

Detective Abrams reached out and took it from Blair. The two men shared a knowing look.

"What?" I said.

"You realize we couldn't use this in a court of law," David said.

"Why not?"

"Because there was no chain of custody established," Detective Abrams said. "There's no way to guarantee where this came from or that you didn't somehow compromise the evidence."

"Or plant it," Rudy said with a disappointed sigh.

Detective Abrams shrugged. "Right. But it still might be helpful. Where did you find these?"

"There's a flat rock out in those trees," I said. "Maybe halfway through."

"A place that's hidden from view, but that just happens to have a perfect view of the Inn," Rudy added.

"We think whoever it was sat there and waited until most of the lights went out in the Inn," I said.

"We also found this in a small parking lot on the other side of Goldie's home," Rudy said, producing the second bottle. "The path from the parking lot leads directly to the beach in front of her home and then picks up again, running through the grove of trees to the Inn. We think he parked there."

She placed the bag on the table and slid it across to Detective Abrams. He picked it up and just stared at it, before sneaking a second glance at David.

"What?" I said again. "C'mon, you guys know something you're not saying."

Detective Abrams sighed. "We found a bottle just like this hidden behind a bush at the library yesterday morning. We had no way of knowing who left it there. But it's the same brand."

"Wow," Blair whispered. "We really *did* find evidence."

"But that also means that Ahab *was* stolen because of Trudy's murder," Doe said.

"That's why I said what you found might still be helpful," Detective Abrams said. "This is a very rare beer. In fact, there's only a couple of places in Seattle that sell it. You didn't happen to get a look at the guy who attacked you last night, did you?"

"No," I said with a sigh. It was too dark, and he was behind me most of the time. I got a whiff of his cologne though. And Minnie bit him in the face."

"That could be good," David said. "Do you know what the cologne was?" David asked.

"No, but a kid that just checked out today was wearing it."

I told them about Mr. Dalton. David took notes, but they weren't encouraging that Mr. Dalton was our suspect. After all, his face was unblemished. In other words, no bite marks from an angry Dachshund.

"So the odds are high that the same person left the bottles behind, don't you think?" Rudy surmised. Detective Abrams nodded. "We didn't touch the bottles," she said. "You might still be able to get fingerprints off them. We picked them up with the baggies. But they're fresh."

David nodded. "We think the one we found at the library was too. But that one was pretty badly compromised because of the storm that night. These," he said, nodding toward the two on the table, "might give us more information."

Blair grinned. "So, we did good?"

A brief smiled flashed across Detective Abram's handsome face. "Yeah, you did good." He leaned forward and rested his elbows on the table. "We also found a note caught in the bushes up at the library. We can't be sure it has anything to do with Ms. Bascom's murder, though."

"What did it say?" I asked him.

He paused before saying, "Ain't karma a bitch?"

"That's weird," Blair said.

"That doesn't ring a bell to any of you?" he asked.

We all shook our heads.

"Well, now we need to figure out who might have made that comment about Mrs. Finkle in front of Ahab. Think back," he said to me. "Who was at the Inn that night that might actually want to kill her?"

I shook my head. "I've already done that."

"Besides, *everyone* at that party probably wanted to kill her," Blair said.

He sighed and leaned back again. "It's true. She isn't well-liked. We've been researching her background on the island, and she's sued half the people who live here."

"Including me," I said with a smirk.

"But has she ever hurt anyone?" Rudy asked. "I mean to the point that someone would want that kind of revenge?"

David shook his head. "No, not that we can find. Most of her lawsuits are pretty frivolous. She's been successful in extracting some money from a few people, but more often than not, the suits are dropped. But we're still interviewing people. And we're looking into her background."

At the mention of her background, I flinched. I snuck a glance at Rudy, who gave an almost imperceptible shake of her head. We weren't going to admit to the trash run.

"She's actually more irritating and exasperating than anything," Doe said. "Not worth going to prison over."

Detective Abrams pushed his chair back and stood up. "We'll see what the bottles show us," he said. "Meanwhile, keep thinking about who might have made that comment in front of Ahab."

They both stopped at the door to the hallway.

"And next time something happens, call us," David said firmly. "The patrol guys don't know the difference between a routine break-in and what might be connected to a murder case."

"Okay, but I hope there won't *be* a next time," I said.

CHAPTER FOURTEEN

Shortly after the detectives left, Roger reappeared.

"The keypad is up and running," he said. "But you really should equip your upstairs windows with alarms, Julia. After what happened, I'll give you the labor for free. What d'you say? I could schedule it early next week."

I nodded. "Let me talk to my bookkeeper. I should have done it right from the beginning. I'll give you a call."

"Well, again, I'm so sorry about Ahab. Everything is still under warranty, so there's no charge, but…well, it doesn't make up for your loss."

I caught a tear forming and reached up to swipe it away. "Thanks."

He reached out a long arm and placed a hand on my shoulder. "If you only knew how badly I feel, Julia. Please, let me know if there's anything I can do."

"I will. Thank you."

Roger gave me a weak smile and left. I turned to the girls who were waiting in the breakfast room.

"C'mon, Julia," Rudy said. "Let's get going. I'm booked this afternoon."

We each grabbed our beverage of choice and headed for the garage, which sat between the Inn and the guest house. As we came around the corner, we encountered Jose´. He had the garage door open and was staring through the van's open back doors.

"Um, I can explain," I said, coming up behind him.

He turned dark eyes my way, his handsome features twisted into amused curiosity. "You told me to pick up a bachelor's chest from the early 1900s today, but it looks like you cleaned up trash along the highway instead," he said with a smile.

We had formed a half circle around him, all staring at the mess of bulging garbage bags and dirty plastic bags in the back of the van.

"Very funny," I replied. "But there's a reason all of that mess is in there."

"And I'm sure we're waiting to hear it," a voice cut in from the back.

We all turned to find April standing behind us, wrapped up in a faux fur-lined coat. Her arms were crossed over her chest, and she had a muffler around her neck. Instead of a pleasant smile though, she had a look of restrained patience on her face.

"When you said last night that you hoped I wouldn't need the van today, I assumed you meant that you had a pickup or a delivery. But apparently, you've joined Doe in the business of picking up other people's garbage."

"No, just Dana Finkle's," Blair blurted.

Rudy shot Blair a look of reproach as April's eyes expanded with recognition.

"Ah, I see," she said, stepping forward to stare at the jumble of cardboard boxes, empty paper bags and trash that littered the back of the van. "Let me guess. You think you're going to find something in there that will help you solve Trudy's murder."

"We need to know more about Dana," I said. "And why someone might want to kill her."

"And you think you're going to learn that from her trash." April's dark eyes glinted with skepticism.

Blair was standing closest to the back of the van, and she reached out a manicured fingernail to poke the label on a flattened shipping box. "Well, who knows, maybe we'll find the receipt for a bunch of sex toys in there."

"And that would be important because…" April let her sentence draw out.

"More likely we'll find an empty tube of Preparation H," Doe said cynically.

I let out an exasperated sigh. "Look, we'll be done here in about an hour. Then you can go pick up that chest," I said to Jose'.

He shrugged his shoulders. "Doesn't matter to me. I have plenty to do." He ambled away, and I turned to April. "By the way, we went out and searched the beach area like you suggested, and we found a couple of empty bottles from a rare kind of beer in the trees. The detectives were here and said they found one just like it at the library."

Her eyes fluttered. "So whoever took Ahab really might be the guy who killed Trudy."

I nodded. "It looks that way. We still need to figure out who it was that said they'd like to kill Dana in front of Ahab, though. Can you think back on that night? Try to remember if you saw anyone hanging around his cage?"

"Sure. By the way, I just heard on the news that Dana has formally dropped out of the mayoral race. She had a short press conference downtown. Meanwhile, I'll leave you to it," she said, nodding to the back of the van. "Don't catch any diseases." She left us with a wave of her hand as she disappeared around the corner of the garage.

"Dana doesn't have any diseases, does she?" Blair asked.

Rudy sighed. "No, Blair. She just has a diseased mind. C'mon, let's get started. I have a fast-pitch meeting this afternoon."

"Let me get some big plastic bags," I said.

I ran over to a workbench and pulled out a box of leaf bags. I handed bags to everyone and shook mine open.

"Here. Why don't we shove all the torn up boxes into this one?"

As the girls began to pick through the trash and toss cardboard into my bag, my mind wandered back to Dana and the campaign.

"So, she actually did it," I said.

"What?" Rudy asked.

"Dropped out of the race. I wasn't sure she would. I think she wanted to be mayor more than anything," I said.

"Because it would give her what she doesn't have," Doe said. "Power."

"Exactly," I replied.

We worked in silence for a moment, and then Doe addressed Rudy. "You think your new knee will handle fast-pitch this year?"

"I hope so," Rudy said as she separated out a bunch of paper goods and stuffed them into a second bag. "I miss it. And I can't keep up my skills if I don't play."

"Are you going to try out for pitcher again?" Blair asked.

"Not sure," Rudy replied. "My shoulder has been acting up. I've been getting some PT to loosen it up."

Doe was folding up a box to fit into the bag. "The whole team is over 50, isn't it? You guys should be taking it easy."

"That's why it's called *senior* fast pitch," Rudy said with a sneer. "Instead of an 80 mile an hour pitch, I can only do 60 now. But I can still heat up the catcher's glove," she said with a seductive wink.

"Is Colin Peters still your catcher?" Blair asked, referring to the retired athletic coach from one of the high schools. Rudy nodded. "Well, I'd like to warm up more than his catcher's mitt," Blair said as she tossed something into the bag.

"Blair," Doe scolded her.

"Hey," she replied with a lift to her eyebrows. "Rudy enjoys *her* game with soft balls, and I enjoy mine."

Rudy let out a belly laugh. "Well no surprise there."

"Okay, c'mon, let's take this stuff over here," I said.

We dragged the bags to the front of the garage, where we had a large table set up to sort through boxes we sometimes picked up at storage facility sales. I pulled out some folding chairs, closed the garage door and turned on a space heater, while we all sat down and began to sort through the bags.

"Okay, why don't we divide this stuff up?" I suggested. "Let's collect receipts here," I said, indicating a spot in the middle of the table. "And letters and invoices over there," I said, gesturing to my left.

"Here's a box for things we don't know what to do with," Rudy said, lifting up a box and placing it at the end of the table.

"Okay, ready, set, go," I said.

We spent the next fifteen minutes sorting and organizing what was in the trash bags. Anything that was obviously junk was thrown into a garbage can I dragged over from the back of the garage.

"Hey, this is interesting," Blair exclaimed. "It's a letter from an attorney warning Dana to cease and desist." Blair looked up and handed the letter to Rudy, who skimmed it.

"It's regarding someone named Eloise Radle," Rudy said. "That's not a name I recognize."

"Me neither," I said. "What else does it say?"

Rudy studied the letter. "It says that if Dana doesn't stop harassing his client about her back porch light, the attorney will get a court order to force her to back off."

"The back porch light?" I said, shaking my head. "What in the world is she complaining about?"

Rudy looked up from the paper in her hands. "This woman lives next door to Dana and has a spotlight in her backyard that shines into Dana's kitchen."

"Her kitchen?" I said. "Where she's probably never trying to sleep. God, sometimes I think Dana is just a ridiculous woman. Where's the attorney located?"

Rudy glanced back at the sheet of paper. "Seattle."

"I think we ought to set that one aside and check into it," Doe said.

"I don't know," I said. "It seems awfully petty to me."

"But not to this woman," Rudy said, setting the letter on the table. "After all, she hired an attorney. We shouldn't judge at this point. Just gather information."

Several more minutes went by until I found something that raised my eyebrows.

"Hey, how about this?" I said, waving a receipt in my hands. "Dana bought a gun."

"You're kidding!" Doe said. "When?"

"Um…two months ago," I replied. I glanced around at everyone. "I don't think I like the thought of Dana Finkle with a gun."

"That's cuz *you're* always in her cross hairs," Rudy said.

"Very funny," I said with a grimace. I glanced at Doe, wondering if she'd told Blair or Rudy about her own recent purchase. But she seemed oblivious to the reference.

Blair snickered and then said. "Up until now, Dana has only taken pot shots at people with her mouth. A loaded gun in the hands of a woman like that puts a *whole* new meaning on the phrase, 'pistol packing mama.'"

"Maybe Clay bought it," I said with a smile.

"Well, I just found a receipt for Viagra," Rudy announced with a grin. "Maybe up until now he's hasn't been able to discharge his gun at all."

Blair snorted with laughter. "Yes, but now that he has both a gun *and* Viagra, Dana would be like, 'Is that a gun in your pocket, Clay? Or are you just glad to see me?'"

"Oh God," Doe said, laughing. "Can you imagine the two of them having sex?"

"No," Rudy said, making a face. "She has the slimiest personality I know, and he's the most stoic."

"Uptight is more like it," Doe said, throwing something into the middle of the table. "He always seems like he's constipated."

"Would you smile if you were married to Dana Finkle?" I asked, as I sorted through more old receipts.

"I wonder if Dana even knows how to use it," Rudy said.

"What? The gun they bought? Or the one Clay was born with?" Blair asked with a mischievous smile.

"She probably couldn't tell the difference," Rudy quipped. "She'd be like 'How does this thing work, Clay?'" Rudy sniped, attempting to sound like Dana.

"'But Honey, where's the trigger?'" Doe said, joining in with a hearty laugh.

We all began laughing so hard, we had to stop what we were doing. It was a full ten seconds before Blair added between snatches of breath, "Or...or, in the throes of passion, Clay might say, 'Pleeeze honey, forget the trigger...and just...just bite the bullet."

We finally lost it and just doubled over in laughter. My stomach hurt, and Blair rolled out of her chair and onto the garage floor. It took a good sixty seconds until the frivolity died down. Blair dusted herself off and climbed back into her chair wiping moisture from her eyes. The rest of us took deep breaths to quell the mirth and went back to work.

"By the way," Doe said, getting control of her laughter. "Why isn't Clay a suspect? Don't they say they always look at the family first?"

"He must have a good alibi," I said. "But boy, she sure does spend a lot of money," I added, reading several of the receipts in my hands. "Here's a receipt for $500 worth of vitamins."

"Is Dana a health nut?" Doe asked.

"Hard to believe," I said. "She doesn't look healthy. But here's another receipt for a fancy kitchen range." I looked up at my companions. "The bill was for over $10,000!"

"For a stove?" Rudy exclaimed.

I nodded. "Hey, maybe Clay wanted to kill her just so he wouldn't go broke."

Rudy sat back in her chair. "You know, I've always wondered where the Finkles get their money. I mean, I suppose a collection agency could do pretty well. But Dana's antique store can't pull in much, and yet they live in a million dollar home, drive expensive cars, and although Dana dresses like a birthday party clown, her clothes are expensive."

Doe shrugged. "It could be family money."

"Is there a way to look into their finances?" Blair asked.

"I'm sure the police are doing that," I said. "But if it *was* Clay, it wouldn't be the first time someone wanted to kill their spouse for the life insurance money because they were overextended. I think I heard that he's opening another office somewhere."

Doe raised an eyebrow. "Think there's any way you can find out what's going on from David?"

Before I could answer, Blair cut in, "Hey, I may have found the smoking gun...no pun intended," she said, looking around at us.

"What is it?" Doe asked.

She held up an empty white envelope. "The return address is the Blankenship Law Firm in Seattle."

"Let me see that," Doe said, reaching out for it.

She took the envelope, studied the return address and then dropped her hand to the table.

"Cora Blankenship is a divorce attorney," she announced.

"One of the best around," Blair agreed. "I've used her twice."

"So Clay is divorcing Dana?" I asked.

"No," Doe said bluntly. "Cora only represents women."

I inhaled. "So it's *Dana* who wants a divorce?"

"Wait a minute," Rudy interrupted. "Maybe this attorney just sent Dana a campaign check."

"No," Doe said. "I know Cora. We sat on the opera board together for many years. She doesn't support political campaigns. She says it's because she never knows who her next client will be." Doe glanced at the envelope again. "No, I'd bet my mother's ruby engagement ring that Dana has hired Cora to divorce Clay."

"So maybe Clay wanted to kill her before she took all of his money in a divorce," Rudy said.

"You don't know the half of it," Doe continued. "Cora Blankenship's whole reputation is built on the fact that she breaks the husband's bank accounts. These women walk away with millions. She's a ball buster."

The three of us turned slowly to look at Blair, whose eyes lit up in defense.

"No, no, no. I didn't have to do that. My boys all wanted to take care of me. I just went to Cora because…well, because she's so good."

"Maybe your *boys*, as you put it, took care of you *because* you went to her," Rudy said with a sarcastic twist to her mouth. "Sometimes a threat is worth more than bringing in the actual artillery."

"I wonder if that's why Dana wouldn't let Clay hire a detective," I said. "She didn't want to be indebted to him."

"Well, this changes things if Clay knew about this," Doe said.

"So maybe everybody really *does* have a reason to want Dana dead," I said.

Rudy had just opened a manila envelope and dropped out a stack of photos. Doe leaned over to glance at them.

"Those are pictures of kids," Doe said in surprise, pulling a couple of them toward her.

"But I thought she didn't have any kids," Blair said, grabbing one to study it.

I picked up two of the photos, too. One was a young boy about eight years old. He had coarse, black hair, a round face and dark eyes. The other picture was of two boys. One looked to be about eleven or twelve. He was overweight and had light brown hair. He wore glasses and had his arm around a younger boy. The boys looked like brothers, but the younger one had a birthmark across one cheek that looked like the Nike swoop. He was very thin and vaguely familiar.

"These aren't Dana's kids," I said.

"Then whose are they?" Doe asked.

We passed ten photos around. They were all pictures of young boys. Some were action shots of the kids playing sports or games at parties. Others had them posing in places like a living room or bedroom.

Meanwhile, Rudy had continued looking through the small plastic bag Dana had brought out the night before. "What the heck is this?" she asked. She pulled out a handful of photo paper that had been cut into strips. "It looks like someone cut up some photos."

She laid some of the strips of paper on the table.

"Can you tell what the photo was?" I asked, craning my head to look across the table.

"No," she said, moving the slips of paper around. "But it looks like they came from more than one picture."

"Hold on a minute," Blair said. "I found some of those strips over here, too." She was sitting at the end of the table and had found similar strips of paper in a different bag of trash. "I wonder what they are."

Blair put hers on the table and shoved them down to Rudy. Rudy leaned over and spread them all out. Blair scooted her chair around and began moving strips back and forth on the table like she was working a jigsaw puzzle. For the next several minutes, she and Rudy worked together until a couple of the photos began to take shape.

"Uh, oh," Doe said, reaching over and grasping a single strip of paper. "This doesn't look good."

"What do you mean?" I asked.

She glanced up at me and turned the thin strip of paper around so that I could see it.

"Oh!" I exclaimed.

The strip showed the bare upper thigh of someone and the tip of a penis. I glanced down at the table. Another strip showed the side of a boy's face.

"Wait. That boy looks like one of the kids from the photos that haven't been cut up," I said.

"Yeah, the kid with the birthmark," Doe agreed.

"What the hell?" Rudy exclaimed. "Oh, my God!" she said, sitting back in her chair, the muscles in her face tensed.

"What is it?" Doe and I said in unison.

Rudy put the strip in her hand down with the half completed photo on the table in front of her. We all stood up to get a better view, and then all three of us gasped.

It was the picture of a naked boy posing with one hand on his hip in front of a pin ball machine.

"Oh no," I said, dropping back down in my chair.

"No wonder she wanted to get rid of this stuff quickly," Doe said. "I wonder if there are more."

It took another twenty-five minutes to assemble a dozen photos of nude boys. I had found a roll of clear tape so that we could affix them together and then we sat back, the enthusiasm for discovery destroyed.

"I wonder who the pictures belong to," Rudy said. "Are they Dana's? Or Clay's?"

"Who would have guessed Clay was a pedophile?" Blair said.

"We don't know these are his," I said. "If they are, he may have never acted on his impulses. Maybe he just likes looking at them."

"Isn't that still a crime?" Doe asked.

"Not necessarily," Rudy said. "I covered a child pornography case once and there are differing views on what constitutes pornography."

"You mean just having pictures of nude kids might not be illegal?" I asked.

"Right. It's all in how they're used. If you distribute them for someone else's pleasure, then that's pornography. But the case I covered was a guy who had taken photos and videos of his young daughter, but never did anything with them. He kept them all for himself. She was only seven at the time, and the defense attorney tried to make the case that parents often take pictures of their children taking baths and the like."

"Were these pictures of her in the bathtub?" Blair asked.

"No. He'd used a telephoto lens to take pictures of her from the backyard when she was getting dressed and also set up a video camera in the closet of her bedroom."

"That's disgusting," Blair spat.

"He didn't get off, did he?" Doe asked. We all turned to stare at her. "No, I didn't mean it that way," she said quickly. "I meant that he wasn't acquitted, was he?"

"No. Not in the end. But it was interesting how the defense presented their case. They tried to make the argument that since he hadn't distributed them to anyone else, he hadn't committed a crime."

"Even though he was probably *getting off* as you say, just by looking at them," I said.

"Right," Rudy replied. "It's just like now with cell phones. You've seen those cases where a couple of kids will take nude selfies. They only get in trouble if they send them out to anyone else. Did you know that approximately 1 in 16 kids will suffer some form of sexual abuse?"

"Those aren't good odds," Doe said.

"No. And around 80% of the kids abused are abused by a parent," Rudy said with a raised eyebrow.

"In this case, maybe a foster parent," I said.

"I wish there was some kind of radar that could tell you when someone was a predator," Blair said. "It would make things so much easier. Put them in jail *before* they ruin some poor kid's life."

"Well, these all look like pretty old pictures," Doe said, fingering the corner of one of them. "Several of them are Polaroid's and the colors are faded."

"And look at the clothes and hair styles," I added, pointing to them. "I bet these pictures are at least…I don't know, thirty years old."

"Wait, look at this one," Blair said, gesturing to a reconstructed photo sitting near her. "There's a man in the background."

The picture was of the boy with the Nike swoop. He was on the floor on his hands and knees in front of a full-length mirror, with a dog collar around his neck. In the mirror was the reflection of a man holding the camera and taking the picture.

"That's not Clay," Doe said. "Clay is small. That guy must be at least six feet tall. And his face is hidden behind the camera."

"Maybe this is her first husband, when she lived in Vancouver," I said, studying the picture.

"Could be," Doe said. "Or maybe these aren't even hers."

"But why would she have them?" Blair asked.

"The bigger question now is what do we do with them?" Rudy said. "Should we give them to the police?"

There was a moment of silence.

"No," I said. "First of all, we were just told that the bottles and cigarette butt we found can't be used as evidence because we broke the chain of custody. We certainly broke the chain of custody on this one."

"But didn't we also just establish that it may be a crime to have these?" Doe asked. "I mean, I'm not sure they should even be in *our* possession."

"But if we take them to the police, we'll have to tell them how we got them," I argued. "I'm not sure I'm ready to admit that. And besides, we could be implicating someone for nothing. Frankly, we don't know who these belong to. Let's see what else we can find out first."

Rudy didn't look convinced, but she relented. "Okay. This gives me more ammunition with my newspaper friends down in Vancouver," Rudy said. "I'll drive down there tomorrow and do some checking around."

"Do we care about this Eloise Radle?" Doe asked, picking up the cease and desist letter from the attorney.

"No," I said. "I don't think so. Somehow wanting to kill someone over a porch light seems extreme. But let's keep her name just in case." Doe nodded in agreement. "Okay, I have to get down to City Hall and talk to Tony. Meanwhile, is there any way we can find out more about why Dana contacted the divorce attorney?" I asked.

"Cora is tight-lipped when it comes to her clients," Doe said. "We'd have better luck talking with some of Dana's friends."

"And just who would that be?" Rudy asked cynically.

I smiled. "Believe it or not, I think she just joined the 'Others.'"

"Oh no," Blair exclaimed. "I don't know who went to the dark side first, her or them."

I waved my hand in the air. "Oh, for heaven's sake, they're just another book club."

"Not anymore," Blair was quick to say. "First they criticized us for reading what they called trashy genre books, and now they've admitted Dana to their ranks. They really *are* our rival book club."

"Well, speaking of book clubs, now that I'm not running for mayor, we don't have an excuse not to get ours started again," I said.

We began throwing things back into the trash bags.

"I agree," Rudy said. "There's a new book out about the downfall of the Russian aristocracy I'd like to read."

Blair glanced up. "Oh, gee, I can hardly wait."

Rudy gave her a scowl. "Don't tell me…you'd rather read *Fifty Shades of Grey*."

Blair shrugged. "Already read it…twice."

"Well, I didn't know Dana liked to read," Doe said.

"She probably doesn't," I replied. "But she knows the Others don't like us, and so of course, she likes them."

"The enemy of my enemy is my friend," Doe murmured.

"Well, enemies or not, I think we hit the jackpot today," Rudy said, picking up one of the taped photos. "Now we just need to figure out what it all means."

CHAPTER FIFTEEN

We put the photos of the boys back into the envelope, but kept out Cora Blankenship's envelope and the letter from Eloise Radle's attorney. Doe told us to leave the rest of the trash in bags outside the garage and her guys would pick it up the next day. Then, everyone left, and I went inside to fix some lunch.

By two o'clock I was entering City Hall, heading for the City Administrator's office. I'd called ahead and made an appointment with Tony, but ran into Mayor Frum just as he was leaving.

"Hello, Julia," he hailed me as I stepped off the elevator. "What brings you down here?"

"I have a meeting with Tony," I said, not wanting to divulge the reason for the meeting. "Where are you off to?"

"Another ribbon cutting," he said with a broad smile. "One of the highlights of my job is welcoming a new business to town."

"Oh? Who's moving in?" I asked.

"Island Florists have finished remodeling the old Potter building," he said. "So now we'll have a lovely florist and gift shop right downtown."

I smiled. "That's wonderful. I'll have to stop by and order something."

"You do that, Julia. Well, gotta run."

With that, he grabbed the elevator and disappeared behind the closing doors. I entered the outer offices of the Mayor and City Administrator and announced myself. Tony's door was open and he quickly came to greet me and guide me into his office. Even though he was left-handed, he extended his right hand, since his left hand was one of those prosthetics that looked like a real hand, but wasn't very functional.

"Good to see you, Julia," he said with a smile.

Tony was medium height, with dark hair, hazel eyes, and smooth, dark skin. While somewhat shy, his broad smile and intense gaze enveloped you and made you feel you were the only person in the room. He lived in a modest house on the island with his wife and young daughter.

He offered me the chair across from his desk and then sat behind it. Because his lower left leg had been blown off by a land mine in Afghanistan, he wore a prosthetic there, too. But he didn't let it slow him down. He kept active by skiing in the winter and kayaking in the spring and summer.

"What can I do for you, Julia? If it's about my endorsement, you have it," he declared. "I think you'd make a fine mayor."

I laughed. "No. It's not about that. In fact," I said, pausing. "I...uh...well, I've decided to drop out of the race."

"Oh no, I'm sorry to hear that," he said with a genuine look of disappointment.

I sighed. "Yes. You probably heard about Trudy Bascom's murder."

He grabbed a pencil and began tapping it on the desk. "Yes. Tragic."

"You know the target was actually Dana Finkle?"

He nodded. "The Chief of Police gave us a briefing. I'm not surprised by that. I didn't really know Mrs. Bascom very well, but she seemed like a very gentle person. I can't imagine anyone wanting to harm her."

"Not like Dana?" I added.

He winced. "Let's face it. You know better than anyone what she can be like. Last month at the City Council meeting she said that people with disabilities were forcing the rest of the general public to make too many changes that interfered with their freedoms. She knew perfectly well I was sitting right there."

"She has her moments," I lamented. "But no one should try to kill her."

"No," he said, rolling the pencil into his fist. "I suppose no one should do that." He dropped his gaze to his desk and seemed lost in thought.

"Anyway," I said, bringing his attention back to me. "I'm here for another reason. Dana agreed to drop out of the mayoral race if I would."

He looked at me curiously. "Really?"

"Yes," I said. "I never really wanted to run for mayor. But I was convinced if I didn't run that Dana would win. And I couldn't stand for that."

I felt my temperature rise at just the thought of her amphibian gaze contemplating me from behind the mayor's desk, had she won.

"I know what you mean," he said with a shake of his head. "I'd already started looking for a new job. So, now what?" he asked. "I don't remember anyone else filing."

I shifted in my seat. "No one else has filed that I'm aware of. That's why I think *you* should do it."

He stared at me for a moment, his facial muscles frozen in place. He finally took a breath and said, "You've got to be kidding."

"I'm not," I declared with certainty. "Tony, you're the most competent city administrator we've ever had. You're smart. You're hard-working. You're good with people. And you love this island. What more could we want?"

"But I'm not a politician."

"Neither am I, and yet you and many others were willing to overlook that and endorse me."

He got up and moved awkwardly to stare out the window. "After the military, I thought I'd have my own company. My uncle owned a construction company, and I worked my way up through the trades when I was younger. I could hammer and plaster with the best of them. I thought since I'd worked in so many areas of construction, I'd come back after my service and build up my own crew over time." He held out his left hand and glanced down at it. "But Afghanistan changed all of that," he said, flexing the prosthetic fingers. "I had to have a lot of rehab as a result of my injuries, and I suffered from PTSD. I had to spend a lot of time in counseling. My chance was lost." He turned to me. "So I went back to school and got a degree in business and came to work for the city. I'm happy with the job I have. But it's not what I really planned to do. And I'm not sure I *want* to be mayor."

I stood up. "Just promise me you'll think about it," I said. "The filing deadline isn't for a couple of weeks. And my guess is that once it becomes known that both Dana and I have dropped out, a long list of wannabes will quickly file. We need someone who knows what they're doing, Tony. That's you." I gave him my warmest smile.

He nodded. "I'll think about it," he said.

"Good. Now I've got to get going," I said, standing up. "By the way, I hope we'll see you at the reception for Jason Spears on Friday."

"Yes, I plan to be there. I'm not sure I believe in ghosts like you do, but it should be interesting. Is he going to read from his book?"

"I think so. But they're also bringing all of their equipment to do some ghost hunting. I just hope our ghosts cooperate," I said with a smile.

He walked me to the door of his office. As we emerged into the reception area, we were confronted with none other than Detectives Abrams and Franks getting off the elevator. I thought they were following me until I saw the look on David's face as they entered the outer offices. Both he and Detective Abrams stared right past me and at Tony. Detective Abrams reached behind his back, extracted a pair of handcuffs and stepped forward.

"Mr. Morales," he said, "You're under arrest for the murder of Trudy Bascom."

I'm sure he must have finished the whole Miranda warning as he clasped on the handcuffs, but all I heard was a buzzing sound. Everyone in the office stood like statues, staring at Tony with a mixture of fascination and horror. Poor Tony's face had disintegrated from initial confusion to fear. I felt lightheaded enough that I had to reach out to steady myself by grabbing onto the nearest desk.

"But…what do you mean?" I stammered. "He couldn't have done it."

Detective Abrams gave me a stern look. "The evidence proves otherwise."

He took Tony by the arm and escorted him out the door. David followed, but I caught up to him.

"David! What are you doing?"

He turned to me with a look of apology. "The text to Dana came from his IP address, and we found the murder weapon in his garage. It's a good arrest, Julia."

"But he didn't do it!" I pleaded.

"You don't know that," he said, inching closer to me. "Now stay out of this and let us do our job."

And with that, my new-found boyfriend was gone, along with the best mayoral candidate we had.

CHAPTER SIXTEEN

I slow-walked out of City Hall in a virtual daze. Even the incessant drizzle of rain that threatened to flatten my hair wasn't enough to make me pop open my umbrella; I had too much on my mind. The man I had just nominated to be our next mayor had been arrested for Trudy Bascom's murder.

I made it to the car, got in, and sat there in stunned silence. Tony Morales had fought for his country, been injured, earned a Purple Heart, and come home a hero. Even though the military had taught him *how* to kill, I couldn't imagine he could brutally murder someone. That took a different kind of person.

I pulled out my cell phone and called Doe to relate the news, but she'd already heard it from her niece, Kayla, who worked in the mayor's office.

"They must've had a good reason for arresting him, Julia," Doe said.

"David said that it was someone from Tony's IP address that hacked my email. They believe it's Tony. I just can't believe that," I said. "Tony is my friend. Why would he willingly implicate me in a murder?"

"To save himself," Doe retorted. "That's what murderers do."

"David also said they found the murder weapon in Tony's garage."

"He didn't say what it was?" Doe asked.

"No. But, God, Tony just told me that he grew up in the construction trade and that he used to be good with a hammer."

"Well, I have other news about Tony," Doe said.

The doomsday tone of her voice forced my heart rate to speed up. "What is it?"

"Kayla said she overheard an argument between the mayor and Tony last week. Something having to do with Trudy."

I exhaled. "Trudy?"

"She didn't hear much. But she said it sounded like the mayor was chewing Tony out for using Trudy to spy on Dana."

"You've got to be kidding!" I said. "Why in the world would he want to spy on Dana?"

"Maybe for the same reason he'd want her dead," Doe said. "You may have to accept this, Julia."

I took a deep breath to calm myself. "I'm not giving in yet. Did you find out anything more about Cora Blankenship?"

"Blair said that Cora's assistant is in her yoga class. She's going to try and pump her for information tomorrow."

"We have to find something. I don't think it's Tony; there's just no reason. Although, come to think of it, Dana has openly challenged him multiple times at City Council meetings on everything from the city budget to certain contracts."

"You're rambling, Julia," Doe said.

I sighed. "I know. I'm upset. Okay, well, I have to stop at the store, and then I'm going to head home. When is Rudy going to Vancouver?"

"Tomorrow morning," she replied.

"Then let's all get together at the Inn tomorrow night. I'll make a big pot of minestrone soup."

"Sounds wonderful. I'm going to do some checking on that Eloise Radle, just in case. I have some contacts downtown. Maybe I can find something out."

I left city hall and headed toward the Albertson's store downtown. At the last minute, I passed right by the store and decided to make a slight detour to SE 27th, where the Finkle Collection Agency was located next to Starbucks. Clay Finkle was just coming out to his car. I pulled to the curb, honked my horn and rolled down my window.

"Hi Clay!" I waved my hand. He turned toward me, squinting through his glasses. "It's Julia. Do you have a minute?"

He threw something onto the front seat of his Saab and closed the door. Clay was a finicky guy and hurried over, holding a notepad over his head. I couldn't imagine why. His gray hair was cut so close it looked like a second skin, and he was wearing a rain coat.

"Hello, Julia. What's up?" he said, leaning over my window.

His long nose protruded through the open window and his bottle-lens glasses made his brown eyes as big as saucers.

"I was wondering how Dana is doing," I lied, leaning away from him. I wondered if he even knew we were helping her with the investigation.

"She's nervous," he said. "Who wouldn't be? This is all a nightmare. And I have to go out of town soon, so I hope they find the son-of-a-bitch."

"Out of town, really? You'd leave her all alone?"

"I don't have a choice," he said, his brown eyes blinking behind those bottle glasses. "I'm closing a deal at the end of the week for a new office up in Bellingham. I told her she could go with me, but she refused. She said she'd be a sitting duck up there, without any protection. I guess it will be okay. The police have added extra patrols around the house, and she's going to have someone come stay with her."

"Well, you must have added security, too," I said.

He nodded, making his enormous eyes bob up and down. It gave me a headache.

"Yes. We're having the whole alarm system upgraded," he said. "But Dana is stubborn, you know. I offered to hire a detective, but she won't accept any help from me."

His face had flushed, and I wondered if he knew Dana was thinking of divorcing him. I contemplated broaching the subject, but decided against it.

"Maybe you should get a gun," I suggested, knowing full-well they already had one.

"We *had* a gun," he said. "Actually two of them."

"Had?"

"Someone stole them. I reported it to the police this morning." He sighed and shook his head. "Anyway, thanks for asking, Julia. I know you haven't been the best of friends."

I smiled. "I suppose that's an understatement. But I hope she stays safe."

I was about to say something about Tony's arrest, but decided against that, too. The police would let them know soon enough. I waved goodbye as he ran back to the car.

I pulled away from the curb and wound my way back to the store. I meandered up and down the aisles throwing a few things into my cart, my mind a million miles away. I ambled over to the produce section and stopped to study the lettuce. I have to admit that my eyes had glazed over somewhere between the iceberg and the romaine, until I heard Tony's name mentioned. I snapped to attention and looked up. Two women were huddled up on the other side of the produce bin, their carts nose to nose.

"I know why they arrested him," a tall brunette said. "There's some big secret about his wife."

"Really?" a short blond replied. "Like what? She's so prim and proper."

"I don't know," the brunette replied, glancing around at me.

I reached out past the lettuce and grabbed a tomato, pretending to study it for bruises. I was surprised the gossip tree on the island had operated so quickly and efficiently. But then I remembered that the town's lead gossiper was Lizzy Forney, the receptionist at City Hall.

"Trudy told me not too long ago that Dana had something spectacular on Tony Morales' wife that could end his career," the brunette said with a conspiratorial nod.

"And now Trudy is dead," the other woman said.

She pressed her lips together in an ugly grimace, but the enthusiasm with which she spoke betrayed any compassion she felt for the dead woman.

"Yes, but didn't you know? Trudy was killed by mistake. Whoever killed Trudy meant to kill Dana."

The blond woman gasped, just as two children ran up screaming at each other over something. The conversation ended. The women said goodbye and took off in different directions.

I looked down and frowned at the tomato in my hand. Someone had pressed two fingerprints into it. I put it back, and then I took a turn around the store to finish my shopping.

On the way home, my brain was a-buzz with a myriad of thoughts. Dana Finkle apparently had something on Tony's wife. That was just like her. She would dig up dirt and use it against people, especially in her lawsuits. If Tony *had* tried to kill her, maybe that was the reason why. It would have to be something pretty spectacular to actually threaten his career; after all, politicians kept their jobs these days after being accused for all sorts of crimes. Perhaps that was also why Tony was asking Trudy to spy on Dana.

Oh dear, I thought. *This was getting complicated.* Tony had a reason to want Dana dead. Clay had a reason to want her dead.

Eloise Radle had a reason. And so did half a dozen others who Dana had sued. Including me.

By the time I returned to the Inn, I was exhausted and longed for a nap. Then I saw Blair's car in the driveway. She was in the breakfast room waiting for me.

"What are you doing here?" I asked her.

"I just talked to Mr. Billings, and he told me something very interesting," she said with a knowing smile.

"Your husband has a first name, you know," I said. "What do you call him at home?"

She smiled. "Honey."

I sighed. "Well, follow me to the apartment so I can put this stuff away."

We traipsed down the hallway and into my small apartment kitchen. While I put away my few groceries, she continued.

"You know Mr. Billings takes all his cars to Emory's Auto Shop in Bellevue. Well, he was in there this morning and came back talking about one of the guys who looks like he's had his face rearranged. I guess he has a bandage across his nose, and his face is scratched up."

"Really? How tall is he?"

Blair shrugged. "I have no idea. Does that make a difference? I thought you didn't get a look at the guy who attacked you."

"I didn't. But I've been thinking a lot about him. I kept bumping up against his chin, as if I fit right underneath it. And I remember his arms around me. They were thick and heavy. It was like being hugged by a bear." I put a carton of milk away as I said this last part.

"You want to go take a look?" Blair asked. Her pretty blue eyes were alight with youthful enthusiasm.

Blair's love for adventure was one of the things I liked best about her. On the other hand, she had a tendency to throw caution to the wind, and that made me nervous.

"Sure," I replied with just a slight hesitation. "But what's our excuse?"

Blair smiled, put a hand on her hip and gave me one of her, 'you've got to be kidding' looks.

"Of course," I said. "It's a business filled with men. What was I thinking?"

She smiled appreciatively. "Let's go. I'll drive."

I always hesitated getting in a car with Blair. She'd once been married to a racecar driver. While I imagine that she taught him how things moved in the bedroom, he taught her the finer points about how cars moved on the road. It was enough to make my stomach turn.

"Let me check in with April, and I'm all yours," I said.

April was in the bakery with her hands wrist deep in bread dough.

"David called," she said when I popped in. "I don't know what it was about, but he wanted you to call him."

I frowned. "I just saw him at City Hall. He arrested Tony Morales."

April stopped kneading the dough. "What for?"

I related the story about Tony's arrest. "But I'm having a hard time believing it," I said. "If someone could hack my emails, what's to stop someone from doing the same thing to Tony?"

"Nothing," April said with a shrug. "This sounds like it's going to get more complicated before it's over, though."

I pulled my phone from my purse, clicked the button and frowned. "My phone is dead. I guess that's why David called you. I'll call him back later. Besides, I don't want him asking questions right now."

April's eyebrows arched. "What do you mean? Stealing Dana's trash wasn't enough?"

I shifted my weight. "Blair and I are just taking a little trip to Bellevue."

April pulled in her chin. "You know," she said. "You've just barely healed from a car accident. And as I recall, Blair was driving then, too. Tell her to take it easy."

The memory of the night Blair and I were fleeing killers as they chased us in a Hummer was never far from my mind. I'd had several nightmares about it, especially the moment we'd gotten sideswiped by a bunch of kids out joy-riding. That had put us both in the hospital.

"Don't worry. We're just going to check something out."

"Does this have anything to do with Dana?"

I couldn't very well lie to April. I never could. She knows too much. With her sixth sense, she's like a truth-o- meter.

"I'm not sure. But it *is* about Ahab."

"Do you know where he is?" she asked. Her dark eyes flashed with hope.

My shoulders slumped. "No. But we may have a lead on the guy who took him."

She straightened up and stood back from the table a moment. "Julia," she said. "Don't do anything rash. This guy could have killed you."

"I know that. We're just going to try to get a look at him. He works in Bellevue."

April wiped her hands on a towel and reached into her pocket. She pulled out her cell phone.

"Here," she said. "Take my phone. Just in case. Give me yours and I'll charge it."

These were cell phones paid for by the Inn, so they were duplicates. We switched phones.

"Thanks. I shouldn't be gone long," I said.

I found Blair waiting for me in the breakfast room munching on a piece of cheese and a cracker from the tray April put out for guests.

"Careful, you might gain an ounce," I said.

"No I won't," she replied lightly. "Even if I do, I'll work it off – one way or the other."

Once again, she flashed one of her seductive smiles as I turned for the front door. I grabbed the door knob, but the door knob wouldn't turn.

"What the…?"

I tried again. This time, the door knob turned, but I couldn't pull the door open. I stood back when I heard a soft giggle.

"Chloe!" I called out. "Stop playing games." I tried the door knob again, but no luck.

Blair moved up close to my ear. "Maybe she can't hear you."

I turned to her. "Why are you whispering?"

"I don't know. Why are you talking to a ghost?"

I turned back to the door. "Chloe, we're going to try to find out who stole Ahab."

The door popped open.

I turned and gave Blair a know-it-all look and then stepped through the door.

Blair was driving her own BMW sedan today, which made me feel a little more secure. It only took twenty minutes to get off the island and across the water to the auto shop, which sat on the outskirts of downtown Bellevue. I took the time to fill her in on Tony's arrest.

Bellevue looks a little like the Emerald City of Oz rising out of the surrounding business district. It's an affluent area, filled with financial institutions, high-end stores, expensive restaurants, and hi-tech companies.

The auto shop sat on the other side of I-405 freeway, near Overlake Hospital. Joe Emory was the mechanic of choice for anyone who owns a high performance car. He used to take care of my Miata before one of Martha's killers forced me off the road. The Miata was totaled. I missed that car. It fit me. It was small. And I'm small. Although I liked my new Nissan Pathfinder, it felt a touch overwhelming. On the other hand, I felt much less vulnerable in it.

As we pulled into the parking lot of Emory Auto Shop, the butterflies in my stomach were a sure sign I was questioning the decision to make this trip. What if this guy really was the man who had attacked me? And if he was the guy who attacked me, he might recognize me. Even come after me.

Blair killed the engine and grabbed her purse. When I didn't move, she turned to me. "Why are you just sitting there? Let's go."

"Are you sure this is a good idea?" I asked, my eyes searching the front of the shop.

"We're not going to do anything dangerous. All we want to do is ID him. Heck, it's probably not even him. There's nothing to be afraid of. Besides, I would never knowingly put your life in danger."

She reached for the door handle as I said, "Why doesn't that make me feel any better?"

CHAPTER SEVENTEEN

Blair unbuttoned her wool coat so that it hung open when we got out of the car. Then she arched her back.

"What are you doing?" I asked from the other side of the car.

She looked sideways at me over the hood and just smiled. Then she stepped forward and threw open the door to the shop. I followed her inside.

The waiting room at the Emory Auto Shop felt more like a boutique than a place where auto mechanics hung out. But then, Joe Emory was a smart business man – he knew the kind of customers he attracted, and they didn't like grease and grime. So the furniture looked like it came out of a Modern Home magazine, the floors were spotless, and there was music playing overhead. They sold designer key chains and fancy aromatics for your car. There was a high-end Keurig machine, fresh pastries, and free Diet Pepsi. I was in heaven every time I went in there.

"Hey, Joe," Blair said with a big smile as she stepped up to the counter.

Joe Emory looked like he could have been a jockey at one point in his life. He was small and wiry and in his mid-50s. He'd done well for himself. He owned three shops, this one and one in Lynnwood and in Kent.

He looked up from the counter at Blair's greeting, and the expression on his face changed from blank to open and friendly. "Hey, Mrs. Wentworth. What brings you here? I hope that BMW isn't giving you any trouble."

"Well there *is* this little ping," she lied, using her manicured fingers to illustrate the *little* part. "I hear it every once in a while. I was wondering if one of your guys could take it for a spin around the block. Maybe it's nothing," she said leaning over the counter, giving him full view of the deep cleavage that left most men speechless.

Watching her made me think of a time in high school when a couple of my friends decided I needed some help in the seduction department. They stuffed two water balloons into my leotard moments before a boy I hoped would invite me to the homecoming dance came out of the science lab. My job was simple, just sashay past him without saying a word. But true to form, I panicked and tripped, landing face down at his feet. The water balloons exploded, drenching me *and* his new Wingtips. Needless to say, I never made it to the homecoming dance.

I shifted my attention to Joe Emory, who was openly staring at Blair's water balloons. He hadn't even noticed me. What he didn't know was that Blair's were as false as mine were in high school, just a little more durable. Still, from the look on his face, I thought it was a good thing he was standing behind the counter.

"Let me get Peter," he said, running his tongue along his bottom lip. "He can take it out for a spin." He dragged his eyes away from Blair and turned to exit through a door behind him.

"So what do we do now?" I asked.

"I know Peter," she said, pulling back from the counter. "He's not the one we're looking for. So let him take the car, and we'll wander around."

A moment later, Joe was back. Like a homing pigeon, his eyes sought out Blair's chest. "Peter will be right here," he said, drawing his eyes up to meet Blair's.

She smiled sweetly. "That's great. Here are the keys," she said, dropping them on the counter. "Mind if we wander around while he's out with the car? I just love being around fast cars," she said with a raised shoulder.

He smiled. "Of course not. The guys love having you here."

I started to laugh and then coughed to cover the indiscretion. *Of course the guys loved having her here*, I thought.

Joe finally noticed me and said, "How are *you*, Mrs. Applegate?"

"Just fine, Joe," I replied.

Peter came through the door and picked up the keys before approaching Blair. "Can you tell where the noises are coming from?"

Peter was one of the few men who didn't seem fazed by Blair's feminine wiles. And Blair knew it – you could tell by her physical reaction. Around 90% of men would turn her into an undulating, breathless woman that reeked of sex. With the other 10%, she seemed to know immediately that her physicality would be lost on them, and the sex appeal that seemed to seep from her pores only moments before would evaporate.

"I'm not sure," she said, standing up straight. In heels, Blair was almost 5 foot 11. Standing next to her, I often felt like her little sister. "I thought maybe if you would just drive around the block a couple of times, you might hear it," she said.

He shrugged. "No problem. I'll be back in a few."

Peter left in the BMW, and Joe returned his attention to the computer, leaving us to do what we'd come there for. We went back out the front door and turned towards the car bays. The big rolling door was all the way up, revealing a large auto shop with three hydraulic lifts and a full wall of counters and drawers filled with tools in the background.

A thin man in blue overalls leaned over the engine of a Volvo. Blair looked at me with a lift to her eyebrows. I glanced at him, but shook my head. This guy was too short and didn't have a bandage on his face.

We wandered past the Volvo to a red Mercedes sports car. The Mercedes was up on the lift, with two mechanics tinkering beneath it. Blair jerked her head in their direction. I paused, but couldn't get a good look. I bent over and studied each one as they worked.

"No," I murmured.

We continued on as if we were perusing dogs at a dog show. Blair had her hands clasped behind her back, her purse draped over one shoulder. This helped to present her best feature to the admiring eyes that followed us.

We stopped in front of the third hydraulic lift. The lift was down, but a vintage Mustang sat there with its hood up. A couple of mechanics were working on it, but since we were standing at the tail end of the car, we couldn't see either one of them.

"Hello, Mrs. Wentworth," a voice called out.

"Hey, Jake," she replied, smiling at a young man coming around the back end of the Mercedes.

Jake was in his mid-twenties with a scraggly beard. He wasn't our guy. I knew Jake. He'd worked on my Miata a couple of times. He noticed me and smiled.

"Hi, Mrs. Applegate. How's your Miata running?"

I frowned. "I'm afraid it's dead. It was killed by a Hummer."

"Too bad," he said. "Those Hummers are monsters on the road."

"How is that new baby of yours?" Blair asked him. "Are you getting any sleep?"

While Blair kept Jake busy, I ambled past the rear of the Mustang and then turned towards the back of the shop. I came up along the wall, skirting around a huge, rolling tool box. I stopped behind the first man. He was holding a wrench for his partner with his left hand and leaning on the hood with his right. Long slender fingers with short fingernails filled with grease rested on the hood of the fender.

As I moved forward, the man turned his head and a lock of blonde hair fell out from under a baseball cap worn backwards.

"Can I help you?"

I paused. It was a woman.

"Uh…my friend is having her car checked out," I said. "Joe said we could wander around."

"Sure, no problem," she said.

I was looking through the open hood when the man next to her looked up. I glanced at him and my heart skipped a beat. He had dark hair and deep-set, dark eyes. His nose was covered in white gauze and tape. Across his left cheek were several deep and recent scratches.

The man's eyes flared the moment he saw me. He straightened up and took a step backwards. "Shit! I'll be back in a minute," he mumbled, and then turned for the office.

My heart was racing. I wanted to run after him, but I had to get more information.

"That guy didn't seem too friendly," I said. My fingers were clasping the straps of my purse in a death grip.

The female mechanic glanced around at the retreating image. "Oh, Big Al? He's not so bad," she said. "He's only been here a short time."

"Seems to me like he could use a little customer service training," I said.

She chuckled. "Yeah, I suppose. But you don't get much customer service training in the joint, if you know what I mean."

"Is that where he got injured?"

"No. He said a dog attacked him." She wiped her hands on a dirty rag. "Had to be a pretty big dog," she said with a laugh. "After all, he's a pretty burly guy."

All of a sudden I felt like I had to pee. That often happens when I get nervous.

"Julia," Blair called from behind me. She hurried up and put a hand on my shoulder. "We have to go. Right now!" She grabbed my arm and dragged me out of the shop. Her BMW was back, and she had the keys in her hand. "Get in. Fast," she ordered.

I did as I was told and fifteen seconds later we were pulling out of the parking lot.

"What's going on?" I asked, holding on as she whizzed out onto 116th Ave.

"I saw the guy with the facemask," she said with excitement. "He came in and told Joe he had to go home for something. I saw him get into an old beat-up pickup truck. I want to follow him."

"But how do you know where he is?"

She pointed a long, manicured fingernail ahead of us. "He's right up there," she said with satisfaction.

A battered old green truck was just turning onto the overpass. Blair wheeled around a minivan in front of us and screeched around the corner hot on his tail. We watched him take the exit onto I-405 South. The light in front of us turned red, and Blair roared right through it. A moment later, we were just two cars behind him on the freeway.

"Did you get a chance to see him?" she asked me.

I was gripping the armrest so hard my fingers were going numb, but I managed to answer. "Yes. I think he could be the guy. The moment he saw me, he took off. But according to the female mechanic, he's only worked there a short time and was in prison before that."

Blair shot a surprised glance my way. "No shit!"

"That's kind of what he said the moment he saw me," I replied. "But that's not all. I asked the girl how he got injured. And she said he told them he'd been attacked by a dog."

"Wow," Blair exclaimed. "We got him, Julia."

"Well, let's not get ahead of ourselves," I cautioned her, using the same expression Doe had earlier. "But I have to admit that I think it's him. He seemed to be about the right height and the right size, and I could've sworn that that was his voice."

We followed the old pickup truck down 405, past the Seattle Seahawks training facility on the shores of Lake Washington. We took the exit for Renton Technical College and pulled under the freeway. Renton was a former coal mining town that had grown into a burgeoning business community with the help of a Boeing plant. Downtown Renton sat in the valley, while a good two-thirds of the town sat on the east hill, called the Highlands.

The truck pulled up the hill, past Mt. Olivet Cemetery on the right and the sprawling Renton Technical College campus on the left. Greenwood Memorial Park Cemetery sat kitty-corner to the college. It was the gravesite of the famous rock star, Jimi Hendrix, one of Renton's claims to fame.

The truck stayed on NE 4th Street and passed the cemetery. Then it took a right into the parking lot of an apartment complex behind the cemetery. Blair and I pulled in and parked across the lot. We watched Big Al get out of the truck and hurry into a ground floor apartment. Blair opened the glove compartment and pulled out a small pair of opera glasses. I gave her an incredulous look.

"What?" she said with raised eyebrows. "You never know when these are going to come in handy."

She used the opera glasses to see the number of the apartment in which Big Al had disappeared. "Number 12," she said.

"Now what do we do?"

There was a part of me that wanted to run from the car, bang on the door and burst in, hoping to find Ahab. But I knew that was a bad idea. And that he might already be dead.

"I say we go talk to him," Blair said.

I stared at her in disbelief. "You're kidding!"

"No. This may be your one chance to save Ahab," she said. "That guy might be in there right now trying to kill him."

My heart rate sped up. "Let me at least call David and have him on the phone when we do this."

She shrugged. "Okay by me. But let's get closer first."

I reached for my phone just as a familiar song began to play. I glanced down at the screen, and my stomach clenched. It read, "Out of the area." That usually meant it was my mother.

I glanced over at Blair as we exited the car, hoping I could take this call without notice. As we began to cross the parking lot, I clicked on the phone and said hello.

"Julia! Be careful," my Mom said. "I can tell you're about to get in trouble."

"How do you do that?" I asked, stopping mid-stride.

Blair turned and gave me an exasperated look. Then she mimed, "Who is that?"

I ignored her. "We're trying to rescue Ahab," I said into the phone.

"Yes, but something's wrong," my mother said.

"Like what?"

"I can't tell."

"Not a big help, Mom," I replied as I followed Blair to hide behind a car. "But you might want to stick around in case there's something you can do."

"I'm not supposed to get involved," she said.

I threw up a hand. "Then why do you keep calling me?"

She sighed on the other end of the line – wherever that was. "I fudge a little, that's all. Now don't do anything stupid." And she hung up.

"What are you doing?" Blair whispered, turning back to me. "Let's go."

"Wait a minute," I said. "Are you sure we should be doing this?"

Blair gestured around us. "There are several people out here in the parking lot," she said. "What could go wrong? We have witnesses."

I turned around. A woman was just getting out of her car, while a mother and daughter were coming out of a nearby apartment. At the far end of the building, a maintenance man was fixing a window.

I turned back. "Okay," I said. "I'll dial David."

My fingers punched in David's cell phone number as we approached apartment 12. We got right up to the door and stopped. Blair turned to me with her hand poised ready to knock. I nodded. As she pounded on the door, I put the call through. I had the phone to my ear when Big Al threw open the door. The look on his face said it all. We were the last people he expected to see on his front doorstep.

"Shit!" he exclaimed again.

He tried to slam the door closed, but Blair stuck the pointed toe of her high-heeled boot in to stop it. The door bounced open again, and she burst through the door. At that moment, David answered the phone. I said hello and then heard, "People come and go so quickly around here. Squawk!"

It was Ahab in a small cage on the counter in the kitchen.

"Pay no attention to that man behind the curtain!" Ahab's little tinny voice squawked.

Al was reaching for the cage as Ahab bounced back and forth on his perch. Blair didn't miss a beat. She grabbed a golf umbrella from the kitchen table and began hitting Al over the back of the head with it. He turned around and grasped the umbrella and tried to yank it away from her, but she was stronger than I thought. They started a tug-of-war game, while David was trying to get my attention on the other end of the phone.

"Julia! Julia!" he kept saying.

But I couldn't answer, because it was pandemonium in Big Al's apartment.

Ahab had begun screeching. Al and Blair knocked furniture over as they swung each other around the room, yelling obscenities at each other. I dropped the phone and began looking for a weapon of my own. I grabbed a lamp, ripped the cord out of the wall and began following Al around the room from behind. I kept trying to hit him over the head with it, but two things prevented me. First, he was too tall, and second, he kept moving.

Al finally swung Blair up against a bookcase, and she let go of the umbrella just as his stereo began blasting *Purple Haze*. Startled, he stopped and looked around, allowing Blair to grab a beer bottle that was sitting on an empty shelf behind her. She raised it to strike him, but he whirled around and lunged for her, forcing her sideways and over a chair. Since she was momentarily incapacitated, he turned and went for Ahab. But this time, I was quicker. I rushed over and grabbed Ahab's cage and ran for the door.

"No you don't," Al growled.

He grabbed me from behind and yanked me off my feet. I dropped the cage and the cage door flew open. Blair came out of nowhere and swung the umbrella at the side of his head with all her strength. The force of the blow knocked him to one knee, just as a blender, the TV and the coffee grinder all started whirring. Lights flashed on and off and his phone started to ring. He pulled himself up and glanced around in confusion.

"What the…?"

It had to be Mom. She'd somehow learned to manipulate electronics from the other side during the last murder investigation; apparently, she was getting better at it.

Blair took the opportunity to grab her purse from where she'd dropped it and started swinging it at Al. It was a big purse and made him duck twice. Then, he caught it, ripping it out of her hand.

I scrambled off the floor and grabbed a small potted plant. I heaved it at his head. He ducked, giving Blair just enough time to wield the most lethal weapon she had. She kicked out with one of those 3-inch heels and caught him in the crotch. He let out a yowl and doubled over just as Ahab flew the coop. Literally.

I tried to grab him as he flapped past me, but he was heading for the open door. Before I could stop him, he was gone.

I ran outside, for the moment forgetting Blair. I cried out Ahab's name, but he was already up and over a nearby tree and out of sight.

"Damn!" I cursed. I'd forgotten to clip his wings the weekend before. Too late now.

As I turned back to help Blair, Al barreled out the door knocking me into a planter. With a few choice words, he jumped into his truck and peeled out of the parking lot.

I groaned as I extricated myself from a prickly bush, and hurried back inside. Blair was on her hands and knees, breathing hard. Her bleached blonde hair had been pulled out of her pony tail and looked like she'd styled it with an egg beater. Her face was flushed. Her lipstick smeared. And one crimson fingernail was hanging off her finger. But she was smiling.

She took a deep breath and sat back on her heels. "God that was fun."

"No, it wasn't," I admonished her. "Ahab is gone!"

Her smile disintegrated into a frown. "Oh, no," she cried. "Won't he come back?"

"We're in Renton," I snapped. "As far as I know, Ahab has never *been* to Renton. And I doubt he knows the freeways."

Her shoulders slumped. "I'm so sorry, Julia. But at least we know he's okay. Can't the police put out an APB on him or whatever they call it?"

"For a *parrot*?"

"Why not?" she said. "If not the police, maybe the Humane Society."

"Oh, no. Speaking of the police, I forgot about David. He's on the phone."

I looked around and found my phone under a chair. I picked it up and spoke into it. "David? David?"

No answer. It didn't matter. The sound of sirens told me all I needed to know.

"Oh, dear," I said, dropping into a chair. "I have a feeling this won't be good."

CHAPTER EIGHTEEN

When a police squad car pulled up, I assumed one of the neighbors had called them. After all, there was now a small crowd of lookie-loos craning their necks to see what was going on in apartment 12. I hadn't even tried to call David back. I felt sure I'd get a lecture from him soon enough.

Two officers emerged from their squad car – a good-looking black man and a stocky Caucasian woman with short blond hair and a burly demeanor. They hurried over to the open door, where I was attempting to pull a twig out of my hair.

"Everything is okay, officers," I said casually, grabbing the twig and yanking it free. "The man is gone."

"What man?" the male officer snapped, his hand on the butt of the gun at his hip.

"The man who lives here," I replied innocently.

He gave me a quizzical look, his dark eyes shifting between me and the interior of the apartment. "The man who lives here is gone. But you're here. What happened?"

Blair appeared in the doorway behind me, trying to adjust her hair and her boobs at the same time. She took a deep breath and said, "There's been an altercation."

"With who?" the female officer asked. "And why?"

"That's kind of a long story," I said.

The two officers motioned us to step aside and strode past us into the apartment. We followed them.

The male officer turned to me. "I'm Officer Mosley, and this is Officer Hager," he said, gesturing to his female partner. "Now, did someone try to rob you? Something obviously happened in here," he said, taking in the mess and over-turned furniture.

"Well, no, no one tried to rob us. We don't actually live here," I said.

His confused expression melded into a look of irritation. "Then what are you doing here?"

"The man who lives here stole something from me."

The officers shared a look and then Officer Hager snapped. "You just said no one tried to rob you."

Officer Hager stood with her feet planted firmly apart, one hand on the club strapped to her belt. She looked like she was ready to take down someone twice her size and I stepped back.

"Uh…no, not here," I replied.

"Then where?" Officer Mosley asked.

"From my home on Mercer Island."

"Then what are you doing here?"

"We came to get it back," Blair said, sitting down on the arm of the couch. "Possession is nine-tenths of the law, you know." She was focused on her broken nail, as if having two police officers interrogate us was no big deal.

"Look, one of you needs to start making some sense," Officer Hager said. "We got a call from one of the neighbors that someone was in trouble here."

"Yes…that would be us," Blair said, flipping off the broken nail and looking up. "But we're okay now."

Officer Hager glanced at her partner again and rolled her eyes. "Whose apartment is this?"

"Um…we don't actually know that," Blair replied, twirling a strand of hair around her finger.

The female officer stepped forward. "What are your names?"

"I'm Julia Applegate and this is my friend, Blair Wentworth."

"And you both live on Mercer Island?" the officer asked, eyeing Blair's high heels and cashmere sweater.

"That's right," I said.

"Do you know the person who lives here or not?" she asked.

"No," we said in unison.

"Then how do you know he stole something from you?" Officer Hager asked. "And the answer better make sense."

I glanced down at the now empty bird cage lying on its side. "Because the thing he stole from me used to be in that cage," I said, pointing at it.

Both officers followed my gaze. Officer Hager sighed and whipped out a notepad and pencil, her lips drawn into a straight line. Her patience was wearing thin.

"Let's step outside," she ordered.

We moved to the walkway by the front door. The group of lookie-loos had grown.

"This is all a mistake," I said nervously, conscious that we were being watched.

"A misunderstanding," Blair clarified, leaning against a pole.

"Which is it?" Officer Hager asked.

"Both!" we said in unison again.

Officer Hager sighed.

Officer Mosley had been eyeing me and finally asked, "So, you're Julia Applegate? Any relation to…"

"Yes," I replied. "He's my ex-husband."

He shot a warning glance to his partner, who was oblivious to this new piece of information.

"Okay, Mrs. Applegate," he said, with a slight emphasis on my last name.

But Officer Hager was flicking her pencil, ready to write. "Why don't you start from the beginning," she said. "And don't leave anything out."

Her partner sighed and folded his arms across his chest.

I explained what happened at the Inn the night Big Al had taken Ahab, and then how Blair and I had identified him. I spoke a little too fast and little too loud, but at least everything made sense this time. When I was done, I looked over at Officer Mosley in anticipation, as if he would be grading my performance.

"So this guy broke into your home and stole your…parrot," Officer Hager said. "And you figured out who he was and followed him to this apartment, where you found your parrot. Do I have that right?" she said, reading back from her notes.

"Yes," I replied.

"But there's no parrot here now?" Officer Mosley said with a tilt to his head.

"No. But he *was* here," I assured him. "I dropped the cage and the door popped open. He flew away."

Blair must've thought it was time to take over. She leaned forward, inviting Officer Mosley's gaze.

"Officer," she said sweetly. "Let me explain."

He glanced at her chest and then away, his face a blank canvas. *Uh-oh*, I thought. What were the odds that we'd encounter the 10% twice in one afternoon? Blair must have known it too, because she leaned back again.

"At first, all we wanted to do was to find out who this guy was. But then we hoped to find out where he lived," she said. "When we did, we heard frantic squawking coming from this apartment. We thought he was killing the bird to get rid of the evidence. So we had to do something."

I glanced at her in surprise. In what universe had we heard frantic squawking before we knocked on the door? Somehow lying to the police didn't seem like such a great idea.

"But we didn't break in," she said. "We knocked on the door, and he opened it."

Officer Mosley's expression seemed to balance precariously between the serious and the comical. "Go on," he said.

"Well...*then* we might have overstepped our bounds," Blair said with an apologetic nod. "He swore at us and tried to slam the door in our faces."

"But before he did, I saw Ahab in the background," I added quickly, pointing through the open door to the kitchen counter. "The cage was in complete view of the front door."

"And you're positive it was your parrot, not just some other parrot?" Officer Hager asked, the cynicism practically oozing from her lips.

My eyebrows shot up. "Of course it was my parrot! I would know him anywhere."

"How?" she asked. "What color is he?"

"Gray," I replied, realizing I had just exacerbated the problem. Ahab didn't really have any distinguishing marks. He kind of looked like any other gray parrot. And then I remembered. "But he greeted me."

Officer Hager looked surprised by that. "By name? As in, 'Hello, Julia?'"

"Well, no. He quoted a line from the Wizard of Oz," I said, as if that was as good as giving his Social Security number.

There was a long pause, during which both officers merely stared at me, their expressions blank. Finally, Officer Hager furrowed her brow and said, "You're kidding, right?"

"She *never* kids about the Wizard of Oz," Blair said with a toss of her head.

Officer Mosley used his right hand to rub his forehead as if he had a headache. "Okay, what happened next?"

"The guy who lives here tried to grab Ahab," I said.

"The guy you followed?

"Yes, and so I hit him with an umbrella," Blair said.

Officer Mosley turned and leveled a curious look at Blair. "And you thought that would stop him?"

"Yes, but instead he came after me," she continued. "We struggled over the umbrella, and then all the electronics in the apartment started going off. The TV, the stereo, the blender…"

"Why?" he asked.

We both stopped short. I glanced at Blair. Her pert mouth was halfway open, as if she was about to say something, but then stopped.

"Uh…I don't know," she said, glancing at me.

I had nothing to say.

"What happened next? Did Santa Claus show up?" Officer Hager asked. Her bland features were riddled with sarcasm.

"No," I snapped. "I grabbed Ahab's cage, but Al threw me on the floor and the cage flipped open. Ahab flew out the open door."

She stared at me, suppressing a smile. "He just clicked his heels three times and flew away, is that it? Cuz, you know, there's no place like home." A single chuckle erupted from her throat.

I straightened up. "This isn't a joke. That man almost killed me last night." I pulled down my turtleneck to expose the bruises. Her eyes flinched, and she sucked up her laughter. "Call Detective David Franks at the Mercer Island Police Department. He'll confirm my story," I said. "I was on the phone with him when this all began."

"No need to get upset. We'll call Mercer Island and clear this up," Officer Mosley said.

Officer Hager glared at him, but he pulled out his cell phone and gestured for her to follow him. They stepped to the side as he whispered something to his partner. She glanced back at me. She'd just been put on notice that she was insulting the ex-wife of the Governor.

Officer Mosley talked to someone on his phone for a few minutes and then put his hand over it to relay some information to his partner. He spoke once more into the phone and then turned and came back to us.

"Detective Franks would like to speak to you," he said.

I felt suddenly cold all over. But I stepped forward and took the phone.

"Detective Franks," I said into the phone. "I'm sorry to have disturbed you."

"Give it a rest, Julia. You shouldn't have gone after this guy alone. You should have called me first."

"But we didn't have time, David." I noticed the look of surprise on Officer Mosley's face at the familiar use of David's first name. I turned away. "He recognized me," I said in a softer voice. "He knew who I was. I was afraid he was going to kill Ahab."

"It doesn't matter. You need to leave these things to the police. And you need to stop following after Blair."

"It wasn't her fault," I said.

"Look, they could charge you both with trespassing, maybe even breaking and entering. Leave this to us. Now go home and take care of the business you're actually in."

He hung up and I could feel the sting of his last remark as if he'd slapped my face. I handed the phone back to Officer Mosley.

"What now?" I murmured.

"We're going to let you off with a warning," he replied. "And we'll try to track down the gentleman who lives here and…"

"He's no gentleman," Blair interrupted him. "He could've killed us."

"You *were* standing in *his* apartment when we got here," he reminded her.

Blair shrugged. Officer Mosley continued. "We'll see if we can verify that he's the one who took your parrot," he finished.

We thanked the officers and left, climbing back into the BMW. We drove back to the island feeling chagrined and defeated.

"Sorry about that," Blair said after a while. "I didn't mean to get you in trouble."

I sighed. "It's not your fault. But I don't think I'm destined to have a relationship with a cop."

"Well, not if you continue to get involved in murder investigations."

I gave her a weak smile. "What are the odds we'd go right from one murder investigation to another? Dead women are piling up all around us."

I told Blair about meeting for dinner the next night as she pulled down the Inn's drive. She said she would call Rudy and let her know about the dinner.

I dragged myself through the front door feeling on the verge of tears. I had not only embarrassed myself in front of my new boyfriend, I had lost my one chance to rescue Ahab. Now he was out in the world alone, using quotes from old movies to fend for himself. I pictured him flapping his wings, staring down at the freeway and saying, "Just follow the yellow brick road. Just follow the yellow brick road."

Despite the loss, the thought brought a smile to my face.

CHAPTER NINETEEN

I slept little that night, flinching every time a tree rustled or the building creaked, wondering if the noise was Ahab outside trying to get in. I rose the next morning, threw on my robe and hurried out to the breakfast room, hoping against hope that I would find him in a tree outside.

The weather had soured overnight, filling the sky with clouds pregnant with rain. A strong breeze brought whitecaps up on the lake's surface and the temperature had plummeted again, making me wrap my arms around my chest for warmth.

I pulled open the drapes and searched the trees that surrounded the back of the Inn, but no Ahab. After all, how could a little parrot find his way so far north and across the lake to one building tucked on the other side of Mercer Island?

I returned to my apartment depressed and disappointed. Time to get ready for another busy day at the Inn.

After breakfast, I sent a notice to the *Renton Reporter* about a lost parrot. By mid-morning it had started to rain, and the sky had turned a deep charcoal gray. Around noon, a family of four checked into our only suite, which was located above the breakfast room. Their last name was Kohl and they had two boisterous eight-year old twins, Barry and Sherrie – who kept chasing each other around their exasperated mother.

"We're here for my mother's eightieth birthday tomorrow night," Mrs. Kohl said, reaching out to grab her son by the collar. "Stop," she ordered, turning to stare hard at him. He slunk away to toy with the ship's wheel by the front door. "Sorry," she said, turning back to me. "But do you have any suggestions for things to do today?"

"We have some brochures in the rack over there," I said, pointing next to the staircase. "But I'd recommend Pike Place Market or the Space Needle. There's even the Pacific Science Center, if you'd rather be out of the weather."

The door opened and Mr. Kohl came in with the bags, shaking his head to dispel the moisture. He stepped up to the counter.

"Are we all set?" he asked his wife.

"Yes," she replied.

"You'll be at the top of the stairs and all the way down to the right," I said, handing her two keys.

"Does it ever *not* rain up here?" Mr. Kohl said with a slight frown.

"I thought you'd want to bottle it and take it with you," I said with an amiable smile.

His frown deepened. "What's that supposed to mean?"

"Uh…the drought," I replied. "Aren't you rationing water in California?" He glared at me, so I attempted to save the moment. "Well, a little rain never hurt anyone. I'd take umbrellas just in case, though. It's always good to be prepared."

Just then, the front door blew open with a gust of cold air. Everyone turned, and their daughter whimpered and huddled up close to her mother.

"Is it the ghosts, Mommy?" she whined.

Mrs. Kohl turned to me with a concerned look. "We read that the Inn is haunted. Is that true?"

The door slammed shut, making everyone jump. The little girl screamed and attempted to tuck herself under her mother's elbow.

"Um…well…there have been some incidents," I replied, glancing at the door.

"Cool," the little boy said, rushing over to look out the sidelight window.

Mrs. Kohl turned to her husband, who was staring at the door.

"Mrs. Applegate," he began, turning to me. "I'm not sure I'll appreciate any tricks being played on us or on the children while we're here."

I stood up a little straighter. "I assure you, Mr. Kohl, that we don't play tricks, as you say, on anyone. The ghost activity is real. We've had it documented by a paranormal group that stayed here for two nights a year ago. I'll understand if you'd prefer to stay somewhere else. I have to warn you however, that you would lose your deposit."

He bristled at that. But I was on firm ground and he knew it, since the ghost activity was mentioned in all of our promotional materials and on the website.

"So was that one of the ghosts?" young Barry inquired, coming back to the desk.

He was a short, stocky kid, with bushy eyebrows and a straight nose, just like his father. I imagined he'd be a bully by the time he was a teenager. Sherrie looked more like her mom. She had a delicate face and high cheek-bones.

I paused before answering, not sure whether to be honest and further irritate the parents. On the other hand, Mr. Kohl had raised my hackles.

"Most likely that was Chloe. She was about your age when she died in a fire here, back in 1962. She likes to play tricks on people. Especially children."

Barry's eyes opened wide. "That's awesome! Dad, can I stay up all night? Maybe a ghost will appear."

His father looked slightly apoplectic. "Of course not. There's no such thing as ghosts, Barry. There's some other explanation for what goes on here. Let's just go to our room so we can get out and do some sightseeing."

He gave me an openly hostile look, took his room key and grabbed their bags. Mrs. Kohl followed the kids up the stairs, as I moved away from the desk. They were halfway up the stairs when the reception bell rang. I ran back and put my hand over it, and then glanced over at the family, who had all stopped on the staircase to stare at me.

"Sorry. I must have hit it by mistake," I lied.

They continued up the stairs, while I shivered at the drop in temperature around me. I heard another lighthearted giggle. Chloe was nearby. I waited to chastise her until I heard the door to the suite upstairs close.

"Chloe!" I whispered. "Be good, or you'll get me in trouble."

The desk bell rang twice more, so I grabbed it and put it in a drawer. Just then, April appeared around the corner.

"Is our bell malfunctioning?" she asked with a smile.

"No. Chloe is malfunctioning. I don't think she likes the new kids that just arrived."

"She does pick her favorites," April said, bemused. "Maybe she just wants them to play with her." She handed me a slip of paper. "Here's the receipt for the food I bought for the Jason Spears reception. By the way, a man stopped by yesterday while you were gone to see if we had a room available, but Crystal told him we were all booked up."

"Was there a problem?"

"No. Not really. It's just that he asked if we knew where Dana Finkle lived."

That got my attention.

"What did he look like?"

"I don't know. I didn't see him. Crystal's in the laundry, though, if you want to ask her."

"Thanks," I said.

Since I had to leave the desk, I decided to chance it and pull out the desk bell again in case anyone came in. Then I hurried down the hall. The hallway angled to the right and around a corner to a back room we'd turned into a laundry. It had a commercial size washer and dryer, a sink and a folding table, and was wall-papered in a cheery red and yellow flowered paper. Crystal was standing at the counter folding some towels.

"April told me a man stopped by yesterday asking about Dana," I said to her. "Can you tell me what he looked like?"

Crystal was in her late twenties, with bright blue, intelligent eyes and light brown hair she usually wore tied into a loose ponytail. She had worked for us for almost two years while taking night classes at the UW. I trusted her implicitly, especially her instincts. She never failed to read guests as they checked in and could tell whether they would pose a problem or not. So I was interested in getting her impressions of this guy.

"He was tall and overweight," she said, laying down the last towel. "Maybe in his fifties or early sixties. He wore glasses and had large hands with the tattoo of an eagle on the back of one. I thought maybe he'd been in the service at one time."

"How did you see his hands if he didn't sign in?"

"He laid a hand on the counter. Anyway, he said he'd just gotten into town and needed a place to stay. But we were full."

"And he asked about Dana?"

"Yeah," she said with a shrug. "He wondered if I knew her and wanted to know if she lived close by."

"Did he say why?"

"No. But I asked him if he was a reporter or something...you know, because of the murder investigation. He said no, that he just used to know her. And then he left."

"What time was that?"

She thought for a moment. "Close to 3:00."

"Did you get any other impression about him?"

She shrugged. "Just that he seemed...I don't know...angry. I had a feeling he didn't like Mrs. Finkle much."

"Thanks," I said. "I'm going to pay some bills, so I'll watch the front desk for a while."

I did my duty this time and called David to let him know about the guy looking for Dana. Then I took a phone call from Jason Spears, the paranormal writer, about his upcoming event on Friday. We'd planned a small reception, after which he would read a chapter from his latest book and then his wife, who was a medium, would attempt to contact the spirits at the Inn.

I was understandably nervous about the event. I felt a certain kinship to Elizabeth and Chloe. I wasn't sure they would cooperate and make an appearance. But if they did, I had this unnatural sense of protection, as if I didn't want them exploited.

The rest of the day went by without incident, until David called that afternoon to let me know they had ID'd Big Al. His full name was Al Dente, which by anyone's standards was funny. But his record wasn't. Dente had gone to prison for armed robbery and had only been out for six months. And although they'd staked out his apartment, he hadn't returned.

÷

By 6 o'clock that night, the girls were all positioned around the old farmhouse kitchen table. We had extended the flaps so that April could join us. I thought it was time to bring her in. She was smart and inquisitive, and if nothing else, we needed her sixth sense.

She came with a fresh loaf of bread, and I had a pot of my mother's minestrone soup on the stove. Doe walked in with a cold bottle of Chardonnay, and Blair brought brownies left over from the senior center, where she'd spent the afternoon trying to dig up dirt on Dana.

Rudy rolled in around 6:15, straight from her trip to Vancouver. It was still raining, so she came in shaking water off like a wet dog. She hung up her coat and grabbed a glass of wine.

"I have news," she exclaimed.

"So do we," Blair blurted. "Julia and I got into a fight yesterday with the man who stole Ahab, and almost got taken to jail."

Rudy shook her head. "Wait a minute. Slow down. What?"

"Hold it," I said. "Let's get our food first and then we can start at the beginning."

We took a few minutes to fill our soup bowls and get beverages. Then we came back to the table.

"Okay, let me have it," Rudy said. "It sounds like your day was much more eventful than mine."

Since Doe hadn't heard the whole story either, Blair and I filled them in one step at a time. By the end, both Doe and Rudy looked worried, while April cast an admonishing look my way.

"So who is this guy?" Doe asked.

"His name is Al Dente," I said.

Rudy almost spit out some wine. "Is that a joke?"

"No," I said, smiling. "Apparently his mother wasn't a cook. Either that or she had a wicked sense of humor."

"I can't help but wonder why he would steal Ahab," April said. "No one here seems to know him. How would he even know you *had* Ahab? It's not like he had ever been out to the Inn and he certainly wasn't at the party."

"Right," Rudy agreed. "So someone must have hired him."

"That's what I'm thinking," April said with a nod.

"It must have been the person who made that statement in front of Ahab," Blair said.

"But who is that? That's the million-dollar question," Rudy said.

There was silence for a few moments, while everyone concentrated on the food, keeping their thoughts to themselves. Finally April spoke up.

"You know, I've noticed on a couple of occasions that Ahab only has to hear something once before repeating it. I've been thinking about this a lot. And I remembered that last month there were two teenage boys here." She looked at me. "You remember the O'Reillys, don't you?" I had just taken a sip of soup and so nodded.

"Well, I noticed one morning that the two boys were playing video games, and one of them said, 'Smokin', man!' I didn't think much of it until that afternoon. He came back into the room for some lemonade and Ahab immediately repeated that very same phrase."

"As soon as the kid walked into the room?" Rudy asked.

"Yes. He remembered who said it and repeated it the moment he saw him. He probably does that more often than we realize."

"Wow," I said, exhaling. "So it could be that someone said they wanted to kill Dana in front of Ahab days *before* the party. Then, when he or she came into the room that night, Ahab saw them and repeated it, almost on cue."

"I doubt it's a guest, then," Rudy said. "None of the guests that are here now were here for the Christmas Eve party, right?"

April and I shook our heads no.

"And none of the guests that were here then, would ever have had to come back," she said. "So why would they worry about Ahab?"

"That's a good point," April conceded.

"If it's not a guest though, it means it's someone I must know well," I said grimly.

"Yes," Rudy said. "And someone who would be likely to come back to the Inn again for some reason. That's why the bird had to go. Whoever this is couldn't risk coming back a second time and having Ahab repeat that line."

"So we eliminate the guests," Doe said. "Now, all we have to do is figure out who said it in the first place."

I got up and went to the refrigerator and pulled out the butter dish and brought it back to the table. But when I put it down, my hand was shaking. I plopped down in my chair.

"I can't believe this. Whoever killed Trudy is someone who has access to the Inn and has a reason to be here. It all makes sense. I just never thought of it that way."

"Let's be honest," Blair said. "There are an awful lot of people who could say something like that about Dana, though, just out of frustration if nothing else."

"Yes, but if they said something like that just as a joke, or even as a random comment, why would they hire someone to break in and steal Ahab?" Doe said.

"The more I think about it," I said. "Ahab doesn't pick up just anything. It has to stand out to him. Like what that kid said. He either picks up things that are repeated over and over, or specific comments made right in front of the cage. Otherwise, he'd be repeating everything everyone says all the time."

"God, it just seems crazy that someone would stand right in front of Ahab's cage and say that they want to kill someone…anyone!" Doe said.

"But they had to be talking to someone else," April said. "And if it was said with enough intensity, Ahab would've picked it up."

Doe gave a fake shudder. "That gives me the chills."

"Look, you guys," Rudy spoke up. "We've known since Ahab was stolen *why* he was stolen. Why are you so shocked now?"

"It just feels different when you put it all together," Doe said.

"Okay then," Rudy said. "Think back to the weeks *before* the Christmas party. What other events or meetings did you have here? When someone might have been left alone in the breakfast room?"

I sighed. "Oh dear, let's see. We were planning the reception for Senator Pesante. But of course that was canceled. I did hold a library board meeting here during that time. And Mr. Mulford was here to do the books."

"Don't forget, Roger's son was here to install the new alarm system after Martha's murder investigation wrapped up," April said.

"That's right," I said. "That was the day before the party. And the caterer did a walk-through for the reception that never happened, and then she came back again with one of her caterers to discuss the Christmas Eve party."

"Anything else?" Rudy asked.

I thought back to those days just before and just after Martha was murdered. "Nothing I can think of right now."

April got up and went to the drawer in the center island and pulled out the same notepad and pencil I'd used earlier. "Let's write it down," she said, coming back to the table. "Who all is on the library board with you?"

I gasped. "Are you kidding? Those are all upstanding Mercer Island citizens. None of them would kill someone."

"So were the gang of murderers who killed Martha," Blair said solemnly. "And you and I just nearly got arrested as upstanding citizens," she reminded me.

"Okay," I relented. I recited the list of library board members. They included business owners, a fireman, a teacher, a nun, a college student, Roger Romero and, of course, Tony Morales.

"Was Tony here for that meeting?" April asked solemnly, writing down the names.

"Yes. We met in the dining room." I paused, thinking back to that afternoon. "And as I recall, he left a couple of times to take phone calls. But he always does that," I said, defending him.

"So, he could have come into the breakfast room and talked to someone on the phone within earshot of Ahab's cage," Rudy speculated.

"Yes," I replied reluctantly.

"What do you know about Mr. Mulford?" Doe asked.

I slapped both hands on the table. "Oh, for heaven sakes," I exclaimed, scaring everyone. "Mr. Mulford couldn't kill anyone unless it was with his bad breath."

That sparked a few smiles around the table.

"No one is accusing anyone of anything at this point," Doe said. "But we need to at least eliminate people."

"I hate to say it," Blair said. "But I heard something about Mr. Mulford today while I was at the senior center. Apparently, he used to audit the collection agency Dana's husband owns. Something happened between them and Clay fired him."

"But Mr. Mulford probably loses business all the time," I said defensively. "If he killed all the people who left him for another CPA firm, he'd be a serial killer."

April reached over and placed her hand gently over mine. "Calm down, Julia. We're on your side. And Mr. Mulford's. And Tony's. Let's just get everything down so we know what we're looking at."

I exhaled. "It's just so hard to go through this again. We're talking about people we know and care about."

"Speaking about people we know," Doe said. "What about the caterer? She does business all over the island, and she's probably done business for Dana."

"Yes, but I was with her the entire time she was here," I said. "And during the Christmas party she was in the kitchen the whole time. She had staff who stocked the tables in the breakfast room."

"Maybe it was one of her staff," Blair said.

"But how? She had two people with her, and I never saw them together. They were always working independently of each other. It would have had to have either been a heated discussion between two people right in front of Ahab's cage, or someone talking on their cell phone."

"That would make sense," Blair said. She turned to me. "Do you remember ever seeing anybody standing in the breakfast room talking on their cell phone?"

"Guests, maybe. They're on their cell phones all the time, making plans for the day. So we're back to Dana," I lamented. "We need to know more about her." I turned to Rudy. "I guess it's your turn. What did you find out in Vancouver?"

She took a sip of wine and smiled rather wickedly. "Dana had quite the reputation in Vancouver," she said. "My sources down there remember her well. That's where she must have acquired her fondness for lawsuits. And remember those photographs of the naked boys?"

"Whoa!" April demanded. "What naked boys?"

So much had happened over the last couple of days I had forgotten to tell her about that. "We found some photographs of young naked boys," I said.

"I think I got that part," she said. "Where? And what do they have to do with Dana Finkle?"

"Well, we kind of found them in her trash," I said. "After she demanded that I help her, I said we'd need to know everything about her. She backed off so quickly, she almost left skid marks on the kitchen floor."

"She *said* she was in the middle of a project at home and had to finish it first and would call us the next day. We figured it had something to do with trash pickup the next day," Rudy said.

"And we were right," Doe said. "We picked up her trash and found the pictures."

"Again, what pictures?" April exclaimed.

"Wait a minute," I said.

I got up and ran to my apartment and got the folder with the pictures. I came back and handed it to April. First, she shuffled through the pictures of the boys fully dressed and then the ones we'd taped together of the naked boys. The expression on her face deteriorated quickly until she began to look ill.

"Oh, my," she said as she exhaled. "And you found these in Dana's trash?"

"Yep. In fact, we saw her bring the bag out of her house and drop it at the street," I said.

"She had cut the photos up and put them in two different bags. We pieced them together." I pointed to the picture with the reflection in the mirror. "We don't know who this guy is in the background, though."

"But I think I do," Rudy spoke up, holding up her wine glass. "That's what I was about to tell you. I'm pretty sure that's Dana's ex-husband, Vince Fragel."

"She went from being a Fragel to being a Finkle?" Blair quipped.

"Yes," Rudy replied, frowning at Blair. "He was a banker. He made a lot of money, and they owned a big home overlooking the Columbia River. After a few years, they decided to start fostering children."

"So those are foster kids?" Doe asked with alarm.

"I think so," Rudy replied. "And they only fostered boys – a bunch of them over a period of about five or six years. But then rumors began."

"Oh, God, I think I'm going to be sick," Doe said, turning away.

"Sorry," Rudy said to her. "But it has to be said. Apparently good old Vince liked little boys more than he liked Dana."

"Well, that's understandable," Blair sniped.

"Blair!" Doe said.

"Sorry. That was tacky," she said with an apologetic gesture.

"Was anything ever proven? Did he go to jail?" Doe asked.

Rudy pushed her empty bowl forward and placed her elbows on the table. "No. He was accused, though. I guess he was just a little too friendly and rumors began. I guess the police even questioned him. But there wasn't enough evidence, because none of the boys would admit to the abuse."

"But if Dana had these pictures," April said, gesturing to the folder. "Then she had to know about it."

"Right. The pictures would have been the proof the police needed," Rudy said. "That's what's so strange about this."

"So she protected him. You don't think she was in on it, do you?" Doe said with distaste.

Everyone squirmed a little in their seats.

"God, I hope not," I said. "Even though I can't stand the woman and think she's capable of most anything, I'd hate to think she's capable of that."

"The rumors never included Dana," Rudy reported. "But that's not all. One boy killed himself while in their care. Right after that, Vince disappeared."

"You mean as in – never found?" I asked.

"As in never found," Rudy confirmed. "No one ever saw him again. Eventually, Dana had him declared legally dead and moved up here. Which at least tells us where some of her money comes from."

"Because she gained legal control of his assets," April said.

"Right," Rudy confirmed.

I had picked up the photo of the boy on all fours, with the man in the background reflected in the mirror. His face was obscured by the camera he was holding, but the frames of his glasses poked out one side.

"Uh, oh," I said, staring at the picture. I looked up at my fellow sleuths. "I don't think he's dead, legally or otherwise."

"What do you mean?" Rudy said.

I put the photo on the table. "I think he might be very much alive and ready to make trouble right here in River City," I said, quoting a line from the *Music Man*.

"What do you mean, Julia?" April asked.

"Look at his hands," I said.

I explained what Crystal had told me about the man who had stopped by the Inn the day before, asking about Dana. Then I pointed to the picture.

"Wow," Blair said. "His hands are huge."

"And he has the tattoo of an eagle," I added.

"Wow is right," Doe agreed. "We need to tell Dana."

"And the police," April said. She glanced at me. "Dear God, here we go again."

"But wait," Rudy said. "Do we really think the husband has resurfaced and is the one who tried to kill Dana? Why would he do that?"

"Maybe for the money," April speculated.

"Or revenge," Blair said. "If she had these pictures, she must've known about the abuse, but she got off scot-free *and* with all his money, while he's been running from the law all of this time."

"I think it's time you brought in the police," April said to me. "They'll need to know about all of this."

I looked at her as if she had just asked me to swallow a spider. "But then we'll have to tell them how we found the pictures."

She lowered her chin and looked at me over her glasses. "What did you expect when you decided to steal Dana's trash, Julia?"

CHAPTER TWENTY

I excused myself and called David to report what we knew. The moment I admitted to how we had obtained the pictures, I heard a deep sigh on the other end of the phone, but no verbal reprimand – at least not yet. He said he would send out a patrol officer to pick up the photos. And then, he added, "It's time to stop now, Julia. You need to leave this to us."

"But if we hadn't stolen Dana's trash, you never would have found out about these boys," I argued.

"You don't know that. In fact, Detective Abrams is down in Vancouver right now researching Dana's background. I'm sure he'll find out about the accusations."

"But now we have proof!"

"Which you've completely compromised."

I swallowed. "I…well…"

"Leave it to us, Julia. Please. Now, I have to go."

We hung up, and I returned to the kitchen feeling defeated all over again. Just as I was coming through the swinging door, my phone rang and I answered it.

"Julia, it's Dana."

Heaven knows I didn't need her to identify who she was. I would recognize that croak anywhere.

"Yes," I said with irritation.

"You can come over. I'm ready to talk."

I glanced up at the girls with a less-than-enthusiastic expression. "Actually, Dana, we've been told to back off the case."

"But you promised. I dropped out of the campaign!"

I returned to my seat at the table, while four pairs of questioning eyes watched me. "Why do we have to come there? Why don't you come over here?"

"You have people coming and going there all the time. I'd feel more comfortable here."

"You realize I won't be coming alone."

"I understand," she said.

I sighed. "Okay, we're just finishing dinner. We'll be there in about thirty minutes." I hung up and rolled my eyes.

"What's up?" Rudy asked.

"She wants us to go over to her house. She says she's ready to talk."

"What about the police?" Rudy asked. "Did I hear you say they want us to cease and desist?"

"Yes. David was quite clear on that."

"Then why are we going over to Dana's?" Doe asked.

I hesitated before replying. "Because Dana insisted, I suppose."

Doe and Rudy shared a cautious look. "Are you sure you want to do this, Julia?"

"We did make a promise. Let's hear what she has to say. Then we can decide."

Doe began gathering up the photos and sliding them into the folder. "How are you going to approach these?"

She handed me the folder. I handed it to April. "David is sending over a patrol officer for these. Can you handle that?" She nodded reluctantly and took the envelope. I turned to the others. "I say we play it coy in the beginning. Let's not let on that we raided her trash."

I gave Blair a warning look. She raised her perfectly penciled eyebrows in response.

"I agree," Rudy said. "But if she brings up anything related to her husband and the boys they fostered, technically it's fair game."

"What do you mean?" Blair said. "I thought Julia just said we couldn't talk about anything we learned from her trash."

Rudy gave her a sly smile. "But I learned most of the same information from my trip to Vancouver."

"Good point," Doe said.

April pushed back her chair and took her soup bowl and utensils to the sink. "Well, I'm happy to bow out of this one. I have lemon bars to make for tomorrow, and the thought of another conversation with Dana might just curdle more than my stomach. I'll bring the ingredients over here, so I'll be here when the police arrive," she said.

April left, and we did the dishes and put food away. Twenty-five minutes later, we were pulling into Dana's driveway in Doe's big Mercedes.

Dana and Clay had bought a home owned at one time by a Microsoft executive. It was a rather ugly, split-level mishmash of glass, steel, and plaster, garishly painted a bright, taxicab yellow. It fit Dana's personality to a T.

She answered the door dressed in electric blue slacks, a blue and black sweater with a bold geometric design splashed across the front, with a contrasting blazing orange scarf tied around her thick neck. My eyes momentarily blurred.

We followed her into the living room. Doe and I sat on the sleek leather sofa, while Blair perched primly on the piano bench. Rudy took a straight-backed chair near the fireplace, while Dana plopped into a leather wingback chair next to the window.

"I should have assumed you'd all be together when I called," she said with a stiff lip.

"Why wouldn't we be?" I said. "We were talking about you."

Her eyes flared. "I should have known. You all…"

I held up a hand. "Hold on, Dana. You're the one who asked for our help. So why wouldn't we get together to talk about your case?"

She seemed to relax. "I guess you're right."

"Okay, enough chitchat. Let's hear it," Blair blurted.

Dana shot her a glaring look and then inhaled and held her breath. Blair drew her Botoxed lips into a sweet smile. "You can't hold your breath forever," she said.

Dana released her breath and allowed her shoulders to relax. "Okay, what do you want to know?"

"Everything," Doe said.

"I've already been interviewed by the police, you know," she said.

Her stubbornness forced me to let out a frustrated sigh. "Dana, you said you wanted our help. So, do you or don't you?"

She paused and glanced at each of us. Her hands were clasped into a tight ball in her lap, and moisture glistened on her upper lip.

"Yes, I do," she finally said. "I know the police are doing everything they can, but…you guys have ways of finding out information in town that they don't. I think I'll need that."

I glanced up at the girls thinking, *if she only knew*.

"Okay, let's start with what you told the police?" I asked.

"I told them about all my lawsuits."

"Jeeze, how many are there?" Blair exclaimed.

Dana hesitated before responding. "Six."

"You have six open lawsuits?" Rudy asked, leaning forward.

Dana shrugged. "Yes. There's the suit I filed against Julia, of course."

She had filed a lawsuit against me a few months earlier because I had tripped in front of Starbucks and spilled hot chai tea all across her broad back. She accused me of doing it on purpose.

"Who else?" I said with a clenched jaw.

She shifted her eyes in my direction. "I have a suit filed against Swedish Hospital because they botched a small procedure they performed on Clay."

"What was the procedure?" Blair asked.

"None of your business," Dana said with a snap of her head in Blair's direction.

"Okay, okay," I said. "What else?"

She sighed as if this was a big waste of time. "I also have a suit against Kentucky Fried Chicken in Kirkland. I found a fingernail in my mashed potatoes last May."

"Ewwww," Blair whined.

Rudy shot Blair a glance of reprimand. "Go on," she said to Dana.

"A year ago I bought a blouse from Nordstrom's in Bellevue Square," Dana said. "And the first time I put it on I got a deep scratch from a pin that was left in one of the seams."

"Well, that wasn't their fault," Doe said. "They didn't make the blouse."

"But they sold it to me," Dana retorted with a raised chin.

"And they have deep pockets," Rudy added. "Keep going. That's four. What are the other two?"

"The last ones are a suit against a remodeling company for a mistake they made on my kitchen counter, and one against Emory Auto Shop for putting a hole in my radiator."

There were several gasps around the table, which had Dana looking back and forth at us with curiosity. "What?" she asked.

I hesitated before responding, because I wasn't sure how much I should tell her. "Dana, do you know a man named Al Dente?"

She crinkled up her forehead. "Is that a cooking joke?"

"No," I replied. "He works at Emory Auto Shop."

She shrugged. "No. I've never heard of him. Why?"

"Two days ago, he broke into the Inn and stole Ahab." Her eyes widened, but she kept silent, so I continued. "Yesterday, Blair found out he worked at Emory's. We went to check him out and then followed him to his apartment...where we found Ahab."

Dana let out an exasperated sigh. "What does that stupid bird have to do with me?"

I glanced at Rudy, who nodded at me to continue. "We believe Ahab was stolen because of what he said the night of the Christmas Eve party. Don't you remember? You and I were standing in front of his cage, and he squawked, 'I want to kill Dana Finkle?'"

"Yes, of course I remember that insult. You taught it to him," she said with an angry edge to her voice.

"No. I didn't. That's the point. He heard it from someone else." I stopped talking and watched as the gravity of that statement took hold.

"Oh my God! You mean someone at the party?"

"We think it was someone earlier in the week. Someone who was standing close to the cage, perhaps talking on the phone to someone else," Doe responded.

"But how will you ever figure out who it was?" she asked.

"That's one of the things we were discussing when you called," I said.

She shifted in her seat. "So, have they arrested this...Al Dente?"

My shoulders slumped. "Um...no. He got away."

"Great," she said with a sharp look. "But do you think he's the guy who tried to kill me?"

"You mean the guy who mistakenly killed *Trudy*," Rudy admonished her.

"Yes...of course that's what I meant," she said unapologetically. "Yes, poor Trudy. Well if you think this guy was involved, what about Tony Morales? After all, they arrested him. I think he's probably the killer, don't you?"

Rudy sat back and crossed her legs. "No. We don't. But if you're convinced that Tony is the killer, why did you ask us to come here tonight?"

"I'm not sure what you mean," she said.

I watched Dana's reaction. Besides the fact that she averted her gaze, her voice lacked any conviction of the truth. In fact, she reminded me of every time I'd ever lied to my mother when I was a teenager.

"Yes, you do," I said. "You don't think Tony is the killer, because he doesn't have any *real* reason to want you dead. I mean, after all, why would he?" She didn't answer, so I asked again. "Why in the world would Tony Morales want to kill you, Dana?"

She pursed her big lips as if she was afraid an errant remark might slip out.

Rudy slapped the table, making everyone jump, including a glass candy dish that bounced. "C'mon Dana," she spat. "Out with it. What do you have on Tony?"

"Okay, okay," she snapped
. "I know something about Tony's life."

I cut her off. "Don't you mean his wife?"

She opened her mouth to say something, but stopped. "Yes. I know something about his wife. Where did you hear that?"

"Doesn't matter," I said. "Keep going."

"I suppose you're going to think I'm small-minded," Dana said. "But I found out that his wife used to dance at a striptease place. She was in college at the time."

"So?" Rudy responded.

Blair laughed out loud.

"That's the big thing you have on Tony?" I said. "Who cares if his wife worked at a striptease joint? Especially when she was so young?"

She straightened up to her full height and puffed out her chest in indignation. "I care. Women who work in striptease places are immoral."

"Damn, Dana, you don't look like you were born in Victorian England," Rudy quipped.

Dana turned an evil eye in Rudy's direction.

"Maybe she didn't strip. She could have just been a waitress," Doe said.

Dana shifted her weight uncomfortably. "I don't know for sure."

"Either way, there is nothing wrong with a woman working in a striptease joint," I said to her.

"Tell that to Tony," she retorted. "When I told him I might go public with it, I thought he might kill me right then and there."

"And just out of curiosity," Doe said. "Why would you go public with something like that?"

She paused. "He was opposing me on rescinding an exception to one of the zoning laws."

"Ah." I exhaled and sat back against the sofa. "The exception that allows *me* to have both the bakery and the antique business on the same property as the Inn? Isn't that right?"

"Yes. You know I don't think an exception should be made just because…,"

"… I'm the ex-wife of the Governor," I said, finishing her sentence.

"I was going to say an exception shouldn't be made just because you live so close to the downtown area."

I arched my eyebrows in disbelief. Her motives were as false as Blair's breast implants.

"And besides," she continued. "Tony doesn't like me."

"*No*body likes you!" Blair said.

"Let's face it Dana, if disliking you was the prime motive for wanting you dead, then half the island would be under suspicion," Rudy said.

"So, if Tony isn't the killer, it means the killer is still out there," Doe said quietly.

Dana slumped back into her chair. "I don't know if Tony is the killer or not. But if the police think he is, they might stop looking, and then what? That's why I need you guys."

Rudy had gotten up and wandered over to a floor-to-ceiling bookcase that flanked the fireplace. She seemed to be browsing the books, but suddenly turned to Dana. "Listen, Dana, it's time to cut the crap. What's the deal with your ex-husband and little boys?"

Well, that sucked all of the air out of the room. I thought Dana was going to turn blue, since she had her mouth shut so tightly.

Count to three.

She finally exhaled and said, "Oh, look at the time. I'm supposed to be meeting Clay." She started to rise, cutting our meeting short.

Crash!

Everyone jerked around to where a glass frame had fallen off the fireplace mantle and shattered on the flagstone hearth. Dana's hand flew to her mouth, and she ran over to scoop up the broken pieces. Rudy stepped back and crossed her arms over her chest.

"You did that on purpose," Dana said to her, placing the broken pieces back onto the mantle.

Rudy shrugged. "I must have bumped it by mistake."

"If I were you, I'd answer the question," Doe said, throwing a warning glance at Rudy.

Dana paused and looked around the room. "How did you find out about the boys?" she asked. The look of fear in her eyes was palpable.

"Again… It doesn't matter," I said. "We know."

"Actually, you were quite the media darling in Vancouver," Rudy said, running a finger along the spines of the books. "Tell us now, or I'll just do more digging," she said, picking up a heavy cut glass vase from one of the shelves.

Dana quickly reached out and took the vase out of her hands and replaced it on the shelf. "Okay, okay, just leave my things alone."

Rudy put up her hands in submission and backed away, while Dana returned to her seat, looking back every few seconds to check on Rudy. Convinced that Rudy would behave, she began to speak very softly.

"When I was married to my first husband, we found out that I couldn't have children. He came from a large family, and so he talked me into fostering kids. But…he only wanted to foster boys. He said he'd always wanted a son, so that he could teach him how to play baseball and soccer." She paused as if the memory were painful. "Anyway, we had a large basement, which he outfitted with pinball machines and other kinds of games for the kids."

She looked genuinely uncomfortable as she relived the memories. I almost felt sorry for her. Then I remembered who was doing the talking.

"And that's where he would abuse them," Rudy stated.

It looked like Dana was going to deny it, but then she changed her mind. "Yes," she said in barely a whisper. "Eventually rumors began. Then we were visited by the state office, and then by the local police. It was humiliating." She dropped her head.

"And you knew about it? The abuse?" Doe asked.

Again, she inhaled as if to deny it. But then she exhaled. "Not in the beginning. But finally, like everyone else, I suspected it. When I confronted him, he blew up."

"Have you told Detective Abrams or Franks about this?" Doe asked.

"Of course not. Do you think I'm crazy? I'd never live it down."

"Are *you* crazy?" Blair blurted. "Someone's trying to kill you."

"Dana," I said in my most reassuring voice. "Haven't you considered that perhaps the person trying to kill you is one of the boys abused by your husband?"

She looked up and put her hand to her throat, as if she were having trouble breathing. "That was so long ago. And the boys were so young."

"But they wouldn't be young now," Doe said. "I think you need to talk to the police."

Now she was wringing her hands. "I...I can't. What if it became public?"

"That's the least of your worries," Doe said.

"But I had nothing to do with harming those boys. Honest. So why would one of them come after me?"

"Why indeed," Blair murmured.

"Don't you understand? If this comes out, it will ruin my life," she said to Blair in a pleading tone.

Her expression was pitiful. She actually believed her reputation was more important than her life – or, apparently, more important than the lives of Trudy Bascom and those abused boys.

"Dana, it's better to be embarrassed than dead, don't you think?" I said to her.

She looked at each of us in turn and then seemed to make a decision. "Okay, I guess you're right. I'll go talk to them first thing in the morning."

"So what else?" Rudy said. "We want it all."

"That's all," she said. "There's nothing more. You have it all. The lawsuits. Tony's wife. And my husband's indiscretions."

She didn't look anyone in the eye, but instead, glanced toward the hallway and then down to her hands again. Doe picked up on the cue.

"You're lying," she said.

Dana's head jerked up. "I am not!"

"Yes, you are," Rudy said. "You're so obvious."

"You're hiding something," Doe kept pushing her. "What else are you afraid we'll find?"

"Nothing. Nothing at all. And if you don't believe me, you can search my house. Any time." She stood up, facing Doe and me on the sofa. "Now, I really *do* have to go."

"What?" Blair exclaimed, standing up. "You're the one who invited us over here."

"Yes, but I told you all that I know. I have to pick Clay up in Bellevue. His Saab is in the shop. And then we're grabbing a late dinner."

She glanced at her watch and began walking toward the front door. Behind her, I saw Rudy fade back into the hallway that led to the back of the house. Rudy and I locked eyes, and she nodded for us to follow Dana out the front door. Then she disappeared into the darkened hallway.

We converged by the front door, everyone grabbing coats and purses, including Dana. Dana was in such a hurry to get us all outside, she didn't even notice Rudy wasn't with us.

"Well, thank you for coming," she said, locking the front door and turning toward her car. "I hope I've been helpful. Now I have to go."

With that, she left us standing in a huddle on her front step while she scuttled down the brick path to where her car was parked next to Doe's Mercedes in the driveway. She opened the door, got in, and left.

We all just stood there watching her tail lights disappear up the street.

"What a witch," Blair said, turning to look at us. "Wait a minute, where's Rudy?"

She and Doe both looked around as if they'd lost something. Just then the front door opened, and Rudy emerged with a Cheshire cat grin spread across her face.

"Why don't you girls come on in from the cold?" she said.

Doe nervously glanced up the street, as if Dana might come back. "But…what if…"

Rudy swung the front door wide. "You heard her. She said we could search her house anytime we wanted. I choose now."

Blair clapped her hands together like a child at Christmas. "Oh Rudy," she exclaimed. "You are a devil in disguise."

We all quickly climbed the steps and reentered the home, closing the door behind us.

CHAPTER TWENTY-ONE

"So what's the plan?" Doe asked once we were inside with the door closed.

We shed our coats and threw them onto a bench by the front door, draping our purses over the side. I glanced at my watch.

"If she's really going to dinner, then she'll be gone at least an hour and a half. That should give us enough time to search," I said.

"Okay," Rudy said. "We need to find out what else she's hiding. Knowing Dana, she could have things stuffed almost anywhere. So, Doe, you take the kitchen and the hallway. Julia and I will take the living room and the study. And Blair..."

"I'll take the bedrooms," she said with a wave of her hand. "After all, I know my way around a bedroom better than most people know their way to the bathroom."

"She has us there," Doe said. "Let's just make sure to leave things exactly as we found them."

We nodded and split up. We spent the next 45 minutes opening and closing drawers, looking under cushions, looking into jewelry boxes, magazine holders, closets, and wastepaper baskets. It was almost 9:00 when we heard Doe exclaim from the foyer, "Aha!" Blair ran down from the second floor, while Rudy and I hurried in from other areas of the ground floor.

"Look at this," Doe, said with enthusiasm, holding up a manila envelope in one hand and a sheet of paper in the other.

We met her at the base of the stairs and she handed the piece of paper to Rudy. Rudy glanced at it briefly and handed it to me. Doe looked over my shoulder as I read the note.

Leave $25,000 in cash under the baseball bleachers at Liberty Park in Renton tomorrow afternoon at 3:30. Come alone. If you don't, more than your life will be in jeopardy.

It looked like a threatening note from an old Charlie Chan movie. Each letter had been cut out from either a magazine or a newspaper and pasted onto a blank sheet of paper. It would have been comical if it weren't for the message itself.

"Why wouldn't Dana tell us about this?" Doe asked.

"The bigger question is why wouldn't she tell the police?" Rudy said.

"Well, technically we don't know that she hasn't," I said.

"Yes we do. If she'd told the police, they would *have* the note."

"That's true. Where did you find it?" I asked Doe.

"In the drawer in that table," Doe said, pointing behind her to a sleek table set against the staircase.

"But now what do we do?" Blair asked. "We have the note, but we don't know who it's from or why it was sent."

"And we just got our fingerprints all over it," I said dismally.

Doe leaned in over my shoulder and said, "Wait a minute. Hand it back. Let me smell that."

I handed her the note, and she took it by its corner. She waved it back and forth in front of her nose. We watched curiously.

"What are you doing?" Rudy asked.

"Don't you smell it?" she said. "It smells like barbeque sauce."

As she waved it, I stuck my nose up and inhaled. It actually did smell like barbeque sauce.

"You're right."

Blair reached out and grabbed it and stuck it to her surgically enhanced, perfectly shaped nose. "I can smell it, too."

"But how is that going to help us?" Rudy demanded. "How in the world are we going to be able to tell who sent it?"

"Because I recognize the barbeque sauce," Doe said with confidence.

Rudy threw out a narrow hip and put her hand on it. "Seriously? There are maybe a million different barbeque sauces in the world."

"Exactly. That's what I mean," Doe said, her dark eyes glowing. "I could swear this comes from a little restaurant up in Renton. I had lunch there last month. It's well known in the area for their special barbeque sauce because it has some secret ingredient in it. Trust me. It's a smell you don't forget."

I looked up at my elegant friend. "I can't picture you eating barbeque."

Doe was a picky eater and almost obsessive about how she looked. Her thick, salt-and-pepper hair never seemed to move, even in a stiff breeze. Her clothes were always perfect – never a button missing, a stain, or a wrinkle. And when she ate, she never dribbled, spilled, or shed a flake. It was hard to picture her eating greasy barbeque. But I also remembered that she was a wine expert and could tell the bouquet of certain wines just by smelling them. She had a good nose.

She smiled. "Don't worry, Julia. I didn't eat the barbeque. We have a satellite office over in the Highlands in Renton. My manager selected the restaurant, and I had a salad. But I asked them about the sauce, and they told me they use a flavored liquid smoke. I didn't even know there *was* such a thing."

Rudy stepped in and took the threatening note. She held it to her nose as she said, "And you can tell that this is the same barbeque sauce?"

"I'd bet on it," Doe said. "It's distinctive. So distinctive that the smell was trapped in my car for days."

"Okay," I said. "Let's take a picture of the note with one of our cell phones and then return it to its hiding place."

"And then what?" Blair asked, as Rudy pulled out her phone and clicked a picture.

"Then I say that tomorrow a couple of us take a trip out to Renton for lunch."

As Rudy snapped a picture of the note, a car's headlights flashed across the front window. Fortunately, the drapes were closed. The four of us froze.

"What do we do?" Blair screeched.

"Shhh," Rudy hushed her.

She returned the note to its hiding place and gestured all of us to follow her back into the living room.

"Okay, everybody take your places exactly as you were before Dana left."

"But…" Blair started to say.

"Just follow my lead," she said.

It wasn't 10 seconds before we heard someone stomp up to the front door and throw it open.

"What the hell are you still doing here?" Dana demanded, coming into the living room.

Doe and I were sitting placidly on the sofa, while Rudy stood near the bookcase with an open book in her hand, and Blair sat at the piano picking out a tune. We all looked up.

"You left us here," Rudy said calmly.

Dana's eyes grew wide and her mouth dropped open. "Whaaat? I left you all standing on the front steps."

Rudy glanced over at us, her face a picture of angelic curiosity. "No… I don't think so. We're all still right here, where you left us."

I smiled inwardly. I'd hate to play Rudy in a game of poker.

"That's right, Dana. We were wondering what time you'd get back," I said. I glanced at my watch. "You said you were going to dinner in Bellevue, but you've been gone less than an hour. Where did you eat? Jack In The Box?"

Her beady eyes narrowed, if that were even possible. She wasn't buying it. And coming in behind her was Clay. His face lit up with surprise at seeing us.

"Nice to see you, Julia," he said, as if it were the most normal thing in the world to see me in his living room uninvited. He hung his coat and climbed the stairs.

Dana watched him disappear at the head of the stairs and then her head swung back in our direction.

"You're not fooling me," she said. "How the hell did you get in here?"

Rudy snapped the book closed. "You're the one who told us we could search the house at any time," Rudy said with innocence. "Perhaps we took you up on your offer."

Those beady eyes flew open in surprise. "You wouldn't!"

She glanced at each of us, as if to see if we were holding onto any secrets. Then she spun around and marched toward the hall table that held the note. She opened the drawer and pulled out the envelope and glanced inside without saying a word. She was about to replace it, but quick as a wink, Rudy scooted across the living room gesturing for us to follow. By the time Dana was ready to slip the note back into the drawer, we were all standing right behind her. Blair tapped her on the shoulder. She whipped around with a look of surprise that almost made me laugh.

"What's that?" Rudy asked a phony innocence. She snatched the envelope from Dana's stubby fingers with lightning speed and pulled out the sheet of paper. She allowed her eyes to scan the page. "Oh look you guys. It's a threatening note."

Doe grabbed the note and held it to her nose. "Gee, it has a funny smell," she said. "I do believe that's barbeque sauce."

Dana reached for the note, but not before Blair grabbed it, turned and walked away with it. While Dana protested from behind, Blair read the note out loud, and then she whipped around to face Dana. "Dana, this could be important evidence. Why haven't you given it to the police?"

Dana snatched the piece of paper away from Blair. "Because I just received it yesterday afternoon," she said. "And…and I hadn't decided what to do about it. Besides, it's none of your business."

"What do you mean it's none of *our* business?" Rudy demanded coming up on the other side.

We had formed a complete circle around Dana now, and she was looking mighty uncomfortable.

"You're the one who asked us to help investigate Trudy's murder, and you're the one who invited us over here tonight to discuss it," Rudy said.

"That's right," Doe said. "You promised that you had told us everything."

Blair leaned in and wagged her finger at Dana like a nasty teenage girl. "You're holding out on us, Dana. I wouldn't do that if I were you."

Dana backed toward the staircase and bumped into a wastebasket, knocking it over. Some loose paper fell out, along with a big wad of cash.

"What's that?" Rudy said, quickly slipping behind Dana. She grabbed the roll of bills before Dana could stop her. "Well, I guess we missed this," she said. "Is this the blackmail money?"

Dana stared at Rudy, her lips pressed together. She glanced nervously up the stairs, as if afraid that Clay might hear, and then exhaled like a deflating balloon.

"Yes. That's what I was doing this afternoon. Like I said, the note just came yesterday. I don't know who it's from… I…there's no stamp or return address on it. Someone must have just left it in the mailbox."

"So you withdrew the money and were going to hand it over?" I asked in surprise.

"Wouldn't you? Whoever this is, is trying to kill me."

"And you think by paying them off, they'll stop?" Rudy asked.

She slumped back against the table. "I don't know. Probably not. That's why I wanted you to keep digging."

"Oh, save it, Dana," Rudy snapped. She handed Dana the money and marched over to the bench where our coats and purses were. She grabbed her coat and threw it around her shoulders and then grabbed her purse. "You've been wasting our time from the beginning. And I for one have a whole lot of other things I could be doing rather than sitting around your house on a weeknight waiting for you to come home. Let's go, girls," she said, starting for the door.

The three of us swept past Dana and also grabbed our coats and purses. Rudy had the door open, and we were just about to leave. Dana stopped us.

"Wait!" she said with a raised hand. "Don't go. I do need your help. This note scares me. This whole thing scares me. I'm sorry. I don't know what to do. I'm not making good decisions."

Rudy used one hand to swing the front door closed again. "Okay. Then besides the abuse, why else would someone blackmail you?"

Dana's eyes shifted from one to the other of us as she contemplated her answer. Then her entire body relaxed in defeat.

"Because when I was very young…I was responsible for someone's death."

CHAPTER TWENTY-TWO

It was after ten-thirty, and we were back in Dana's living room. Her husband, Clay, was still upstairs. Dana was in the wingback chair, this time looking a little green around the edges. It must be hard to have every mistake or indiscretion of your life exposed, and it made me wonder briefly how I would feel. But then, I thought, *nice people didn't do the things that Dana did.*

"Originally, I wanted to be a nurse," she said. "So right out of high school, I trained to become a home health aide, while I saved for tuition. I was actually very good at taking care of other people. And my clients loved me. Especially an old gentleman named Mr. Peabody, who was dying from lung cancer. He was receiving hospice care in his home. He lived alone, with the exception of a housekeeper. He had no other relatives and no real friends." She stopped, took a breath and glanced down at her hands. "We became very close. "

"Oh God, you don't mean…" Blair blurted.

"No, not that!" Dana said, glancing up. "For heaven's sake, give me some credit. I'm not some Anna Nicole Smith."

Blair almost choked at that. I'm sure she hadn't meant to physically compare Dana to the blond bombshell who had married a millionaire in his nineties. Besides the difference in hair color, there was the difference in, well, everything else.

"Let me guess," I said. "The old guy put you in his will."

She glanced at me, her gaze frozen in place. She might as well have had the word *guilt* written across her enormous forehead.

"He…he didn't have anyone else," she said in a wormy sort of way. "And he told me I reminded him of his daughter, who had died very young." She paused, as if deciding whether to go on. Finally, she said, "So he had his will changed, leaving everything to me."

"Oh, my God," Rudy said. She dropped her head into one hand.

"It's not like that," Dana said, glancing at Rudy defensively. "I didn't kill him. He died naturally…well, sort of."

Rudy lifted her head and looked at Dana with suspicion. "Don't tell me. You just didn't save him, did you?"

There was a long pause. A very long pause.

Doe groaned as Blair muttered under her breath, "Sheesh."

"The lung cancer made it hard for him to breathe or even to swallow," Dana said. "So the housekeeper used to cut up his food into very small pieces. One day, she left his lunch in the kitchen and went to the store with instructions for me to give it to him. He…uh, choked on some broccoli. It was awful. He kept trying to get a breath, and then his face started turning blue."

"And you didn't do anything to help him," Rudy said.

This time Dana stared at Rudy. "I was so young. I didn't know what to do," she said in a defensive tone.

"That's not exactly true, is it?" Rudy said, her eyes narrowing. "To become a home health aide, you have to have been trained in CPR and things like the Heimlich maneuver."

Dana turned fearful eyes in my direction, but I didn't come to her rescue.

"How could you do that?" Blair exclaimed.

Dana turned to Blair. "He was in a lot of pain. All the time. He would've died in a few months anyway. This was better, don't you think? More humane."

"Oh jeeze," Blair said, standing up in disgust. "You killed him as sure as if you had stuck a knife in his back. And now it's come back to haunt you. This and your husband's preference for little boys. I, for one, am done with you."

Blair left for the foyer, and the rest of us stood awkwardly and followed. Dana panicked again. "No. Don't…" she said, running after us. "Don't go. I've been honest. That's what you wanted. You promised you would help me."

Rudy turned to Dana as she donned her coat a second time. "I keep looking for a redeeming quality. Something that will make me feel good about helping you, Dana. But I just don't see it."

"So you're all just going to leave? You're going to leave me to fend for myself?"

I had just slipped into my own coat and grabbed my purse. I looked at the girls' faces. What I saw were varying degrees of contempt and anger. But we'd made a promise, and I thought we should keep it.

"We did say we would help," I said to them. "And we forced her to tell us everything. None of us ever expected Dana to be an angel."

"We didn't expect her be a walking encyclopedia of bad behavior, either." Rudy almost spit the words out.

I stood my ground. In situations like these, Rudy would usually carry the day. Her take-charge attitude and her brusque manner would overshadow anyone else's objections. But not this time.

"We made an agreement, Rudy. We need to follow through." But then I turned to Dana. "But you have to give the blackmail note to the police and tell them the same story you just told us."

Her eyes opened in surprise as she took a quick intake of breath. I could feel the objection coming, so I put up my hand.

"Don't even say it. You have no choice in the matter. You either tell the police, or we will. Along with the story about your first husband and his penchant for young boys."

She dropped her head and nodded in defeat.

"All right, then. Do that first thing in the morning. Then meet us at the Inn at 11:00. We'll need to make a plan."

CHAPTER TWENTY-THREE

The next day dawned with a slate gray sky, a light breeze, but no rain. The temperature had risen to a balmy 48 degrees, and there were promises of sunbreaks later in the afternoon.

As scheduled, we met at 11:00 a.m. Dana had delivered the note to Detective Abrams, who was back from Vancouver. He had, in fact, learned much of the same information Rudy had, but he'd also been successful in tracking down some leads on Dana's ex-husband, Vince Fragel. Not the least of which was that he'd been incarcerated for embezzlement at one time under an assumed name.

I'd forgotten to tell Dana about the man who had shown up at the Inn asking about her. Instead, Detective Abrams filled her in. The news put her on edge, and she wondered out loud if he was the one who had sent the blackmail note. But Detective Abrams had instructed Dana to return her money to the bank, and that they would find a female officer to stand in as a decoy at the appointed time for the money drop that afternoon.

"So, I guess there's nothing for us to do," she said as we sat around the kitchen table. "We'll just have to wait and see who they pick up."

Rudy was tapping her fingers on the table, gazing out the window. The Brewsters stood at the end of the dock, each with a cup of coffee. Rudy's competitive nature had led to a college scholarship in women's track and field, and she'd been the pitcher on the women's softball team. Now, she played fast-pitch. But even as a female jock, she'd won the state spelling bee in high school and earned a bachelor's and master's degree in Communications from the UW. Add to that a short stint on the debate team, and you can see why I called her "The Boss." Her verbal skills matched her pitching arm, and right now I could almost see her brain churning as it stewed on our current situation.

"What are you thinking, Rudy?" I asked. "I see smoke coming out of your ears."

She turned her tan, weathered face toward me, her brown eyes narrowed in a squint. "The person who sent that note can't be Dana's ex-husband."

"Why not?" Dana blurted.

"What time did you pick up your mail yesterday?" Rudy asked her.

"Uh…about 1:00, I think."

Rudy looked at me. "What time did Crystal say that guy stopped by the Inn asking about Dana?"

"Around 3:00 p.m.," I replied. "Oh, I get it. You're right."

"You get what?" Dana asked, looking back and forth between the two of us.

"Your ex-husband was asking where you lived yesterday afternoon at 3:00. But you'd already picked up the ransom note at 1:00. In *your* mailbox."

I saw the lightbulb in Dana's head sputter. She was a little slow to pick up on things.

"Dana," Rudy said. "At 3:00 your ex-husband didn't know where you lived. So how could he have been the one to leave the ransom note in your mailbox earlier that day?"

The lightbulb popped on full force. "Oh! So, it must have been someone else," she said. She looked even more uncomfortable at this revelation. "So Vince is looking for me, but someone *else* is blackmailing me?"

"And don't forget someone's trying to *kill* you," Blair said with a helpful smile.

Dana grimaced. "Thanks. Now what?"

"What time were you supposed to drop off the money?" Rudy asked Dana.

"At 3:30 this afternoon," she said.

"Hmmm…that could be right after the shift change at the restaurant," Rudy said thoughtfully. "Okay, why don't we see if we can ID the blackmailer first?"

"How do we do that?" Dana asked.

"The restaurant," Rudy said.

Doe turned to me. "Are you sure you want to do this, Julia? Remember what David said about staying out of this."

"What? I can't go have lunch?" I said. "I *like* barbeque."

We looked up the restaurant online and scoped out the picture of the building. It sat in a strip mall off Sunset Boulevard in the Renton Highlands. The front of the restaurant was two giant windows, making it easy to see inside. So we discussed our options and decided on a plan.

We gathered our coats and emerged from the kitchen into the breakfast room. The Kohl family opened their door and noisily began to descend the stairs just as we rounded the corner into the reception area. As I came into the entryway, the kids saw me and ran down the stairs.

"I think I saw one of the ghosts last night," Barry said, his eyes alight with excitement. "It was peering in the window."

"He's making it up," Sherrie said, stopping behind him. "He's just trying to scare me."

"I am not," Barry said, pushing her shoulder. "You're just a fraidy cat. The ghosts won't hurt you, will they Mrs. Applegate?"

Their parents had come up behind them.

"Barry, stop that!" Mr. Kohl ordered. "I don't like this nonsense. I told you, it's just a marketing ploy, like Santa Claus."

He had clenched his gloves under his elbow as he reached into his pocket to grab his keys. I watched with amusement as the gloves began to move. It looked as if someone was pulling them from behind his elbow. Another second and they hit the floor.

He looked down in surprise.

"Where are you off to today?" I said, deflecting their attention.

"We're heading over to my mother's in West Seattle," Mrs. Kohl said. "And then we're going to take the ferry over to Bainbridge Island."

"Well, that sounds like fun," I said with insincerity.

Mr. Kohl bent down to pick up his gloves, but they moved sideways an inch before he could retrieve them. He adjusted his stance and reached for them again. Again, they moved. The kids were already arguing over something, while their mother tried to referee. The rest of us just watched while prim and proper Mr. Kohl chased his gloves across the floor.

I finally stepped forward and stomped my foot on them. He glanced up at me, his face red with anger, and then yanked them out from under my shoe.

Rudy opened the door. "Have a great time," she said with a big grin.

Mrs. Kohl and the kids went outside, while Mr. Kohl lingered. He leaned over to me, blowing coffee breath into my face.

"I don't appreciate tricks. And I doubt the Better Business Bureau would either," he said in a threatening manner. He turned and marched out the door.

"Don't fall overboard," Rudy called after them, as they climbed into their rental car.

÷

We took two cars to the restaurant: my Pathfinder and Doe's Mercedes. Once there, Doe and Rudy went inside to order lunch. Blair stayed behind in the Mercedes as backup. Dana and I sat in my car, parked right in front with two pairs of binoculars.

The goal was simple: scope out the restaurant personnel to see if Dana knew any of them. Doe and Rudy purposely picked a table near the window and sat down. A few moments later a young man delivered glasses of ice water and then left. We continued to watch while the girls toyed with their water glasses and the utensils on the table. A young waitress arrived a minute later with a notepad. Dana leaned forward, peering at her through the window as Doe and Rudy ordered.

"Did you recognize either the boy or the girl?" I asked, as the young woman left with their order.

She shook her head. "No."

We sat there for a few minutes watching people come and go. An older man and a woman parked next to us and entered the restaurant. As the door opened, I noticed a middle-aged woman near the back, wearing an apron. She was standing behind the order counter. I nudged Dana.

"What about her?" I said, pointing to the back of the restaurant.

Just as Dana adjusted her binoculars, the door swung closed. She dropped her hands in frustration. "Darn it," she said.

"Come on, keep looking through the window. She's bound to move back and forth and maybe you can see her."

Dana held up the binoculars again, scanning the interior of the restaurant. "I can't see her," she said. "I'll have to get closer." She started to reach for the door handle, but I grabbed her wrist.

"No," I said. "Whoever this is can't see you. If they recognize you and realize that you're here, they're liable to run."

She blew out a frustrated breath. "Fine. Now what?"

"It's time for Blair," I said.

I pulled out my cell phone and sent a text to Blair. I told her to go in and sit at a table in the back of the restaurant, where a middle-aged woman was the waitress. She glanced over at me and nodded. She got out of the car and entered the building.

As I looked through my binoculars, I noticed that Rudy and Doe ignored Blair's arrival, just as we'd discussed. Blair sashayed to the back of the restaurant and took a table in the corner. I could see a person go right over and place a glass of water in front of her and hand her a menu. Blair seemed to study the menu, and then handed it back. The individual crossed back to the counter to place the order. As the person turned back, Blair pulled out her phone and snapped a picture. A moment later, Blair forwarded the picture to me.

"Here, take a look at this," I said to Dana.

I held out my phone. Dana lowered the binoculars and refocused her eyes before glancing down at the picture on my phone. A second later, she'd grabbed it from me to study the picture more closely.

"Oh my God! I know that woman."

"Who is she?"

"Her name is Sonja Kyes. She was Mr. Peabody's housekeeper. I can't believe it. *She's* the one who's blackmailing me? That bitch!"

"But why would *she* blackmail you? I thought she was gone that day."

But Dana hadn't heard me. She threw open the car door, got out and rushed inside before I could stop her. I followed as fast as I could, coming in behind her. Blair looked up in surprise as Dana blew past tables in the middle of the room and marched up to the cash register.

The woman she'd ID'd as Sonja Kyes was taller than Dana by a good three or four inches, skinny as a rail, with long, stringy black hair way overdue for a dye job. She was about to hand change to someone when she looked up and recognized Dana. Her eyes opened wide, and the coins in her hand clanged across the counter and onto the floor as she backed up a step.

"How dare you," Dana screamed, advancing on her.

Sonja turned, ready to flee, but Dana was fast when she was mad. She circled around the end of the counter and caught Sonja from behind.

"Oh, no you don't!" Dana yelled.

Sonja whirled around and shot out with her fist, catching Dana in the jaw. Dana flew sideways into the short order counter, knocking a plate of barbeque onto the floor. She quickly reached up and grabbed a second plate off the counter and flung it like a flying saucer straight at her opponent. Sonja ducked. The plate skimmed over the front counter, barely missing a young man sitting there. He whipped around to watch the plate slam against the far wall, splattering barbeque and French fries all over the wall, the floor and several patrons sitting close by.

People began to scatter.

Meanwhile, Dana and Sonja had come together like battering rams, slapping and clawing at each other. And then they had their hands around each other's throats and were yanking each other back and forth.

I thought maybe I should try to stop them.

I came up behind Dana and reached around her shoulder to grab her wrist. Blair found a way around the other end of the corner and came up behind Sonja. There was a lot of pulling and pushing, grunting and groaning, but Blair and I finally got their hands loose.

I was pulling Dana back, when her right hand slipped out of mine and slapped Sonja hard across the face. Sonja yanked her right hand away from Blair and slapped Dana. Dana howled and pulled away from me.

She slammed into Sonja, knocking her backwards. Blair lost her grip and suddenly, the two women were slapping each other in a mean game of patty cakes. Hands and fingers flew as they each ducked to avoid a slap. I kept trying to grab Dana's right hand, but got smacked in the process, making my eyes water.

Just as the cook came out yelling, Sonja reached out with her foot and pulled Dana's leg out from under her. She and I both went down, but not before Dana grabbed for Sonja, taking her down with us. Before I knew it, Blair had been knocked backwards, and all four of us were on the floor behind the counter, arms and legs flailing.

I caught glimpses of the cook behind me in his barbeque-stained apron and his little white cap. His face was twisted in anger, as he gestured at us with a grease-covered spatula, shouting something that sounded like a mixture of Spanish and French.

Doe and Rudy arrived at either end of the space behind the counter, ready to engage, but clearly holding back. As I glanced up, four customers were craning their necks over the counter, watching us with bemused smiles and cell phones out, taking pictures.

That's when the brief wail of a siren made everyone stop.

"Julia, it's the police!" Rudy yelled.

Breathing heavily, we quickly disentangled. The floor was sticky, so it was difficult to get my feet underneath me. I was about to push off the floor, when a burly voice called out, "What's going on here?"

Blair and I locked eyes. What were the chances?

The four of us stood and turned sheepishly toward the voice, as the four bystanders with cell phones stepped aside.

"Well, well, well…this is our lucky day, wouldn't you say, Roy?"

Just our luck. It was Officers Mosley and Hager again. Officer Hager had her hands on her hips and her mouth set into a grim smile. But her eyes weren't laughing.

"Ladies, it's nice to see you again. I see you brought some friends to the party this time. Care to explain?"

CHAPTER TWENTY-FOUR

The officers split us up and then called for backup. Another squad car arrived. They filled in the new officers on the situation and then cleared one half of the restaurant. They took over a couple of tables on the other side of the room and set up shop to interview everyone.

While one officer watched us, Officer Mosley and a second officer began with the witnesses, including the owner. Officer Hager began with Sonja, while we sat wiping barbeque sauce off our hands and faces, and Rudy sat back to read the local newspaper as if nothing was wrong.

I watched Sonja for a moment, wondering what she must have been like in the days she worked for Mr. Peabody. She must have been pretty once. She had good bone structure and intelligent eyes. But the ever-dutiful housekeeper had aged badly. Her skin was puffy and mottled, as if she had been a heavy drinker. Probably in her late sixties, deep lines pulled her facial features into a haggard look, making me think she'd lived a hard, angry life. I was sure that Dana had been partly responsible for that.

Sonja immediately threw us under the bus, screaming that Dana, Blair and I had all attacked her. Dana tried to break in at one point to straighten out her recounting of the incident, but was shushed by Officer Hager as she gestured for a young, skinny officer to move in closer to keep an eye on her.

Meanwhile, I felt along the upper part of my cheek-bone while I waited. It smarted just below my right eye, and I thought I might have a bruise where Dana had smacked me.

By the time Officer Hager got around to Dana, she was practically hyperventilating.

"That woman is a murderer," Dana exclaimed, pointing at Sonja as she marched over to the table.

Sonja jumped to her feet in defense. "I am not! I had nothing to do with that."

Officer Hager turned to Sonja and pointed at the chair behind her. "Sit down and don't move again."

Officer Hager interviewed Dana for a good ten minutes, while Sonja sat and steamed. We could only hear snippets of Dana's conversation, but she was overly animated while she talked, and I wondered what kind of tale she was weaving, even if she was being honest. At one point, she raised her voice and said, "I'm telling the truth. Just ask Julia." And then she pointed at me.

Officer Hager turned to me. "We'll be talking with Ms. Applegate and Ms. Wentworth very soon," she said. She turned back to Dana, spoke to her softly and then released her. Dana got up and walked rigidly back to her seat, all the time glowering at Sonja.

I was called over next, and since Officer Mosley had finished with the customers, he called for Blair.

"Dana is right, you know," I said to Officer Hager when I sat down. "That woman was trying to blackmail her."

"How do you know that?" she asked.

"I've seen the blackmail note. The Mercer Island police have it now. You can call Detective Abrams at the Mercer Island Police Department," I said. "Dana gave him the blackmail note this morning."

"I'll do that. But let's get back to the altercation...your *second* altercation, I might add," she emphasized. "What happened?"

"To understand all of this, you have to hear it from the beginning."

I explained about Trudy Bascom's murder and the threat to Dana. Officer Hager politely listened and took notes, but finally interrupted.

"Ms. Applegate, what I'm trying to understand is why you and your friends are involved in this investigation in the first place. The Mercer Island police are capable of handling it. They do have trained detectives, you know. I doubt very much that they need your help."

I ignored the affront. "Dana came to us on her own. She thought we might have resources the police wouldn't."

"Like what?" she said without trying to hide her cynicism.

I puffed up at this. "You may think we're just a bunch of old busybodies, but I'll have you know that the Mayor of Mercer Island actually bestowed honorary awards on us last year for helping with a murder investigation."

"Very nice, I'm sure," she said with a slight roll of her eyes. "But I doubt the police will appreciate your meddling. Now let's keep going. How in the world did you settle on Ms. Kyes as your blackmailer? Mrs. Finkle said something about the smell of the blackmail note."

"Yes. Our friend, Doe," I said, nodding in her direction. "She recognized the smell of the barbeque sauce in here." I flared my nostrils and glanced around. "I'm sure you can smell it. It's quite distinctive. Almost overpowering, I'd say."

"So you came over here, and Mrs. Finkle recognized Ms. Kyes?"

"That's right. They have a history."

"What do you mean?"

I shrugged. "You'd have to ask Dana. I'd only be repeating what she told us. But it sounds like Sonja really does have a reason to hate Dana enough to want some kind of revenge."

"According to Mrs. Finkle, you and Ms. Wentworth were just trying to stop the fight. Is that right?"

"Yes. Dana did go after Sonja. I don't think she meant to hurt her, but she was mad, and before we knew it, they were at each other's throats. So Blair and I tried to intercede." I reached up and fingered the goo in my hair. "Unfortunately, we weren't very successful."

Officer Hager sat back and closed her notebook. "All right. You can go back to your friends. I need to talk with Officer Mosley a moment."

She got up and joined Officer Mosley, who had just finished with Blair. As Blair and I returned to our seats, Mosley and Hager huddled up to compare notes. They called the owner over at one point and then once again, Officer Mosley pulled out his cell phone. He had a brief conversation with someone, and then they both turned and came over to us.

"All right. We've confirmed much of what you've told us with the Mercer Island police. They're on their way over and asked that you sit tight until they get here," she said. "Especially you two," she said, glancing at me and Dana. "The owner will be filing a complaint, and you'll have to reimburse him for broken dishes and some lost revenue. We'll be in touch on that. But we have a few more questions for Ms. Kyes," she said, eyeing Sonja.

"What? *She* attacked *me!*" Sonja yelled, standing up and pointing at Dana again.

"There's the little matter of a blackmail note," Officer Hager said.

Sonja's jaw dropped open a notch. "I…uh…don't know what you…"

"Please step over here," Officer Hager said, gesturing for Sonja to return to the interview table.

Sonja turned to Dana. "This is all your fault. You killed Mr. Peabody. Took my inheritance. And now someone is trying to kill you. You deserve it." She almost spit out this last part and then cast a hateful glance at all of us, before slumping her way back across the room.

At least now the police would question her on the real issue. Meanwhile, we were allowed to close ranks. I got up to use the restroom, where I attempted to make myself look presentable in case it was David who was making the trip over to Renton. As I was using a damp paper towel to wipe dirt and barbeque sauce from along my jawline, Blair, Rudy and Doe all opened the door and crowded in with me.

"Where's Dana?" I asked in surprise.

"We told her she had to stay there," Rudy said. "Are you okay?"

I threw the towel away, ran my fingers through my hair and then turned away from the mirror to face my friends.

"Let's face it, we're going to get a tongue-lashing," I replied. "This couldn't have turned out more wrong. Detective Abrams and David were prepared to trap Sonja in the act, and now they can't."

"They can compare fingerprints from the note," Rudy said hopefully.

"Yes, but each one of us also handled that note. So who knows if they'll be able to find a viable print?" I sighed. "We may have really screwed this up."

"Along with your romance," Blair said, leaning against the sink. "We're sorry, Julia."

I looked at my friends. Blair and I both looked like we'd been mugged by a four-year old with gooey fingers, while Doe and Rudy just looked defeated.

"Maybe we're carrying this murder investigation stuff too far," Doe said. "We should have just told Dana no from the beginning."

"Yeah," Rudy agreed. "Let's face it. Once they'd caught Sonja in the act, Dana could have ID'd her. We jumped the gun." We all shifted our gaze to her. "Sorry, no jokes about Dana and guns this time," she said, her hands up in a defensive gesture.

"What do you want to do, Julia? My gut says we ought to get out of here. Technically, they can't hold us."

I sighed. "Yes, but it's not as if the Mercer Island police don't know where we live. I say we wait and take our medicine. And then, frankly, I'm going home to take a shower."

CHAPTER TWENTY-FIVE

It was only Detective Abrams who came to Renton. I couldn't help but wonder why David hadn't accompanied him. Had he just given up on me? Did I embarrass him that much?

Abrams sat us down on the far side of the room, his broad shoulders hunched as he clasped his hands together on the table. "Okay," he began. It was clear he was making a vain attempt at hiding his irritation. "How did we get here?"

"It was Doe's nose," Blair blurted out.

He glanced up at her and then over at Doe, who lifted those graceful brows. "I suppose you didn't notice," she said.

"Notice what?" Detective Abrams said.

"The smell of barbeque sauce on the note," she replied. "It comes from this restaurant."

He shot her a look of total skepticism. "You've got to be kidding."

"Don't you smell it?" Blair asked.

His blue eyes roamed briefly around the room, as if the smell would be plastered on the walls. But I saw his nose twitch, so I knew he was taking a whiff.

"And?" he encouraged us to continue.

"And she was here," Rudy replied. "Just like we figured."

"Sonja Kyes," Dana added. He shifted his attention to Dana, who withered under his gaze.

"And just who is Sonja Kyes?" he asked.

"She was the housekeeper at Mr. Peabody's," she replied.

"Keep going," Detective Abrams said.

Dana looked at all of us, and I felt the other shoe was about ready to drop.

"She…uh…came home that day…the day Mr. Peabody died. She came home just as he was choking on his lunch."

Detective Abrams' eyes narrowed. "Let me guess? And she watched *you* watch *him* die?"

She lowered her head. "Yes. She was too late to help. But then she found out he had also taken her out of the will. She was originally supposed to get it all. She'd been his employee long before I came to work there."

Detective Abrams sat back. "So let me get this straight. She witnessed you doing nothing to save the old man, and then suffered a second blow when you knocked her out of the will? Do I have that right?"

Dana merely nodded.

"And now you think that she's blackmailing you?"

"Yes," Dana said.

"But none of you actually know if she had anything to do with Trudy Bascom's death?" he asked, looking around the table at us.

"No," we all murmured.

He shook his head and stood up. "Okay. We're in the process of fingerprinting the note. Hopefully, that will tell us if she is, in fact, the blackmailer. According to the Renton police, you'll owe the restaurant owner some money to replace items here. You also may face some complaints from some of the people who got caught in the crossfire. But for now, go home and let us take it from here. And I do mean *let us* take it from here," he said, his blue eyes intense. "Think you can do that? Because I could book you for obstruction."

He stood up, towering over us. This magnified the demeaning look he cast about the group. I felt like I was in elementary school and had just been called to the principal's office, where my father was now lecturing me before taking me home. But there were a lot of relieved confirmations from the group as each of us grabbed purses and made ready to leave.

As we stood up, Detective Abrams placed his hands on his hips and leveled a severe look at each one of us. "And this time it's an order. Because next time, I'll let them put you in jail."

÷

Dana and I drove back to the island in silence. I was thinking about David and the fact that he hadn't come to Renton. I felt my relationship with him was falling apart, and it made me sad.

Doe split off to take Blair and Rudy home, while Dana and I continued toward the Inn. Dana finally spoke up as we pulled onto N. Mercer Way to bypass downtown.

"You think I'm a horrible person, don't you?"

I glanced her way. "You do seem to relish taking advantage of other people," I replied. "Why is that?"

She seemed to think a minute, as if deciding how much to say. "Because I'm just like my mother," she said. "She was someone who just never seemed to get enough. She left my father because he couldn't give her everything she wanted. So we moved from place to place, living off one man or another until she'd gotten tired of them, too." She paused and watched the trees flash by on her side of the car.

"So she was a con artist," I said.

She shot me a demoralized glance. "Not really a con artist. She just used people. She grew up in the Depression and had nothing, so she resented anyone who had more than she did and was always on the hunt to take it away from them."

We were getting close to the Roanoke Inn and a couple miles from home.

"In fact, when I was thirteen," Dana said. "We were living with her most recent boyfriend, and…"

There was a loud pop from somewhere off to our right and the rear window cracked. We both screamed. I swerved, nearly hitting an oncoming car. At the last moment, I yanked the wheel to the right. My Pathfinder swiped past the oncoming car with inches to spare, and then I cranked the wheel to the left to avoid a mailbox. The Pathfinder bounced to a stop, crosswise in the middle of the road.

Dana was still screaming. I had trouble catching my breath and threw my right arm out and smacked her in the chest. "Stop it! We're okay."

She sucked it up and went silent, while I took a deep breath and glanced out my window. The car I'd almost hit had stopped fifty feet behind us. Both doors opened and a man and a woman got out and ran up to us. I opened my door.

"Are you okay?" the man asked.

"Yes," I forced myself to say, taking another deep breath. "What happened?"

He glanced at the back window and then grabbed his companion and pulled her in close. "I think someone shot at you."

I stared at a big hole in my back window. All three of us huddled behind the car, while he reached for his cell phone. I told Dana to duck down, just in case.

I peered through the car windows at the dense foliage on the opposite side of the road, searching for someone with a gun. But on this part of the island, roads ran off in all directions and homes were hidden by an abundance of trees and bushes. Whoever had shot at us was probably long gone.

A few minutes later, we were explaining the situation to a patrol officer. We were taken to the Mercer Island Police Station, while other officers stayed with the car and blocked off the road. Eventually, David showed up.

"Julia, are you all right?" he asked, coming over and putting his hands on my shoulders.

Suddenly he was all compassion and concern. Inside, I glowed.

"Yes, I'm fine. Neither one of us was hurt." He reached out and touched my bruised cheek. "No. That was from the brawl over in Renton," I said, flinching.

We gave him all the details we could remember, but there wasn't much to tell. David took notes. "Okay, I'll have an officer take you home, while we process the crime scene. We need to keep your car for now."

"I don't want to go home!" Dana blurted.

We turned to her. Dana's haughty demeanor had evaporated and been replaced by real fear. The last few days had taken its toll. I realized she had circles under her eyes, and she was visibly shaking.

"We'll put a car out front," David said. "You'll be fine."

"No!" she demanded. "Clay left for Bellingham this morning. I can't stay alone."

Her voice vibrated with emotion, and suddenly I heard myself saying something I thought I'd never have to say. "She can stay at the Inn." David looked at me in surprise, but I just shrugged my shoulders. "It's okay," I said. "We had a cancellation this morning, so there's an extra room. But I'd appreciate that car out front. Just not too noticeable, if you know what I mean."

David nodded and stood up. "Okay. Get your stuff. I'll have an officer drive you home in an unmarked car and then stay close by."

He disappeared into the hallway. A few minutes later, he was back.

"Officer Capshaw will meet you in the lobby," he said. "C'mon, let's go."

As we moved down the hallway to the entrance, David reached out and let his fingers briefly grab my hand. My heart almost exploded.

"Are you really okay, Julia? I heard about what happened in Renton."

Our fingers touched for a moment and then we both self-consciously retreated.

"I'm fine. Just a little shaken." I glanced up at him. "How come you didn't come over there with Detective Abrams?"

He pressed his luscious lips together in a grimace. "Because we have other open cases we're working. And Sean has already suggested once that he might take me off this case."

My eyes popped open in surprise. "Why would he do that?"

David stopped with a hand on my arm. We allowed Dana to shuffle her way into the lobby.

"Because he's very aware that you and I are…well, dating."

I tossed my head. "I think you can hardly call it dating. We've only been out together once, and that was interrupted by this murder investigation."

The hurt look on his face made me immediately regret my remark. "Regardless, we have a personal relationship," he said crisply. "And it can prove awkward. As it is right now."

He started to move away, but I grabbed his hand. "I'm sorry, David. I want nothing more than to resume our…relationship. I just have to get Dana…" I said, glancing at her sulking in the lobby, "out of my life."

CHAPTER TWENTY-SIX

Officer Capshaw took us first to Dana's house to get her overnight things. We went inside with him and remained in the foyer, while he checked the house to make sure it was safe.

Dana stood quietly by my side, almost sullen. I glanced sideways at her. Her left eye was swollen where Sonja had connected with the initial punch, and her face was smudged with dark splotches of dirt and barbeque sauce. Those naturally rounded shoulders I often made fun of were hunched with tension as she clasped her arms close to her chest. She was a wreck.

Once Officer Capshaw was satisfied the house was vacant, Dana went to her room to fill an overnight bag. We then went to the Inn.

It was dark by the time we arrived. I'd called April, and she offered to make dinner. I was too exhausted to argue. We left Officer Capshaw in the unmarked car out front and dragged ourselves into the entryway. I went to the reception desk to get the key for Dana's room, but a commotion in the breakfast room made me look over that way.

The Kohls were back from their trip to Bainbridge Island and were huddled around Ahab's empty cage. Sherrie and Barry, the twins, were laughing and pointing inside, which raised my antenna. I pictured them somehow defaming Ahab's cage or in some other way misbehaving and I snapped.

"Excuse me," I shouted, leaving the front desk to march in their direction.

And then I heard the voice I'd been longing to hear.

"I'll get you, my pretty, and your little dog, too. Squawk!"

I nearly ran the rest of the way to the cage, scattering the children.

"Sorry," Sherrie said as she stepped to the side. "He was outside the window, so we opened the door, and he flew right in."

"It's okay," I said to them. "I'm sorry I snapped at you. Hello, little boy," I said, poking my fingers through the cage.

Ahab bounced over and rubbed his beak against my finger. "Happy to see you. Happy to see you. Going my way?" he squawked.

April came through the swinging door of the kitchen, a small towel between her hands.

"Well, what do we have here?" she said with a broad smile.

She came up to the cage and stuck her finger through, too. Ahab bounced over and touched his beak to her.

"Polly want a cracker," he said.

Everyone laughed.

"And you deserve one, too," I said.

We filled his water bowl and his little food dish. He went to work, pecking away. I got out my phone and texted Jose´, who was just getting ready to leave. He hurried over.

I said, "Jose´ can you find a padlock somewhere? And then I want this cage bolted to the floor tonight. I'll pay the overtime."

He grinned. "No problem. Right away."

I looked up at April, tears in my eyes. "I'm so glad."

"I know," she said, reaching out to put a hand on my shoulder. Her features compressed into distaste, and she withdrew her hand, rubbing her fingers together. "What's all over your coat?" Then she got a good look at me. "And in your hair?"

My hand reached up to where a glob of sauce had stuck a fingers-width of hair together. "Famous barbeque," I said with a fake smile, trying to rub the sauce off my fingers. "I don't think I'll eat barbeque ever again."

Dana had remained by the reception desk through all of this, so I helped get her settled into an empty guest room upstairs and then went to my apartment to clean up. An hour later, we joined April in the guest house, where she grilled more than the Panini sandwiches she served us. She wanted a moment by moment account of what had happened that afternoon. I did most of the talking, while Dana stared at her plate.

We left the guest house around 7:30 to cross the drive back to the Inn. I noticed Angela's car out front. "Uh, oh. Prepare yourself," I said to my companion.

"Why?" she said, pulling back a little.

"My daughter is here again. Which means her dog might be, too."

Dana stopped in her tracks, her mouth pulled into a grimace.

"What is with you and dogs?" I asked, stopping with her. "Did one attack you as a child or something?"

Her eyes had come alive again, and I thought for a moment she might pass out. "They lick," she said with disgust.

"Yes? So?"

"And they smell things. I…I can't stand the thought of where their noses have been."

"You mean you're so pristine that you can't be around a filthy, smelly dog?"

She straightened up. "Well, they do…you know…um…lick themselves."

Her lips pinched together and her nose twitched as if she had just smelled cow dung. I whirled away from her in newfound disgust.

"You've got to be kidding me! Didn't you ever hear that dogs' mouths are cleaner than humans?" I continued toward the front door, leaving her behind. She hurried to catch up.

"That's not true," she said. "I don't believe it."

I turned to her. "Yes, it is. Any doctor will tell you that a human bite is far more dangerous because of infection than a dog bite. So frankly, I'd rather share my table with either one of my dogs than you." We entered through the front door and stopped in front of the reception desk.

"So, to be clear," I continued. "We'll make sure to keep all the dogs in my apartment while you're here. But you should know that Angela's dog, Lucy, actually saved my life during the last investigation, and Mickey and Minnie rescued me the night Ahab was stolen. It's uncanny how a dog knows the difference between a friend and foe. I'm not sure that any one of them would extend the same favor to you. I rather think they wouldn't. Regardless, I'll keep them locked up so you won't be offended by their presence. Good night. And don't call me unless your life is in danger…again!"

She started to say something, but I turned my back on her and strode down the hall.

Angela was sitting comfortably on the sofa with her laptop out and the fireplace going. Lucy, the Great Dane, was stretched out in front of the fireplace soaking up all the heat, with Mickey and Minnie tucked in between her big paws. The moment I came in, my dogs jumped up and ran over, bouncing around my feet. Lucy lifted her head and looked at me over her shoulder before lying back down.

"Hey, there," Angela said.

I made an immediate turn into my kitchen, willing myself to calm down. It was odd, that after all Dana had confessed, I was most offended by her aversion toward my dogs. Clearly, the stress had caught up to me, too.

"I heard about what happened this afternoon," Angela said, putting her laptop down and following me to the other side of the counter. "So I decided to come hang out with you for a couple of days." She watched me grab a glass and pour myself some wine. "You okay?"

I took a swig and swallowed before replying. "Sorry," I said. "I'm fine. Just incredibly irritated at Dana right now. I can't stand that woman."

She laughed. "Did you just realize that?"

"No," I said, taking a second gulp. "But believe it or not, we'll have to keep the dogs in the apartment while she's here because she has an intense aversion to them."

Angela rolled her eyes. "I can handle that."

I grimaced at her over the counter. "So, I take it you're here to protect me?"

"Something like that. I came armed."

"With Lucy? Or a real weapon?"

"I came armed," she repeated, locking her gaze on mine.

"Angela, I don't feel comfortable with weapons in the house. Real weapons, I mean."

"Well, you'd better get used to it. You *are* dating a policeman, you know." She smiled ruefully. "Can I have hot chocolate?"

I paused, knowing this was a battle I would lose.

"Marshmallows?"

"Of course." She pulled a stool out and climbed onto it. "So tell me about it."

"You already know," I said, filling a mug with some 2% milk and placing it into the microwave. "We got shot at on the way home."

"That's not what I mean. Why are you helping Dana? You lied to me the other day."

I pulled out a package of hot chocolate and a bag of marshmallows. "No, I didn't. She really did walk into the kitchen accusing me of trying to kill her."

"But…?"

I dropped my hands to the counter and sighed. "But she also asked me…no, let me rephrase that. She demanded that I help her."

"But why would you agree, Mom? Not only do you hate her, it's putting you right in the line of fire again."

I explained the deal I'd made with Dana about dropping out of the campaign for mayor.

"So this was an easy out," I said, ripping open the bag of hot chocolate. "Of course, my solution was to get Tony Morales to run instead, but…"

Her eyes opened wide. "But he was arrested."

"Right."

"Well, if it's any consolation, he clearly wasn't the one who took a shot at you this afternoon, so they've let him go."

"Thank God," I said with a sigh.

"He's not out of the woods yet. He could be an accessory. But he's a lot lower on their list of suspects."

"What about the weapon they found in his garage?"

"I guess he leaves the side door to his garage unlocked. Someone could have easily planted the hammer. Besides, the hammer that was used to kill Trudy was what they call a planishing hammer. It's used for metal working. Tony was a construction worker, but he didn't do any metal work and said he didn't own one. So they're checking local hardware stores to see if they can ID someone who might have bought it recently."

The microwave beeped, and I made Angela's hot chocolate, adding some extra chocolate syrup and the marshmallows. Then we retired to the living room.

"Angela," I said, once I'd settled into my wingback chair with a small Doxie tucked in at each side. "What do you know about the statute of limitations for child abuse?"

She stopped halfway to a sip of hot chocolate. "Oh, the pictures, right?"

Angela was an assistant prosecuting attorney. Since she was dating Detective Abrams, their pillow talk was as good as a direct phone call.

"Yeah. I was just wondering if Dana is in any real trouble."

She put her mug onto a coaster and sat back. "Do you know, yet, why Dana had the photos?"

"No. We confronted her, but she wouldn't say much, other than she had nothing to do with the abuse."

Angela's eyebrows clenched. "And just how did *you* come into possession of them?"

I squared my shoulders. "I'd rather not say."

"Mom," she said. How many times had I heard that tone of voice? "You didn't break any laws, did you?"

"Certainly not," I replied, hoping against hope that I hadn't just lied.

"Well, for most crimes, the statute of limitations is only three years. Of course, murder is the exception. There is no statute of limitations on that."

"What if Dana knew about it? Would that make her an accessory to the crime?"

"Depends on what she knew."

"Well, she had the pictures, so she must have known something."

"Not necessarily. She might have found the pictures after her husband disappeared. Did the pictures show actual abuse?"

I shook my head. "No. They were just pictures of nude boys."

"Well, being in possession of pornographic pictures is much different than actual abuse. You'd have to prove they were being used for someone's sexual pleasure. So Dana was throwing these photos away because she was afraid she'd be culpable?"

"I think so. Or she just didn't want to ruin her reputation. She seems overly concerned with that. The answer to who's trying to kill her could be in those photos, but she's not giving up all the information."

Angela stood up. "Okay, then. Let's go talk to Dana."

"Weren't you the one who said I shouldn't get involved with Dana?"

Angela smirked. "That was before you jumped into the investigation and got shot at," she said. "Let's go talk to her."

"But as I said, she's not saying much about that."

"Yes, but maybe having an assistant prosecuting attorney asking the questions will wake her up a bit."

CHAPTER TWENTY-SEVEN

We left the dogs in the apartment and climbed the stairs to the second floor. I didn't relish another go around with Dana, but I wanted this nightmare over so I could get back to my priorities – like dating David.

But as we reached the head of the stairs, there was a shriek and Dana's door flew open. She burst onto the landing, breathing heavily, her face twisted in fear.

"What happened?" I called out, rushing up to her.

"Someone…was in my room. I…I think it was a…a…it was a ghost," she said, trying to get the words out in between gulps of air.

The door to the suite next door opened and the Kohl family emerged with looks of concern. Barry hung back just inside the door.

I heard a noise a moment later, and the Brewsters appeared on the opposite end of the hallway. It was early enough that no one except Dana had gone to bed yet. She was dressed in a long nightgown.

"Calm down, Dana. It's okay. Let's go back in your room."

"But…but, Julia, I'm not kidding. I was in bed and someone pulled the blanket off. You've always said the Inn is haunted. I didn't believe you. But…"

She began to hyperventilate again just as Barry giggled. I glanced over at him. He had stepped out into the hallway and was standing behind his father with something held loosely in one hand. The moment I eyeballed him, he closed his fist around whatever it was, but I noticed a string extending from the ball of his fist to the floor. The moment he realized that I'd seen the string he abruptly turned toward the wall.

As Angela guided Dana back into her room, I turned to the guests. It was just the Kohls and the Brewsters. Most likely, the other guests were still out for the evening.

"Sorry, she just had a nightmare."

As they shuffled back into their rooms, I stepped forward to follow Angela and Dana, but stopped the moment I noticed something bobbing along the carpet runner at my feet. I leaned over and grabbed it. It was a small claw clasp tied to the other end of Barry's string. I turned to him with a very disappointed look and yanked on it. His parents had returned to their room, so it was just the two of us, standing there holding opposite ends of the string.

"I wouldn't play games if I were you," I said. "The Inn really is haunted, so you don't want to make the ghosts mad."

He chortled. "Yeah, right," he said. "You heard what my dad said. It's all fake."

He yanked the string out of my hand. Since his parents were inside their room, I moved up close to him.

"Well, let's put it this way then. It's not nice to frighten older women. They might die on you, and then the police could lock you up for murder."

His eyes opened wide at the threat, and he turned and disappeared into his room.

I returned to Dana's room with a sly smile playing across my lips. Angela noticed it as I closed the door.

"What?" she said.

"Your ghost, at least this time, was merely the prank of the evil fifth grader in the room next door."

"What do you mean?" Dana said.

"He must've gotten in here after the room had been cleaned earlier. We don't lock the room until a new guest checks in. He would've had time to attach a string to the end of your blanket. Then while you were falling asleep, he pulled it off. Kinda gutsy, actually," I said.

"Really?" Dana said. "You think scaring me half to death is gutsy?"

Angela was sitting at the end of the bed, while Dana was sitting in the middle. I took the straight-backed chair at the small desk under the window.

"Look, Dana, I have to be honest. It's been documented that we have supernatural activity here. But there is nothing to fear. No one has ever been harmed or their safety threatened."

"I don't want to stay here. I want a different room," she demanded.

"Sorry," I replied hurriedly. "I didn't mean to scare you. But there isn't another room available."

"What about your apartment?"

"I could stay up here," Angela offered, trying to be helpful.

"No," I snapped. "Besides, there's Lucy. She'd have to stay with me."

"But…" Angela started to object.

"No, Angela! Like I said, Lucy *has* to stay downstairs." I turned to Dana. "So, if you're comfortable with having all the dogs around you, then by all means, come down to the apartment."

I was afraid the smile I was feeling on the inside was spreading like molasses across my face.

Dana's expression seemed to morph between fear and disgust within nanoseconds.

"No…no, I'll be okay, then. Some little kid isn't going to scare me off."

"Fine. And just remember, that if you do see something, Chloe is a very sweet little girl. Nothing to be afraid of."

"Let's get around to what we needed to talk about," Angela said, cutting to the chase.

Dana turned to her. "What do you mean?"

Angela leaned forward, resting her elbows on her knees. "Let me say first Dana, that I'm with the prosecuting attorney's office in Seattle. So if you're uncomfortable saying anything in front of me, I'll leave. But I'm here to be helpful, not in any formal capacity."

Dana shifted her attention to me. "What's this about, Julia?"

I took a deep breath. "Dana, I told Angela about the nude photos."

She took a quick intake of breath. "What?"

"We need to know why you were throwing them away and what they mean," I said.

"Actually, I'd like to know why you were holding onto them in the first place," Angela interjected.

"How did you know I was throwing them away?" she said, giving me a suspicious look. "You said Rudy found out about the abuse in Vancouver. How did you even know I *had* photos?" Dana stopped and drew in a breath. "Oh, it doesn't matter anymore. None of it matters anymore."

"Dana, why did you hold onto the photos?" Angela asked again.

"Because my husband was an animal. He did more than just abuse them. He dehumanized them. He really was a sick bastard. And if I argued or said I didn't want to go along with things…he'd take it out on me." She hung her head in defeat.

"So you participated in the abuse?" I said in shock.

Her head jerked up. "No! Please, you have to believe me. I never abused anyone. But we argued about it often. I knew what he was doing, and a couple of the boys came to me for help."

"And you didn't do anything," Angela said.

Tears filled her eyes. "No. You don't understand. He was abusive in more ways than one."

"What do you mean?" Angela prompted her.

Dana hesitated. She was chewing the inside of her cheek, a sure sign she was nervous.

"The statute of limitations has run out," Angela said. "You can't be prosecuted."

This didn't seem to relax her, but she took a deep breath and continued. "My husband would hit me if I complained. And… he liked to put the boys in cages as a punishment. He put dog collars on them and forced them to crawl around on their knees like animals."

She had begun to sweat, and I could tell that reliving this was difficult.

"He liked having control over others. I felt as trapped as those boys." She was staring at the floor. Finally, she said, "He forced me to take the photos you saw and to bring the boys food. But I never harmed them or did anything to them. I swear." She choked back a sob. "I'm not an animal," she whispered.

Angela sat back. "But that, Mrs. Finkle, could be why someone is trying to kill you. Abuse is a powerful motivator."

Her head came up. "But it could still be Sonja Kyes. She hates me. I ruined her life. And if my ex-husband is here on the island, it could be him, couldn't it?"

"Maybe," Angela said. "But it sounds more like Mrs. Kyes was exploiting the fact someone was trying to kill you. She used that to blackmail you. And we don't know why your ex-husband is here. Perhaps he's involved. Perhaps not. I think it's more likely we'll find the killer amongst those boys. How much have you told the police?"

"Most of it," she replied.

"Then you need to tell them the rest. Tomorrow."

She glanced up at me. "I'll go back to the police station in the morning," she said. "And then once this is over, I might as well move to Canada, because I'll never be able to show my face anywhere in this country again."

At last, I thought. *Something good might actually come from all of this.*

CHAPTER TWENTY-EIGHT

It was early in the morning when I got up to pee, and April's lemon bars began to call to me on my way back to bed.

Julia. Juuulia!

I did an about-face, put on my slippers and opened my bedroom door. I snuck into the hallway, leaving the dogs behind this time. I tiptoed past Angela's closed door.

No sound.

I kept going.

I opened the apartment door and tiptoed into the main hallway, heading for the breakfast room, wrapping my arms around my chest for warmth.

I should have grabbed my robe, I thought. The hallway was chilly.

I was passing the library, just as the front door to the Inn opened. I flashed back to the attack on the night Ahab was stolen and ducked into the library, hiding around the corner. My heart was pounding. I heard tentative footsteps echo in the entryway.

I peeked around the wall. It was Mr. Campo, a young man in town for his sister's wedding. I sighed with relief. I'd given him the code to the alarm system. He stopped and checked his cellphone and then climbed the stairs unsteadily. *Must have been a great wedding reception,* I thought. I watched him disappear and then leaned into the hallway to listen. I heard his door close and carefully re-emerged.

I stepped into the hallway, shivering from the blast of cold air that had followed him inside. *Should I go back to the apartment and get my robe?* I glanced down to my favorite Mickey Mouse pajamas, realizing that I wouldn't look very professional if I ran into one of my guests. But then, I could taste the burst of lemon in my mouth. It would only take a minute.

I stepped forward and glanced up the staircase, just to make sure I was alone. I moved quietly into the entryway and was just about to turn into the breakfast room, when a door on the second floor opened.

Damn!

I started for the office – changed my mind – turned back for the library. Nope. Too far. I whipped around and ducked behind the registration counter, my heart beating wildly.

The sound of light footfalls whispered across the upstairs landing and then began to descend the stairs. I pushed myself into the farthest corner between the counter and the staircase, to one side of the closed office door. I felt so stupid. I was hiding because of my vanity. But really, maybe it was time to upgrade my pajamas.

Fortunately, darkness shrouded the area behind the registration counter so that I wasn't visible, but I dared not peek to see who was coming downstairs.

The footfalls descended the stairs and then paused at the bottom. Perhaps my visitor was making sure they were alone as well. Finally, the individual crossed in front of the reception counter and came around the corner. I scrunched myself into a ball so that all I saw were two fluffy slippers disappearing into the breakfast room.

There wasn't any food out, and it wouldn't be for several hours. We didn't even have the coffee pot going. But I was ultra-sensitive to anyone who got too near Ahab. I listened and heard the kitchen door swing open.

Someone was raiding the kitchen!

The kitchen wasn't necessarily off limits, but out of courtesy, people didn't usually go in there. And there wasn't really anything worth stealing – other than the lemon bars. But I was more than a little curious about who had the gall to invade the sanctuary of our kitchen in the middle of the night.

Dana!

I crept forward on hands and knees and poked my head around the corner to make sure no one was in the breakfast room. Then I got up and scurried through the entryway to the front door, where I hid behind one of the steamer trunks used in my antique display. I quickly reached up and turned off the small table lamp we kept lit there for late arrivals, so that once again, I was hidden by deep shadow. I crouched down and peeked around the corner of the steamer chest. I wanted a clear view of Dana when she came out of the kitchen. Before she could make her escape, however, another door opened and closed on the second floor.

Really? This was beginning to remind me of a Peter Sellers movie.

I poked my head above the steamer trunk and watched as the twins, Barry and Sherrie, quietly descended the stairs, whispering to each other like co-conspirators. They rounded the bottom of the staircase and tiptoed with stealth, giggling, to the reception desk. Sherrie scooted around to the back of the desk and placed something into a potted fern that sat on top of the counter. Then she reached through the fern and handed something to her brother.

Another string.

Barry ran the string under a heavy table runner that stretched the length of the counter and over to the staircase. Barely containing his mirth, he gestured for Sherrie to come back around to the front of the counter. Just as she did, she glanced my way, making me duck down.

"Aaaargh!" she screamed.

I'd been made.

Barry's matching scream set my teeth on edge.

Damn!

I was about to rise, but a movement to my left stopped me. Elizabeth's unearthly image shimmered in front of the door. She turned her ghostly head to me and then pointed a transparent finger in the direction of the children. The kids screamed again. She made an abrupt turn and flew through the opposite wall.

The kids wailed a third time and ran crying up the stairs as doors flew open on the second landing. I watched as Mrs. Brewster came running out of the kitchen and ran up the stairs behind them. *So it wasn't Dana, after all.*

Mickey and Minnie had begun to bark and the noise grew louder as my apartment door opened, which meant Angela was on her way down the hallway. I had only moments to figure out what to do without anyone seeing me.

Angela appeared and began to ascend the stairs. I scooted out from behind the trunk and stepped in behind her.

"What's the matter?" I called out, as if just arriving on the scene.

Angela turned in surprise, but kept going up the stairs. I flipped on a light switch as I passed, illuminating the entire area.

Everyone was huddled around the kids at the top of the landing. Their father stood behind his wife, pulling a robe around his shoulders. The children blubbered, while everyone murmured their support.

"They say they saw something," Mrs. Kohl said to me as I arrived on the scene. She was leaning over Sherrie, her arms around her daughter's shoulders. The little girl was sobbing and shaking.

"It was a ghost," Sherrie said, her voice wavering. "She walked right through a wall."

Her mother looked up at me for clarification. I didn't have any, so I shrugged.

Mr. Campo had come down the hallway. "Damn, I wish I'd seen it. I just came in," he said with a slight slur.

"Maybe the children just saw you," the mother said hopefully.

Mr. Campo frowned. "I doubt it. First of all, I haven't walked through any walls lately." He laughed stupidly. "And anyway, I was already in my room." He teetered and almost bumped into the wall closest to him.

"No...no, it was a woman in a nightgown, downstairs," Barry sputtered.

Tears streaked his face, and for the first time he looked like the kid he was. The once ballsy boy was tucked behind his mother, clearly frightened.

"What were you doing downstairs?" I asked as innocently as I could.

They both stopped blubbering and stared at me, wide-eyed. Barry, the consummate liar, spoke up. "We thought maybe there'd be some cookies left."

"Ah..." I said. "Well, the excitement is over. Perhaps we should all go back to bed."

Mr. Kohl was being uncharacteristically quiet, and I couldn't help but wonder what he was thinking. Mr. Brewster had come up belatedly behind Mr. Campo and stepped out onto the landing.

"Don't tell me we missed the excitement again," he said.

His wife slapped his arm. "Oh, forget it, Harry. I don't think we're going to see any ghosts. I'm going back to bed."

She wasn't going to confess to her secret trip to the kitchen. She turned and padded back down the hallway. He followed, and everyone turned to go back to their rooms.

"Where's Dana?" Angela said once everyone was gone.

Dana's door had remained closed, even though we were right in front of it.

"I don't know! All that commotion should have woken her up."

I knocked on Dana's door. No answer. I knocked again. No answer.

"Do you have a key?" Angela asked.

"Behind the registration desk," I said.

I was headed back down the stairs, when Dana's door finally opened. She poked her head out. "What's going on?" she murmured.

Her eyes were only half open, and I realized she'd been sound asleep.

"Can we come in?" I asked.

She pulled the door open and we stepped inside.

"Dana, are you okay? Didn't you hear the screams?" I asked.

"I took a sleeping pill."

I relaxed with a sigh. "Well, sorry, then. The kids next door just...they had a fright." The room was freezing and I shivered. "Did you close the heater vent?" I pulled my arms around me again for warmth.

"No. Why would I do that?" she mumbled. She climbed back onto the bed and pulled a blanket around her.

I felt an actual breeze and turned towards the window. "Is there a window open?" I stepped over to the window next to a small desk and pulled the curtains aside. It was wide open. "Dana, why did you open the window?"

"I didn't," she said stubbornly.

"Well, someone did," I said, slamming it shut. I shivered again and allowed the drapes to drop back into place. As I turned to step away from the window, I happened to glance at the floor. What I saw brought the sour taste of bile to my mouth.

There was fresh mud on the carpet.

CHAPTER TWENTY-NINE

Dana freaked out.

Once we'd calmed her down, we convinced her to come downstairs for the night. I just couldn't force myself to call the police out one more time, so I reported the incident to Officer Capshaw, who was stationed in front of the Inn in the unmarked car. He came in and searched the Inn, just to make sure no one had made it past Dana's room. Since the guests had all reacted to the emergency with the children, we didn't feel it necessary to disturb them again. But Officer Capshaw looked into every other room. Since Dana's window was at the back of the Inn with a trellis nearby, we figured whomever it was had come down the side drive past my apartment to the rear of the building and climbed up the trellis. So, this time, I asked Officer Capshaw to camp out in Dana's room until dawn, just in case.

As I returned to my apartment, I smiled despite the anxiety I felt at a second break-in, thinking how surprised Dana's stalker would be if he came back and found a burly male officer in Dana's bed instead of her. *Oh, Grandma, what big teeth you have.*

Angela had gone into the apartment first to make sure the dogs were safely tucked away in the bedrooms. Fifteen minutes later, Angela had retired again, and I was handing off a pillow to Dana for the couch.

"I know you don't like me, Julia," she said sleepily. "And I know this must be a great imposition, having me here at the Inn. So…thank you."

I paused with a folded quilt in my arms. She was right. There was nothing I liked about her. But I had a natural compassion for the underdog and right now, she was the underdog.

I plopped down in a nearby chair. "I *don't* like you, Dana. I think you take great pleasure in causing other people pain and distress. I don't know if you do it in order to make *yourself* feel better, or…I don't know, you're bored. But just because you're mean-spirited, I don't think you deserve to be murdered. Maybe this will be a wakeup call and you'll change."

She dropped onto the sofa, a beaten woman. Everything about her had changed. All of her bravado was gone, along with any sense of confidence.

"I'm not sure I *can* change," she said with an apologetic nod. "It's how I was raised. I told you about my mother. She spent her entire adult life finding ways to get back at people who had more than she did. She seemed to work hard at making their lives miserable, including mine. She once made a formal complaint against a kid in my sixth-grade class who had a glandular problem and weighed about 300 pounds. His parents were wealthy, which just naturally pissed her off. So she made a case to the school district that he should be home-schooled because of his unusual size, which, she argued, made the other kids uncomfortable. Somehow she got two other mothers to join her, and that poor kid finally dropped out of school. My mother gloated about that." Dana took a deep breath and lowered her chin. "You may not like me, Julia, but it's who I am. It's who I was trained to be. I don't know *how* to be different."

"Did your husband really abuse you when you lived in Vancouver?"

Her face tensed, and tears appeared. "Yes. He beat me so badly once I had to go to the ER. I was in the process of making plans to leave him and go to a shelter when he disappeared."

I handed her the quilt. "Well, I'm sorry about that. Really, I am. But at least now you're being honest about things."

She swiped a tear away. "It's not easy being me."

A laugh erupted from my throat. "Well, we finally agree on something."

She glanced up at me, and then smiled. "Touché," she said.

"Look, Dana, somehow we'll get you through this. And then you can go back to being a pain in the neck again. Just hopefully not *my* neck."

She slumped back on the sofa. "You know, I have to admit that I've sometimes been jealous of you."

"Me? Why?"

She glanced around at all of my antiques and *Wizard of Oz* memorabilia. "Partly the Inn. It is lovely, and you get to meet such interesting people. And partly your husband."

"Ex-husband," I said.

"Well, he *is* the governor of the state. But most of all, your friends. You seem to attract people like a magnet. I'm just the opposite."

"Let's face it. We approach life very differently. I smile. You frown."

I smiled. And finally, she smiled too. "Okay," she said. "I get it."

"Now, let's get some sleep. We have a busy day tomorrow. Jason Spears will be here."

CHAPTER THIRTY

Another storm front moved in overnight, so that heavy rain and blustery winds greeted us the next morning. It was just after 8:00 a.m., and Officer Capshaw had just sat down in the breakfast room to eat April's ham and bacon quiche, when David and Detective Abrams marched through the front door, shaking water off as they came. Guests looked up as they strode in, so I guided them into the kitchen, where Dana and Angela were eating.

Dana looked up in surprise. "Did you find out who tried to kill me last night?" she blurted.

"I was about to call you," I said. "I already reported the incident to officer Capshaw."

David put up his hand to stop me. "We know. He called it in last night."

"Whoever it was had disappeared by the time we got there," I continued. "And we were all too tired to deal with it last night. But no one was hurt and nothing was stolen. And I put Officer Capshaw in Dana's room in case whoever it was came back."

"Good thinking," Detective Abrams said. "But once again, someone knew that your upstairs windows weren't alarmed. I think it's time we talk to Roger Romero again, since he installed your system. But do you have any idea how they knew which room Dana was in?"

That stopped me. I glanced over at Dana. "Did you call anyone?"

"I talked to Clay," she said. "But I never mentioned what room I was in."

"That's the only person?" David asked.

"Yes. I wanted him to know I was okay and was staying here at the Inn."

David looked at me. "Anyone else you can think of?"

I shook my head. "I don't think so. I mean all of the guests knew she was here, but that's it."

"Okay," he said, opening a folder and dropping two 8 X 10 photos on the table. "Do either of you know this man?"

David turned the folder around to show us the grisly photograph of a man who had been shot in the head. The body was laying half in and half out of a bunch of bushes. I could feel the blood drain from my face, and I felt cold all over.

It was Big Al.

I looked up at David. He wasn't enjoying this anymore than I was. "Do you know who he is, Julia?"

"Yes," I said a little breathlessly. "It's the man who stole Ahab." I sat down next to Angela and suddenly felt very afraid. She put a hand on my knee. "But I didn't kill him," I said. "After all, Ahab came back. Everything's fine."

"We know that, Julia. We think he was killed either late last night or early this morning." David turned his attention on Dana. "With a .9 mm hand gun."

Dana just stared at him with a blank expression.

"We found a gun in the bushes close by," David said. "It had your fingerprints on it, Mrs. Finkle."

She sucked in a quick gasp. "I didn't kill him."

"But you own a .9 mm," he said.

"Well, yes. That and a rifle. At least we did."

"What do you mean?" Detective Abrams said.

"They were stolen. We didn't notice until a couple of nights ago. I heard a bunch of noise out by the street just after midnight and went to get the revolver, just in case. But both the revolver and the rifle were gone."

"Noise out by the street?" Detective Abrams asked, stepping forward.

Inwardly, I cringed. That would have been the trash run. I drew my hands into my lap and chanced a cautious look at April, who was at the sink. She raised an eyebrow and went back to her dishes.

"Yes. There was a lot of banging out by the street. The next morning we found our trash cans all knocked over, and one was in the street. I suppose it was just kids, but, at the time, it frightened me. So I went for the gun."

"Did you report it?"

"Clay was going to," she replied.

"We'll check on that. We were able to ID this guy through his fingerprints," Detective Abrams said. He looked back at me. "He's the same guy who worked at Emory Auto Shop and lived in that apartment where you and Blair found Ahab."

I glanced at the photo again and pushed it back. "God, who would do that?"

"Someone who is trying very hard to cover his tracks. My guess is that this guy was hired by someone to steal Ahab. He was also probably the one who shot at you yesterday. But since he failed twice, he was eliminated. At least that's our working theory. We haven't been able to find any shell casings or bullets out on the road. We have a team over at his apartment now, though, looking for clues. And they did find one of those same beer bottles there, which makes it look as if he might be the one who killed Trudy Bascom. But it also seems that Ahab is a major player in this case. Can you tell us again what happened that night?"

I let out an exasperated sigh. "We've been over this a million times. Dana and I were standing right in front of his cage during the party." I glanced at Dana, whose face had gone very pale. "We were arguing, like we usually do. And suddenly, Ahab squawked, '*I want to kill Dana Finkle.*'"

"Do you have any idea where he learned to say that?" Detective Abrams asked me thoughtfully.

"No. But April remembered him picking up a phrase from a kid one day, and the next time that kid walked into the room, Ahab repeated the phrase. He picks things up very quickly. Last night I noticed that he kept asking for a cigarette. But no one at the Inn smokes."

"Has he ever said that before?" David asked.

"No. Never. I just assumed he picked it up in Big Al's apartment," I said pointing to the picture.

"Okay, we're going to need the names of every person you can remember that was here at the Inn during the two weeks *before* that Christmas Eve party."

I looked at April and nodded toward the drawer. She walked over, opened it and took out the small note pad. "Done," she said, handing it to Detective Abrams.

He glanced at the names on the paper. "So Tony Morales was here?"

"Yes. We had a library board meeting here," I said.

He handed the list to David. "When is your husband back?" Detective Abrams asked Dana. "We'd like to talk to him as well."

"Uh…tomorrow night," she said.

"Okay, one more question." He dropped another photo on the table. "Do you know this man?"

It was the picture of a man coming out of the Stay America Hotel in downtown Mercer Island. He was tall, about forty pounds overweight, with thinning gray hair and glasses. Dana grew very still and just stared at the photo.

"Mrs. Finkle? Do you recognize him?" David asked again.

"It's Vince, my first husband," she said quietly. She glanced up at the detectives, fear etched into her face.

"Okay," Detective Abrams said with a nod. He glanced at me. "When you told us about the man looking for a place to stay, but asking if Mrs. Finkle lived on the island, we took the description and canvassed all the hotels and motels. We came up with this," he said, gesturing to the photo. "He registered under the name Paul Conner."

"Do you think he's the one trying to kill me?" Dana asked.

"You had him declared legally dead and took all of his money," Detective Abrams said. "He might want it back."

"But how? I mean, how could he get it back?"

Angela spoke up. "He might figure that once you're dead, he'll resurface and go to court to reclaim it. You don't have kids or other relatives, do you?"

Dana shook her head. "No. Clay has a sister and a niece, but I don't have any other family."

"So, maybe he thinks he could fight Clay in court for the portion of the money that came from his estate," Angela offered. "After all, he was never convicted of the child abuse and the statute of limitations has run out. I'm not sure he'd win, but it could be worth a try."

"Except I'd have to die first," Dana spat.

Angela shrugged. "Well, there *is* that."

"Where is he now?" I asked.

"We're not sure," Detective Abrams said. "We have the hotel staked out."

"Do you think he hired Big Al?" I asked.

"We're looking for a connection now," David replied. "There are a lot of unanswered questions. We need you to stay here for the time being, Mrs. Finkle, until we sort this out."

CHAPTER THIRTY-ONE

Friday was the day Jason Spears was scheduled to arrive and hold a séance of sorts. He had not only published a couple of books profiling haunted locations around the country, he and his wife and two cohorts constituted the Salem Paranormal Investigative Team (SPIT), which was located in Salem, Oregon.

We had invited a select group of people to the reception – mostly the Library Board and a couple of bookstore owners, since Jason hoped to attract their attention. I had decided to change out the nautical theme I'd created by the front entrance to lend some ambieance to the reception. By 10:00 a.m., Jose´ and I were moving in an old prison electric chair I'd found at an estate sale. God knows why the family had had it in the first place. But it was so unusual, I felt sure I'd have an opportunity to use it. The ghost hunting event seemed like the right opportunity.

First we draped sheer white fabric down the wall. Then we placed the heavy chair up against it. On either side, we hung framed sepia daguerreotypes – photos from the early 1800s made on a silver or silver-covered copper plate. The images of civil war soldiers, stern Victorian grandmothers, and sunken-eyed children in sailor suits were seriously creepy, if not ghostly. Next to the chair, we placed a round end table graced with a vintage clock, an old, tattered copy of *Murders of the Rue Morgue* and one of *The Ghost and Mrs. Muir*, along with a pair of wire-rimmed glasses and an old pipe. We left the old steamer trunk where it was. A tall, working Tiffany lamp completed the tableau. It was probably as much a murder theme as a ghost theme, but it would have to do.

Mr. Kohl appeared just before noon to check out and stepped up to the desk to settle his bill. I was about to greet him, when the door to the office behind me shut with a bang. We both just stared at each other.

Count to three.

"May I have my receipt?" he said without acknowledging the door.

I turned and went into the office to print out a receipt. As I handed it to him, the door slammed behind me – again. He paused and glanced over at it this time. As he folded the receipt and put it into his wallet, his wife and children came down the stairs. The kids were quiet and stuck very close to their mother. Mrs. Kohl rolled their large suitcase toward the front door.

"Well, thank you for a nice stay," Mr. Kohl said, putting his wallet back into his pants pocket.

The reception bell clanged, making us both jump. He stared at it for a moment without saying a word and then glanced at me. He could see I hadn't moved, leaving the two of us to stand silently staring at each other again.

"John?" his wife said behind him.

"Just a minute," he said without looking away.

The standoff lasted another second or two, before his eyes sought out the bell once more, as if daring it to ring. When it didn't, he turned away, and I retreated to the office.

The bell clanged twice more in quick succession.

He whipped around, but I was already inside the office door.

"Damn!" he said, breathing hard.

His expression made me think he was contemplating taking the bell and putting it through the window, so I held my breath. But he turned on his heel and followed his family out the door.

The Kohls' suite was booked, so we had to turn it right away. A middle-aged couple arrived around one o'clock to check in. Mr. Campo also checked out. Since our housekeeper, Trish, lived in one of the guest rooms, with Dana's room, that left two empty rooms for the paranormal group.

At one point, Dana's husband called to check in on her and to tell her that he would need to stay in Bellingham at least until Saturday. Dana said he seemed glad to know she was staying at the Inn. She didn't tell him about the intruder the night before, or I felt sure he would have come home. They had a strange relationship.

Since we only had about fifteen people coming that night in addition to the guests, April and I had decided to skip the caterer and do the food ourselves. I recruited Angela and Dana to help out in the kitchen, thinking it would take Dana's mind off her situation.

Jason Spears and his team arrived at 3:00 p.m. to begin setting up their equipment. They pulled up in two black SUVs, just as they had when they'd come once before to spend the night and record the ghosts. They'd had limited success that time, catching mostly floating orbs and snatches of what I thought might be Chloe's voice on a recorder. But it was enough to get us featured in his upcoming book.

They emerged into the heavy rain dressed in big waffle coats and mufflers. Jason was a bear of a man – over six feet tall, barrel-chested, with a shiny bald head and a trimmed goatee. His wife was diminutive in comparison, with a head of red curls that hung to her shoulders. His two tech guys, Frankie and Shorty, were polar opposites of each other – one tall and slender, the other short and stocky.

The weather had deteriorated. It was cold and had been raining steadily since before dawn. We'd had so much rain over the past few days in fact, that there were reports of flooding in areas south of Seattle.

I met Jason on the porch and ushered him and his wife inside while their staff began to unload the cars.

"Welcome," I said, giving them a broad smile. "It's good to see you again."

"It's nice to see you again, too," Jason replied. "Especially when so many roads are closed. I wasn't sure we'd make it. By the way, this is my wife, Willow."

I smiled as I shut the door. "So nice to meet you, Willow. You guys can warm up in here," I said, drawing them further into the entryway and rubbing my hands together to warm them up. "We have two empty rooms for you and about fifteen to twenty people for the event tonight." I moved behind the reception desk and turned the book around for them to sign. I grabbed a key and slid it across the desk. "You'll be right at the top of the stairs in #4. Frankie and Shorty will be around the corner in #3."

"Perfect," Jason said.

"The inn is lovely," his wife said, glancing around. "I'm so glad I was able to come with Jason this time. I love the vignette at the front door. Was that for our benefit?"

I grinned. "Yes. I'm not sure everyone will appreciate the electric chair, but it's all in fun."

"I think the whole thing is priceless," she said with a smile. "I touched the chair and felt an immediate buzz of energy."

"Was that the electricity or a ghost?" I asked.

Her ruby lips parted into a smile. "Hard to tell."

"Well, all the antiques are for sale," I said brightly. "It's part of the business."

The door opened behind me, and the two tech guys came in with a horizontal dolly, carrying computers and monitors.

"Hey, wait," Jason said to them. "Let's get some tarps down first so you don't get mud all over the place."

He left to help his guys, while I led Willow into the living room, which was decorated in an early Americana theme. Deep cranberry red drapes offset a sofa upholstered in red and white chintz. A giant picnic basket sat next to the sofa with a blue throw draped out from under one flap. An old framed American flag hung above the fireplace under glass, while a giant, iron star hung in between the bookcases. I'd also had Jose' move some of the larger furniture out and other furniture back against the walls to maximize space.

"I made a space for you under the window over there," I said, pointing to the opposite end of the room.

Willow nodded. "That should work perfectly." She stopped and glanced around. "What a beautiful room. I feel the energy, you know. The spirits. You weren't kidding. There's lots of activity here."

"Well…" I said. "I'll let you get settled, while I get back to work. Let me know if you need anything."

÷

For the next couple of hours, Jason and his team dragged electrical cords across hallways and then covered them with cord covers. They set up cameras in the breakfast room, the main hallway and the living room, and then focused one right on the reception desk and staircase since Elizabeth had been seen so many times descending the stairs.

They put a table near the fireplace with computers and three monitors. On a side table, Jason laid out a number of other devices used in ghost hunting: a special infrared camera, an EVP recorder, an EMF meter, and a thermal camera. I had no idea what any of them would be used for, but figured I'd learn during the event.

At 5:00 p.m., I emerged from my apartment dressed in black wool pants, a rust-colored turtleneck and a charcoal gray boiled wool jacket. We set out the food in the breakfast room. Although it wasn't Halloween, April couldn't avoid the urge to have a little fun. She'd created deviled eggs that looked like disembodied eyeballs, a two-layered white cake embellished with a black spider web and several creepy spiders, and sugar cookies in the shape of ghosts.

April and I were working in the kitchen alone, filling up trays ready to replenish those on the tables. Even though I knew April would hang out most of the time in the kitchen, she'd spruced up in a pair of crisp black jeans and a multi-colored linen jacket.

"So how do you feel about having a medium here tonight?" I asked her.

We hadn't really talked much about the event, other than how it would bring the Inn some good publicity, especially if Jason got some pictures to include in his next book. April glanced up from where she was arranging small quiches to go into the oven.

"You mean, am I jealous?"

"No, I know you too well for that. I was just wondering if you're skeptical or not."

She shrugged. "I suppose I'm skeptical of anyone making a profit off something like this. Makes it seem less genuine."

"Are you going to sit in on it?"

"I doubt it. I'll be busy with the food."

I gave her a conspiratorial smile. "Yes, but wouldn't it be fun to have dueling psychics? You could be her truth-o-meter."

April glanced at me sideways. "Thanks, but no thanks."

The kitchen door swung open, and Blair breezed in, dressed in black wool pants, black patent leather boots with three-inch heels, a black cashmere turtleneck sweater and a red wool cape with a high collar.

"Show me your teeth," I said when she hung up her coat.

"Why?"

"I want to see if you have fangs."

Blair's hair was pulled up into a soft up do, and she wore dangling bat earrings. She gave me a brief smile. "Very funny. I thought it would be fun to dress for the occasion."

"We're ghost hunting, not vampire hunting," I said, stirring a dip.

"Speaking of vampires, where's Dana?" she asked, sticking a delicate finger into the dip.

"Shhh, she might hear you," I said, slapping her hand away. "She was in the breakfast room last time I saw her."

"With the food?" Blair asked. "I didn't see her. I must have mistaken her for the stuffed pig."

I gave Blair an admonishing look. "That's not nice."

"Seriously?" she spat. "You're defending her now? Don't tell me you're best buds all of a sudden."

"No, but she's going through a lot."

"Well, how are *you*?" she asked. "Did you get your car back?"

"Not yet. Maybe tomorrow."

The door opened behind us and Rudy and Doe came in. Rudy took one startled look at Blair and said, "I didn't know we were having a costume contest or I would have worn a sheet."

Blair lifted one shoulder. "You're just jealous."

"Well, if we find a dead body with a couple of little holes in its neck, we're going to come looking for you," Rudy teased her. She turned and hung her coat on the wall rack.

"Hey, depending on whose body it is, that doesn't sound so bad," Blair said. "For instance, is Detective Abrams coming?" she asked, turning to me.

"And by coming, you just mean to the party?" Rudy asked with a deadpan face.

Blair broke into a grin. "I like your style, Mama Bear."

"Mama Bear? What's that supposed to mean?" Rudy asked as she circled around the table.

"If Julia can have nicknames for us, then so can I," Blair said with a lift to her chin.

"Really?" Doe said, grabbing a celery stick. "Who am I?"

"I think of you as 'Miss Spit and Polish,'" Blair said proudly.

Doe's eyebrows arched. "I hate spit."

"Yes, but you're always so pulled together. I mean, look at you in those crepe pants and silk blouse. And Julia, you're 'Miss Rough and Tumble.'"

"Me? You're the one who barged in on Al Dente the other day," I said in amazement. "You went after him like a commando."

She smiled contentedly. "Yes, that's true. But you do whatever it takes to get things done. And, April," she said, pulling April's attention away from the counter. "You're my 'Glow in the Dark.'"

April looked puzzled. "I'm not sure what that means, or even if it's a good thing."

"Oh, it's very good," Blair said with a toss of her head. "Not only do you have the second sight, as people like to say, but you glow with confidence. You're kind of my role model in that department."

April smiled. "Thanks. I think."

"You still didn't tell me what 'Mama Bear' means," Rudy said, drawing her thin lips into a frown.

"Isn't it obvious?" Blair said to her.

"Listen," I said, hoping to deflect the argument I saw coming. "I have news. The detectives were here this morning. Al Dente was murdered yesterday."

Everyone wheeled around in my direction. "Well, that's a bombshell," Rudy said. "You didn't think a phone call was in order?"

"Sorry, we've been too busy today, and we just heard about it this morning. It happened sometime *after* we were shot at yesterday. But not only that, they've ID'd Dana's ex-husband. He's staying in town."

"Wow," Blair exclaimed. "So he could be the culprit. Does Dana know?"

"Yes," I said, giving Blair a sobering look. "And she's been even more nervous all day because of it. Besides that, Clay is up in Bellingham and not due back until tomorrow, so I'd watch your step around her."

"Do the police think the ex-husband is behind all of this?" Doe asked.

"They said they're keeping their options open. I take that to mean that even Tony isn't off their radar yet."

"Speaking of," Rudy said. "Is he coming tonight?"

"No. He called and begged off. He was afraid he'd be too much of a distraction."

"Makes sense," Rudy said, reaching for a black olive. "I'm just sorry to see his entire life rearranged because of this."

"Me too. The sooner the killer is caught, the better," I responded.

The kitchen door swung open and Jason walked in. "We're all set up," he announced.

I took a moment to introduce the ladies. A moment later, Willow came in to join us.

"I've heard all about you," Jason said, extending his enormous hand to Blair. "Especially you, Mrs. Wentworth," he said, lingering on Blair. "I understand you're quite the race car driver."

Blair expected compliments, and so her reactions were usually manufactured. In response to Jason's remark, she dipped her chin, tilted her head to the side and said, "Fast cars and fast men. That's my style, Mr. Spears."

He laughed heartily. "Well, hopefully, tonight it will be fast *ghosts*."

"Do you really expect the ghosts to appear?" she asked.

"I certainly hope so. In any case, we're ready for them if they do. This is my wife, Willow," he said, drawing her forward. "If they're here, she'll know it."

"Did you know that April also has the..." Blair began.

"Let's get out there to meet our guests," I said, interrupting her. I shot April a glance, and she mouthed 'thank you' as I ushered everyone out.

We caught Dana at the food table, stuffing one of the eyeballs into her mouth. Blair cringed and said, "Ick, how can you eat that?"

Dana frowned at her. "It's just a deviled egg. They're really good."

Blair stared down at the plate of halved eggs that were filled with a green egg mixture, topped with a sliced black olive and finished off with red squiggly lines across the egg white to resemble bloodshot eyes.

Blair made a sour face. "I couldn't eat something that was looking back at me." She reached for a carrot stick instead.

Jason and Willow had gone back into the living room, so Rudy sidled up to me. "So, the guy who stole Ahab is dead? And the police think Dana's ex-dead-husband hired him?"

"It's a working theory," I confirmed.

"I think that would be dead ex-husband," Blair corrected Rudy from across the table.

Rudy shot her an irritated look. "Well, apparently he's not so dead anymore."

Dana looked up with a bleak expression, a greasy chicken wing in her hand and barbeque sauce lathered on her lower lip. "I should've known that one day he'd come back."

"Dana, the problem is that there are too many reasons why someone would want you dead," Rudy said.

"Yeah, who could keep track?" Blair murmured under her breath.

Dana had lost all of her bluster by this time and merely bowed her head in defeat.

"Is that why you kept the pictures, Dana?" I asked. "Because you thought he'd come back someday?"

"Yes. It was my insurance, just in case. He was a mean son-of-a-bitch. Whether you believe me or not, what I did in Vancouver, I did out of fear."

"I have a feeling this still goes back to those boys, Dana," I said. "Have you ever seen any of them since then?"

"No," she replied, shaking her head. "Once the rumors began, the boys were taken from us and given to other fosters. I never saw any of them again. They were so young, I'm not sure I'd recognize any of them now, anyway."

Her cell phone rang, and she switched the chicken wing into the other hand to answer it. "Yeah, hi, Clay," she said. "No, I'm fine. What?"

She turned away from us to take the call just as the front door opened and several members of the library board came in.

"I have to go greet people," I said to the girls.

I turned and moved into the entryway to grab people's coats and take them into the library. When I came back, I introduced Jason and Willow. Angela came down the hall from the apartment, dressed in black slacks and a sequined jean jacket. Just as I was about to introduce her to the president of the library board, the door opened again and Roger Romero stepped through, followed by one of the bookstore owners.

"Julia," Roger boomed. "I heard about your upstairs window last night. I warned you. We need to talk…"

"I want to kill Dana Finkle." Squawk!

I whirled around to see Ahab was bouncing back and forth on his perch. Then I turned back to Roger, who seemed rooted in place, his facial features frozen. We stared at each other for a horrified moment.

Count to three.

Roger spun around to flee, but the front door slammed shut in his face. He grabbed the knob and twisted, but it wouldn't budge. Panicked, he turned for the hallway, but Angela jumped in front of him, lifted her left leg and gave him a sharp kick to the solar plexus. He expelled a breath and flew backwards, landing in the electric chair with a thud.

"Damn, Angela!" Blair said with appreciation.

We formed a half circle around Roger, blocking his escape. Hearing the commotion, the rest of the guests flooded into the entryway behind us. Meanwhile, Roger sat plastered against the back of the electric chair, gasping for air, his bony features engraved with fear.

"Roger!" I cried. "How could you?"

He made a feeble attempt to rise, but Angela jumped forward in an attack pose, making him flinch back into the chair.

"Down, dear," I said to my daughter. "I don't think he's going anywhere. Why don't you call Detective Abrams?" Then I turned back to Roger. "Well?" I demanded.

"I…I'm not what you think, Julia. I didn't kill anyone. Honest."

"Then why did Ahab just repeat that line?" Blair asked, stepping forward with her hands on her hips.

"It's true. I did say that in front of him," he replied nervously.

"When?" Blair demanded.

He glanced around at the other library board members, who were all staring at him with unabashed alarm.

"It was back when we had the library board meeting here in December. I took a phone call. A call from someone who was…who was blackmailing me."

"Al Dente," Angela said, putting her phone back into her pocket. "They're on their way, Mom," she said to me.

"Yes," Roger agreed. "Dente approached me about five months ago to see if I would help him…dispose of Dana."

"Why?" Dana screeched, stepping forward. "I don't even know him."

Roger looked up at her. "He said he was one of…one of your boys."

There were a few intakes of breath. Roger looked suddenly old and haggard, as if years of hiding some terrible secret had finally released him from its destructive grasp.

"You don't recognize me, do you?" he said quietly to Dana. She studied his face a moment, and then haltingly shook her head. "My real name is Robert Goode. My brother was Marty."

Dana's stubby little hand flew to her mouth. "Oh my God," she muttered.

She looked faint, and I pushed her toward the steamer chest and eased her down onto it. She sat there speechless.

"So you were one of her boys, too?" I said to Roger.

He nodded. "My brother and I lived there for almost a year. Marty was my older brother, by five years. He was one of her husband's…favorites. In the end, Marty couldn't take it anymore. He hung himself."

More gasps.

"Good job, Dana," Rudy said to her. "You're two for two. Old Mr. Peabody and now Roger's brother."

Dana glanced up at Rudy, but didn't say anything.

Roger wiped perspiration from his forehead and continued. "Anyway, Dente knew I'd lived there, too. I don't know how he knew, but he did. He said he wanted revenge and thought I'd willingly go along with his plan. But I said no, and he threatened to tell everyone about my background and what her husband had done to me. But I still said no. You have to believe me."

"Ahab doesn't agree," Blair said.

"That was the conversation when I said no to him. I told him that, yes, I wanted to kill Dana Finkle. But then I immediately said I couldn't do it."

"So did you arrange to have Ahab stolen?" I asked.

He was wringing his hands. "After Trudy was killed, and it became public knowledge that Dana had actually been the target, my wife reminded me about what Ahab had said at the Christmas party. She had no idea it was me the bird was quoting, or that Dente was trying to blackmail me, but she wondered if it was a clue and if I should mention it to the police. I panicked and contacted Dente and told him we needed to get rid of the bird. He agreed on one condition – that I help him kill Dana." Roger looked up at me. "I felt trapped, Julia. After all, the only person Ahab pointed to was me. I had to say yes."

"Are you the one who shot at us?" Dana asked him.

"No. That was Dente." He took a deep sigh, and I suspected an admission was coming. "But I put a tracking device on your car,

Julia, and one on Dana's. Dente had me follow you all to Renton yesterday. I called Dente when you left the restaurant and headed home. I knew Dana had left her car at the Inn, so you'd have to go back there first. And I could tell right at what point you'd be passing the Roanoke Inn. He was waiting for you."

"And after he missed?" I pushed.

He slumped further into the electric chair. "I told him about the upstairs windows," he said sullenly, dropping his head again. "But that failed, too." He raised his eyes to me. "I tried to warn you about the windows, Julia," he said. "I really didn't want anyone else to get hurt."

"You know Dente was found dead last night?" I said to him.

His body jolted as if the electric chair had sent a shock wave through him. "What? No. I didn't kill him. Oh, God," he whined, dropping his head into his hand. "This is a nightmare."

The sound of sirens and a car sliding to a halt on the gravel outside made everyone glance out the sidelight window. A moment later the front door flew open and Detective Abrams and David came in. Two uniformed police officers followed behind them. They stopped mid-stride when they encountered the small crowd blocking the entryway.

We quickly explained the situation and they took over. David read Roger his Miranda rights and took him into custody. Just before they got Roger out the door in handcuffs, he turned to me.

"I didn't kill anyone, Julia. You have to believe me. It wasn't me."

CHAPTER THIRTY-TWO

"Well, that put a damper on the festivities," Blair lamented after they'd left. "The prospect of seeing a ghost now seems a little anticlimactic."

"I need to go lie down," Dana said. She got up and started for the apartment.

"But, Dana, my dogs are loose in there," I said, moving to catch up with her.

She turned bleary eyes in my direction. "I don't care." And with that, she turned and disappeared down the hallway.

"I'll go with her," Angela said. "I'll put your dogs in your bedroom, and then I'll take Lucy with me. I think I ought to follow the guys down to the regional jail."

"Okay, sweetheart. Thanks."

After Angela left, I glanced into the breakfast room and saw April standing next to the kitchen door. She must have come in when she heard the sirens. She gave me a confirming nod and then stepped back through the swinging door.

I turned to the people filling the area by the front door. "The theatrics are over. Why don't you all go in and enjoy some of April's hors d'oeuvres? We still have ghosts to hunt."

People shuffled off. Jason came up to me, his eyes alight with enthusiasm.

"Julia," he began. "The door," he said, nodding to the front door. "When that guy tried to run, it...uh...closed by itself."

"That's right," I said without much energy.

"And there was no one there."

"No."

"So, it was…uh…"

"Yes," I confirmed.

"You're sure?"

"Yes."

"But who?"

"Chloe. She likes to do that."

"Damn!" He stared at the door for a moment and then turned and nearly ran back into the living room yelling, "We have activity!"

Meanwhile, the party continued. As people milled around the food tables, the girls and I huddled up in the kitchen.

"So, now what?" Rudy said.

I plopped into a chair. "All I know is that I'm exhausted, and I wonder which one of those boys in the pictures was Roger."

"Maybe none of them," Doe said. "I doubt she kept pictures of *all* the kids."

"It's so sad," I said with a sigh. "To start out your life like that, abused and humiliated, only to lose your brother and then get drawn into a murder plot."

"He's no angel, Julia," Rudy said. "He could have stuck to his guns and said no."

"So it's all over," Doe said with relief.

"Maybe not," I said. "Roger said he didn't kill anyone, and I believe him."

"Yes, but it might have been Al Dente who killed Trudy and shot at *you*," she said.

"True, but someone murdered *him*," I replied.

"So there's a third person out there," Blair said. "I wonder who."

"Maybe the ex-husband," Rudy said. "They need to arrest him."

"Dana's not safe until they do," Doe said. "I think they ought to take Dana into protective custody."

"Or station an officer here again," Rudy suggested.

"Hey, maybe David could come and stay," Blair said.

I grimaced. "There's no more room in my apartment," I said.

She smiled wickedly. "Except for your king-sized bed."

I sighed in exasperation. "You guys do realize that I have an inn full of people right now. This needs to end."

The wind had kicked up outside and was slapping the branches of the flowering cherry tree against the windowpanes.

"C'mon," Rudy said. "Let's think this through logically. Up until now, this third guy has been completely in the shadows. There has to be a reason for that."

"Right," Doe agreed. "If it's the ex-husband, he wants her dead in order to get his money back."

"But…if he wants to get the money, he can't be suspected of the crime," Rudy said. "So he would *have* to remain invisible. That means he's also not going to come here after Dana with guns blazing. It will have to be with stealth, like before."

"So, what are you saying?" I asked her.

"You have Dana safely tucked away in your apartment. Why don't we see if we can get the police to put a car at your back door and one at the front door? If we can, I'd call it good."

"And if they won't?" I asked.

Rudy looked around the table. "Then I guess we're all moving in until they catch the son-of-a-bitch."

"Hurray, another slumber party," Blair said with a grin.

CHAPTER THIRTY-THREE

I slipped into the office and called David. He agreed to have a police car stationed at my back door and offered to come and sleep in the study himself once they had processed Roger's arrest.

A half hour later, the breakfast room was filled with guests milling about and chatting. Goldie and Ben knocked on the door off the breakfast room, and I let them in.

"Any news on the big case?" Goldie whispered to me as she stepped through the door. "I heard sirens a little bit ago."

"Uh…, actually, Roger Romero was just arrested."

"Who's that?" she said. "I don't know him."

"Isn't he that security expert?" Ben asked.

"Yes," I replied. "It appears that Roger was involved, although we don't know to what extent. But he *is* the one who tampered with our security system, allowing the thief to get in to steal Ahab."

"Someone should hang him from the rafters," Goldie said with venom. "That's a low-down thing to do…steal a bird. I'm just glad you're okay, Julia, and that Ahab is back."

"Did you ever get your gun back?" I asked, hoping she hadn't.

"Absolutely," Ben said. "It's our Second Amendment right to keep and bear arms. We're not going to let the police take that away."

"Of course not," I agreed. "But perhaps you should have it checked out. It did seem to go off awfully easily."

I inadvertently glanced at my wall, where I'd hung an arrangement of collectible plates to cover the pellet holes.

"The plates look nice," Goldie said. "But if I were you, I'd get that son-of-a-bitch they just arrested to pay to have your ceiling fixed."

The three of us glanced up. Ben's eyes opened wide. "Nice shooting, Goldie."

"Humpf," she grunted. "So how long do you have to put up with her highness?" she asked, meaning Dana.

I sighed. "Just until tomorrow or the next day. Her husband will be back."

"Too bad for you," She glanced around. "Are those good-looking detectives here?" Goldie raised her eyebrows and glanced around.

"They were, but they're downtown now, booking Roger."

"You and that older guy...you're a thing, huh?" she said with a lascivious grin.

"C'mon, Goldie, let's get something to eat," Ben said. He took her elbow and guided her away, giving me a sympathetic look.

I smiled and closed and locked the door, just as Rudy came up behind me. "I think they're ready in the other room," she said.

I nodded. "Okay." I clapped my hands to get everyone's attention around me. "We're ready to start."

People started moving into the living room, where we had extra chairs set up around the perimeter. I turned out lights as I moved into the hallway. We purposely left on the night lights plugged in along the hallways, just in case someone had to go down the hall to the restroom. Then I locked the front door, just in case.

In the living room, we left one hurricane lamp on in the corner, giving off a soft glow. Willow was seated at my antique library table, her hands placed flat on the surface in front of her. Frankie was manning two computer screens at the table next to the fireplace, while Jason sat on a stool. Shorty stood next to him with some kind of meter in his hand.

"Welcome, everyone," Jason said in a melodic voice. "My name is Jason Spears. This is my wife, Willow," he said gesturing to his right. "That's Frankie back there on the computers, and Shorty has the EVP recorder, which can record audible ghost phenomena. We are the Salem Paranormal Investigation Team, or S.P.I.T., and we hunt ghosts." There was a mixture of murmurs and chuckles around the room at the acronym. "My wife is a medium," Jason said. "She can speak to the dead and entice them to appear. That's our goal tonight. We ask that you stay calm and relaxed. Afterwards, if you're interested, I'll be signing some of my books," he said, gesturing to another table. The wind smacked a branch against one of the windows, and Jason turned. "Seems we have the perfect night for a haunt," he said with a smile.

A woman by the window shrieked. Everyone turned, but she slapped the hand of the man next to her. "Sorry," she said. "He pinched me."

"Please," Jason said. "We need all of you to concentrate. I know many of you are skeptical, but we've had some success with this in the past. Let's give it a try. Now, here's what I want you to know. Often, if a ghost is nearby, the temperature will drop. Sometimes, batteries in use will drain."

"Because they draw off the energy?" a young man asked.

"That's right. And you might see what we call an orb. It's a little ball of light. Sometimes, we don't see it with the naked eye, but we'll see it later on one of the cameras. We also have an infrared camera, which detects heat and turns it into an electronic image. So we can sometimes get an actual image of a ghost that can't be seen by the naked eye." He turned to his wife. "Willow will try to contact the spirits known to frequent the Inn. I understand that John St. Claire's wife, Elizabeth, is still here, along with their daughter, Chloe. Is that right, Mrs. Applegate?"

My cell phone began to play *Rock Around the Clock*, just as I heard my name. I jerked to attention. "Yes, that's right. And their dog, Max." I was forced to sacrifice my opportunity to talk about our ghosts so that I could talk to my own ghost. My mother!

I grabbed my phone out of my pocket and clicked it on, turning away from the people closest to me. "What?" I said. "Now's not a good time, Mother."

"It's never a good time with you," she said. "But there's a storm coming."

I glanced out the window to where the trees looked like someone was shaking the life out of them. "What else have you got?"

"Something is about to happen," she said.

Just then the lights in the living room flickered. Several guests gasped.

"You're not helping, Mom. I don't need that right now."

"Need what?" she said.

"For you to play with the lights."

"Sorry," she said. "Not me."

The lights flickered again. Then they went out and came back on.

"Seriously, Mom, I don't need your help right now. Stop fooling with the lights. We're inside and things are fine."

"Again, not me," she said. "Be careful. A storm's coming."

A huge gust of wind rattled windows and slammed against the front door. The lights went out and stayed out.

"Damn!" I muttered. "Hold on, everyone," I called out. "Don't move. I'll get some flashlights."

I used the light from my phone to get to the reception desk where we kept several flashlights for just such occasions. Rudy followed me, so I turned and gave her one and asked her to give one to Jason. April came in from the kitchen carrying a small lantern.

"Can you get some candles?" I asked her.

She nodded and returned to the kitchen. The wind was rattling the upstairs windowpanes and making a whooshing noise that made the hairs on the back of my neck stand on end.

And then someone screamed.

I rushed to the living room and elbowed my way through a number of people who had backed into the hallway. I moved up next to Blair. Elizabeth's hazy outline hovered just in front of Jason, facing me. Elizabeth had her hands to her throat and seemed to be squeezing. She'd done this once before, when she was trying to tell me that Martha had been poisoned.

"She sure is putting on a show tonight," Blair said.

But there was something about Elizabeth that told me it wasn't a show. When squeezing her neck didn't elicit the response she wanted, she turned and walked through the wall into the entryway.

More gasps and screams.

"Are you getting this?" Jason called to Shorty.

"She's out here!" someone called.

All of a sudden, twenty people herded into the entryway, pushing me back into the breakfast room. Elizabeth was by the front door. I squeezed my way back through the crowd. Once I got to the front of the crowd, she took one look at me and walked through the wall into the library.

"What the heck?" I muttered.

The herd followed her, pushing and shoving their way down the hallway. And there she was in the middle of the library. Once again, as soon as she saw me, she turned and walked through the next wall into my apartment.

"What is she doing?" Blair said behind me.

"I don't know. But it looks like she wants us to follow her to my apartment." I inhaled as a thought occurred. "Oh my God. Dana! C'mon!"

I turned and pushed my way through the stunned crowd and ran as fast as I could down the darkened hallway to my apartment. I used my key to open the door and burst inside. A quick check of the apartment revealed what Elizabeth had been trying to tell us.

Dana was gone.

CHAPTER THIRTY-FOUR

"Where the heck did she go?" Blair exclaimed. We were gathered in the hallway just outside my apartment. Jason had steered everyone else back to the living room. "Wouldn't we have seen her leave?"

A heavy blast of wind buffeted the back door. I turned that way, and a thought came to mind. "Wait, she could've gone out the back. C'mon."

We hurried down the hallway and out the back door into a small lot. Only Doe's Mercedes, Blair's BMW, and Rudy's sports car were parked there. The rain had stopped, but the wind blew down the driveway like a train howling through a tunnel, bending the trees in a macabre sort of dance. Lights were out everywhere, leaving us in the dark. The beams from our flashlights cut through the inky blackness, illuminating small swaths of ground as we rotated them back and forth.

"There," Rudy said. She rushed forward to where Dana's orange scarf was lying next to a deep tire track in the mud. Rudy picked it up and turned to us.

"That's her scarf all right," Blair said with a sneer. "But where is she? And where is that cop car?"

"They're probably still booking Roger," I said. The dogs had followed us outside and wandered over to the bushes that hugged the side of the building. For the moment, I ignored them. "Someone must have picked Dana up," I said, glancing around.

"You mean someone took her," Rudy said, wrapping her arms around herself for warmth.

Minnie started to bark, startling us and making Rudy swing her flashlight that way.

"Just ignore her," I said.

"So, what now?" Blair asked, stamping her feet to warm up. "How do we figure out who took her?"

"I don't know, but we need to let the police know." I pulled out my phone and clicked it on. "Damn, the cell tower must be down. I can't get a signal."

"What is the deal with that dog?" Blaire snapped, looking over to where Minnie continued to yap at Mickey.

I flashed my light that way, but all I saw was Mickey's stocky little butt. It was obvious he'd found something under a bush, and Minnie didn't like it. "He's found food, I bet. And Minnie is tattling on him." I marched over to the side of the house. "Come here, you two." I reached out for Mickey and pulled him back. The beam from the flashlight caught the corner of a cell phone lying underneath a bush. I pushed him away and picked it up. "It's Dana's cell phone."

"Why was he eating it?" Blair asked, coming up behind me.

I groaned. "Because Dana was eating chicken wings. And now it's covered in dog slime."

"Turn it on," Rudy said. "Maybe you'll find something."

I wiped my fingers on my slacks to get rid of the slime and then clicked on the phone. When I swiped the screen, her last text message appeared. "Meet me in the back parking lot," I read out loud. "We'll bury our differences, and you can still be mayor." I looked up at my friends. "It's from Tony."

"Morales?" Rudy said. "We need to call the police."

"But how? I can't get a call out," I said. Just then, my own cell phone rang. I pulled it out of my pocket and clicked it on. "Julia!" David snapped. "Roger got away!"

"What?"

"He...away."

"David, your phone is breaking up. What's happening?"

"The electricity...he...out. We're in Seattle...looking...him. Stay put...might come back."

Another blast of frigid air blew through my back lot, nearly blowing me off my feet. Twigs and leaves came with it. I had to lean against Doe's car to steady myself. I shouted into the phone. "But David, it's not Roger, it's Tony. He has Dana!"

"What?" he said.

"Tony Morales has Dana. You have to find them!" And then my phone went dead. I shook it. Pushed buttons. The light stayed on, but there was no signal. "Shoot. It really went out this time. Try your phones!" I shouted.

Everyone pulled out their cell phones, but no one got a signal.

"Now what do we do?" Doe asked, hugging herself. The wind had whipped her hair into a virtual froth, and her crepe blouse was flapping to a quick rhythm.

"Let's go back inside," I said. "I'm freezing."

We returned to the apartment and shut the door. I was shivering so hard, my teeth had begun to chatter. As the four of us tramped down the dark hallway, we met April coming the other way with the small lantern in her hand.

"Dana is gone," I informed her, rubbing my upper arms to warm up. "We think she's been kidnapped."

"I saw something," she said. "That's why I came to find you. Here."

"What's this?" I asked looking down at a piece of paper she'd handed me.

"As soon as the lights went out, I…started getting something. A string of words in my head."

In the small halo of light from the lantern, I could see that she was kneading her temple with two fingers as if she were in pain. I looked down at the paper again.

"Watchtower," I read. "What does that mean?"

"That's just it. I don't know. But I kept hearing that word over and over in my head, followed by something about the wind howling."

Her comment reminded me of my mother's phone call. "I got a call from my Mom earlier. All she said was that a storm was coming."

"I think we know that already," Blair said.

"Something about this sounds familiar," Rudy said, stepping into the light.

"Maybe the Inn is the watchtower," Doe said, peeking over my shoulder.

"No," a deep voice said from the hallway behind us. Jason Spears stepped out of the shadows and reached out his hand. "Willow got a message, too. May I?" I gave him April's note. "Willow got much the same thing," he said, reading it. "This is from a Jimi Hendrix song."

"What the hell does Jimi Hendrix have to do with all of this?" Blair demanded.

"It's from *All Along the Watchtower*," he replied, turning to her. "There must be some kind of way out of here," he sang. "Don't you recognize it?"

"I remember that song," I said. "Said the joker to the…to the…what?" I said, snapping my fingers trying to quote the next line.

"Thief," he replied. "Said the joker to the thief. But the last stanza starts with, 'All along the Watchtower,' and then ends with, 'two riders were approaching and the wind began to howl."

"And Willow got the same message?" I asked.

"Yes," a light voice said from the darkness.

Willow had appeared quietly behind Jason, her red hair glistening in the low light. Jason stepped aside so that she could move into the circle. She had much the same pained expression that April did. "I heard the lyrics in my head," she said. "But I don't know why or what they mean."

I sighed. "We think our friend has been abducted."

"She's the one that had something to do with that guy who got arrested tonight, right?" Jason asked.

"Yes. And April…" I said, gesturing to my partner. "Well, she's a bit like you, Willow."

Willow turned an appreciative glance at April.

"So, do we think this is all connected?" Jason asked. "Because something also happened in the living room. Your stereo just went off. It started playing *Purple Haze*, another Jimi Hendrix song," he said. "I don't mean to make too much of this, but isn't Hendrix buried in this area?"

"Yes, he is. In Renton," Rudy said.

"Actually, right next to where Al Dente used to live," I said. "This keeps going back to Renton."

"Wait a minute," Rudy said, snapping her fingers. "When we were at the restaurant yesterday, there was a *Renton Reporter* sitting on the table. I skimmed an article that talked about moving Jimi Hendrix's grave. There had been some soil erosion under his memorial because of an underground pipe that burst. So they were going to relocate him temporarily until they could get it fixed."

"When?" April asked.

"Tomorrow, I think," she said with a shrug. "There was a picture of the skip loader and the area where they had already dug the hole."

"I don't get it," Blair said in frustration. "What does Jimi Hendrix have to do with Dana?"

I looked down at Dana's cell phone in my hand and read the text again. "Meet me in the back parking lot. We'll *bury* our differences." I inhaled a gulp of air and then looked up at the lamp lit crowd gathered around me. "What if he's going to bury her?"

"Seriously?" Blair said. "Why would he do that? He could just throw her into the lake."

"No, I think Julia's onto something," April said, turning to me. "Haven't you noticed? Every time Roger is here working, he always has 60s and 70s rock music playing, and it's often Jimi Hendrix."

"So he's a fan. So what?" Blair said obstinately.

"So I bet Tony is setting Roger up again," Rudy said, catching on.

"But Roger just got arrested," Blair countered. "He couldn't have abducted Dana."

"But Tony wouldn't know that," I said. "And David just told me that Roger escaped when the electricity went out."

"Could they be working together?" Doe asked. "Roger and Tony?"

I pulled my fingers through my hair in frustration. "I don't know. They certainly know each other. But I still can't figure out why in the world Tony would want to kill Dana in the first place."

There was a scream from the living room and then someone shouted, "She's back! The ghost is back."

"We've got to go," Jason said. He and Willow turned and disappeared down the dark hallway.

"Listen," Doe said, getting our attention back. "Jason said the next part of that Hendrix line was something about a thief. Didn't Detective Abrams say that Dana's first husband had been incarcerated for embezzlement?"

"You're right. You think this is all about him?" I asked.

"It could also be Tony who is embezzling money," Rudy said. "Remember, Doe, you told us your niece overheard the Mayor chastising Tony for having Trudy spy on Dana. Maybe the reason Tony spied on Dana was because she discovered something incriminating about him, and we just never got her to tell us what it was."

"Like stealing from the city?" Doe asked.

"Right."

"Okay, but regardless who has her, the question now is how do we find her?" I said. "*Purple Haze* came on when Blair and I were fighting with Big Al in his apartment, too. Somehow this keeps coming back to Jimi Hendrix and Renton." I glanced at the text message again. "What if whoever has her is going to bury Dana in Jimi Hendrix's new burial site?"

"Then someone needs to stop them," April said grimly.

There was a short silence. I turned to April. "Can you take care of things here?"

"Of course," she replied.

"Let me get my purse." I ran into my apartment, threw on my coat and grabbed my gloves and purse off the counter. I came back out and asked, "Who's driving?"

Everyone looked at Blair. "I've got this," she said. "But we need our coats."

We all hurried to the kitchen. Willow and Jason were in the living room, presumably recording Elizabeth. As the girls got their coats on, I spoke to April in the entryway. "Can you keep trying to get through to the police? Maybe even send someone down there to tell them what's happening. I don't know if David heard me when I told him about Tony, but even if he did, they wouldn't know where to look."

She nodded. "Okay. Just get going. And be careful. It's beginning to snow. Here, take this," she said, reaching behind the reception desk and grabbing my baseball bat.

"Take this, too," Jason said, coming in from the living room. "It's the EVP recorder. It recorded the stereo when it came on. I don't know if it will help, but Willow insisted I give it to you."

I looked past Jason to where Willow stood at the entrance to the living room. April had positioned a bunch of candles on tables, so Willow's face was barely visible, her eyes mere pockets of shadow.

"You need to hurry," she said. "You don't have much time."

"What do you mean?" I asked her.

"They're chattering…the spirits here. They don't like what he's doing. It's an abomination." She paused and then said, "He's going to bury her alive."

CHAPTER THIRTY-FIVE

Blair was forced to drive slowly off the island. Traffic lights swung back and forth, and broken branches flew through the air and rolled across the street as we headed for the freeway. We picked up southbound I–405 and passed patches of lit neighborhoods along the way. But once we left the freeway in Renton, a completely dark environment forced us to slow down even more.

Headlights from a surprising number of cars cut through the darkness as their drivers carefully navigated the streets, stopping at intersections. Given our destination and what lay ahead, it was frustrating. We didn't have time to waste.

We wound our way up NE 4th and crested the big hill again. The darkened Renton Technical College campus appeared on our left. This time we turned at the McDonald's Restaurant at the corner of Monroe Street, where a few patrons lingered in front of the fast food place, perhaps waiting to see if the lights would come back on. Greenwood Memorial Park Cemetery, where the famous rock star was buried, sat across the street on the corner.

There were two entrances to the cemetery. The first entrance led to the chapel, but that was now blocked by a large tree branch that had come down. The grounds were surrounded by a fence, which was lined with bushes and trees. This made it difficult to see into the cemetery grounds. Blair cruised slowly down the street and paused when we reached the second entrance.

The Hendrix memorial sat 100 feet inside the entrance in the middle of a circular lawn, clearly visible from the street, even with the power out. A tall marble pagoda with a domed top was surrounded by slabs of marble that seemed to glow in the dark. I had been there once when Graham wanted to visit the memorial. As I remembered, all four panels of the pagoda had been etched on the inside with images of the famous musician, his signature head band tied around his forehead.

Blair had turned off the car's headlights. If, in fact, Tony had brought Dana here, we didn't want to alert him. The wind had begun to subside, but now snow fell in soft flakes. While Blair concentrated on driving, the rest of us peered through the break in the trees along the street side of the cemetery.

"Back there," Rudy called. "That's got to be him."

Blair slammed on the brakes. A tiny light flickered at the back of the property.

"Okay, if that's him, how will we get to him without him knowing?" Doe asked.

There was a pause, and then Rudy said, "Blair, drive to the end of the road and turn left. The city's maintenance yard is down there."

I swung my head in her direction. "How in the world do you know that?"

"I did an article on the Hendrix memorial back in 2000, on the thirtieth anniversary of his death. This place was packed. I had to drive around looking for somewhere to park. I finally found a place down there and came in through the back."

"Got it," Blair said.

She passed the entrance and then flipped on the lights again. At the end of Monroe Avenue, she turned left. The line of trees continued all along the perimeter of the property, blocking our view. *A good thing*, I thought.

"We can park at the end of the street up here and walk in through the maintenance yard." Rudy said.

"We'll need to be quiet, though," I warned everyone. "If he hears us, he could take off."

"Or kill her first," Doe said solemnly from the back seat. "If he hasn't already."

Blair pulled to the end of the street and parked at the curb. She killed the engine. "You guys do realize it's freezing cold out there?" she said. "And it's beginning to snow."

"Do we have a choice?" I asked.

Blair glanced through the driver's side window. "Damn, I never thought I'd do something so heroic for Dana Finkle."

"I doubt any of us did," I said. "I guess this is what it means to be a Mercer Island Hero."

"Funny," she said. "But I left my medallion at home. Let's get this over with." She started to open the door when Rudy stopped her.

"Wait a minute. We need a plan. He's liable to have a weapon."

"What if we spread out and distract him?" Doe asked.

"And then what?" Rudy countered.

I sat back and unlatched my seat belt, a leaden feeling in my stomach. "No," I said. "I say I go in there alone."

"What? That's not safe," Doe said.

"None of this is safe. But if he thinks I'm alone, maybe I can stall him until the police get here. I told April to send someone down to the station."

"But that could take a while," Rudy said. "Where's that baseball bat?"

I pulled it off the floor. "Right here."

She took it from me. "Okay. It's the only weapon we have."

"What if he doesn't buy that Julia is alone?" Doe asked "We're pretty well known for going everywhere together."

"If he doesn't buy it, then Julia calls the two of you out," Rudy replied.

"But not you," Doe said.

"No. I'll hang back," Rudy said. "I could be out of town or something." Rudy turned to me. "You can do this, Julia. Tony is your friend. Play off that. Just keep him talking."

"What will you do?" Doe asked.

We all turned to Rudy, who was staring out the window at the sliver of light, barely visible from this angle. She handed the bat to Doe.

"I have an idea," she said. "One of you should take the bat, and give me that recorder. Then, just look for my signal."

"Which will be what?" Blair snapped.

"Don't worry, you'll know it," she replied.

Everyone paused and looked out the window towards the solitary light that we believed marked Dana's forthcoming grave.

"C'mon, let's do this," Rudy prodded. "We'll cut through the maintenance yard. Then, Julia, you go first. Doe, you cut around to the left and Blair to the right. You guys take the baseball bat. Maybe between the four of us, we can stop him, stall him, or do enough damage to hurt him."

"I like the sound of that," Blair murmured.

It didn't seem like much of a plan, but we didn't have time for a better one. We climbed out into the cold and assembled on the driver's side of the Mercedes. The wind had dissipated, replaced by light snowflakes. Somewhere a dog barked, and in the background, the sound of traffic on NE 4th Street was dulled, making it feel as if we were on another planet.

I looked gravely at my fellow heroes in the dark, my nerves on alert. "You guys are the best friends a girl ever had."

"Oh, shut up!" Rudy snapped. "We're all going to be fine. Use your flashlight only until you get onto the cemetery grounds. Keep it focused right at your feet, so he's less likely to see it. Once you're through the maintenance yard, you'll have to turn it off."

I nodded and flicked on the small flashlight. We moved up the street to where a locked gate extended across the road. "Now what?" I said, reaching out and fingering a chain and padlock.

"Hold on," Rudy said. She moved to the end of the gate, where it butted up against a tall row of bushes. "Over here," she whispered. "We'll have to slip through." She pushed the bush back, giving us about a foot and a half.

"Are you kidding?" I said in a hoarse whisper. "I'm not that thin."

"Suck it in," Blair said. "You can do it."

I stood up straight, pulled in my stomach and crammed into the narrow space. I got stuck. Rudy pushed, and I popped out the other side, leaving my wool coat a little worse for wear. One by one, the others followed.

Rudy nodded for me to move ahead, so I began moving up a dirt road that led into the maintenance yard, feeling very much alone and vulnerable. I left the hood on my coat down so that I could see and hear better, but my ears quickly started to go numb. The flashlight gave me enough light to avoid killing myself, but it wasn't easy going. The ground was uneven, and I had to be careful I didn't trip – not my strong point.

Blair and Doe followed at a good distance. When I hit a break in the fence, where the paved cemetery road came into the maintenance yard, they held back. I extinguished my small light and walked through, keeping to the edge of the drive.

Tony's light flickered some thirty yards in front of me, partially hidden by a bank of bushes. On the far side was a towering line of trees, now flecked with white. The area was eerily quiet, as the snow picked up and began to blanket the ground.

I took a calming breath and crossed an intersecting road, stopping at the curb on the other side. I turned and glanced behind me. Two shadows followed me through the opening and then split up. I could just make out a third shadow in the background, waiting.

My body was humming with adrenalin. This seemed crazy, but what else could we do? At least we all wore dark clothes, and except for Blair, sensible shoes. Perhaps we could at least surprise Tony. But what then?

I turned back to where the light now flickered a short distance in front of me. The bulky outline of the skip loader sat off to the right, like some monster waiting in the dark. Through breaks in the bushes, I could see someone bending over and then straightening up.

Tony was shoveling dirt.

My heart sank, and I swallowed a ball of spit at the thought that this was really happening. Someone I trusted and cared for was a ruthless killer. This had happened before – after Martha was murdered. How could I keep misjudging people so badly? But then the realization that Tony might already be shoveling dirt back *into* the hole made my chest muscles clench.

I had to hurry.

I stepped up onto the curb and almost met with disaster. My foot twisted into a hole, making me bite off a cry of pain. I stopped, my heart thumping. I took a breath and tried it again, stepping up onto the grass. All was okay, and I continued forward.

My feet whispered through the growing layer of snow. I snuck forward until I was standing behind the bank of bushes. I flexed my fingers, feeling the cold through my leather gloves. I leaned over and peered through the branches, hoping to see Tony. There was a pile of dirt, now covered in white, and the small light that sat on the ground. But no Tony.

I tip-toed to the south end of the bushes and then stopped to listen. I was going to have to get up the nerve to step out and reveal myself, but the thought nearly short-circuited my breathing. I closed my eyes a moment to gather strength, and then offered a silent prayer to keep us all safe. But a shiver ran the length of my spine, as if in warning. When I opened my eyes, I noticed a car parked on the far side of where I stood. My brows clenched in question.

It was a Saab.

"Well, what do we have here?"

I spun around with a gasp. A small figure draped in shadow stood behind me, holding something in his right hand.

"Step around into the light, Julia," he said. "I have a gun."

He gestured with the hand that held the gun. My heart rate went into overdrive, but I turned my back on him and walked into a small clearing surrounded by trees and more bushes.

A hooded camp lantern sat on the ground next to a deep, oblong hole, surrounded by piles of dirt and mud. A large marble monument sat at the corner of the clearing. On the other side of the hole, Dana laid on her stomach, trussed up like a turkey, snow layering the back of her coat. A piece of duct tape kept her mouth shut, but she saw me and started squirming. I felt sick to my stomach. I turned to the man with the gun.

"Why are you doing this, Clay?"

"What do you care?" he snarled. "You hate her almost as much as I do."

"You *hate* Dana?"

"Oh, God, yes," he replied. He came up to my left side. "She's the most awful person I know. But, I suppose after I bury her alive, *I'll* be the most awful person I know." He chuckled as Dana whimpered and squirmed frantically.

"But why bury her alive?"

"Because she was going to divorce me and leave me penniless," he roared. He leaned into me, and in the dark, his eyes gleamed with a seething hatred. He took a breath to calm himself down and a leering grin spread across his face. "Don't you see? This way, I'll have revenge *and* her money."

I glanced at Dana and finally felt sorry for her.

"That's what this is all about? Money. Where's Tony?"

"Tony? Oh, the message. That was a ruse. But first things first. I know you're not alone. So where are the others?"

"I *am* alone," I said unconvincingly. "It's just me."

"No," he snapped, pointing the gun at my chest. "It's never just you. You always have your little entourage with you. So where are they?" He stepped back and glanced around, keeping the gun pointed at me. "Come out, come out, wherever you are," he sang.

There was a long pause as the silence of the falling snow seemed to engulf us. Nothing happened.

"Honestly, I came alone. They're all back at the Inn."

"You're lying. Come out," he shouted. "Or I'll kill Julia now and bury her with Dana." He reached into his pocket and pulled out a long cylinder and screwed it onto the tip of his gun. "See? I even brought a silencer, just in case."

A few seconds ticked by, and I began to shiver, but not necessarily from the cold. Clay moved over and placed the tip of the silencer against my temple. I flinched. A moment later, Doe stepped out from behind a tree on the other side of the newly dug grave.

"No need for that," she called out. "C'mon, Blair. The jig's up."

Blair emerged from behind the large marble headstone. She stepped into the shallow light carrying the baseball bat, snow blanketing her blond hair.

"Drop the bat," he ordered. She tossed it forward, and it fell to the ground with a soft thud.

"Get over here next to your friend," he said, gesturing with the gun.

He stepped back, while Blair moved next to Doe on the other side of the hole.

"Okay, now hand over Dana's cell phone," he said, holding out the flat of his hand to me.

I looked at Doe and Blair, thinking this was the one piece of evidence we had that could tell the police who did it. "I don't have it with me," I lied. "I left it at the Inn."

"I don't believe you," he snapped again. "And if you don't hand it over, I'll shoot you in the knee and then various other parts of your body, until you do."

His hand shook as his anxiety rose. I took a deep breath. His face was like an iron mask in the low light, and his eyes bulged behind those coke-bottle lenses. He was serious.

I reached into my pocket and tossed the phone to him, hoping he'd drop it, and we could rush him. But even though he had to reach for it, he was able to grab it mid-air.

Damn!

"Well, now that that's done, what's next? Oh, yes, I have to kill you."

"But…" I blurted. "What about Tony? Is he part of this, or not?"

I needed to keep him talking. Time was our only ally at this point – well, that and Rudy, wherever she was.

"Oh, for heaven's sake. No," he snarled. "I hacked his email, just like I did yours. It was the best way to get her outside," he said, gesturing to Dana. There was a short, spritely jingle from Dana's phone. He stopped and reached into his pocket and took it out. Even from where I stood, I could tell the phone had lit up. "What the…?" he said. As he studied the phone, Doe inched sideways toward him, while Blair stepped over to where the bat was and got it in between her feet. Meanwhile, Clay ran his fingers across the edge of the phone to turn it off again. "There," he said, looking up. He was about to drop it in his pocket, when once again, it jingled. "Shit! What the heck?" He glanced at the screen and then up at me. "What game are you playing? What did you do to the phone?"

"Nothing," I replied honestly. But I had a sneaking suspicion I knew who was toying with him.

"The text message just changed. It now says there's a storm coming," he said.

I smiled. And then *my* cell phone rang.

"Don't answer that," he ordered with a jerk of the gun. "Give it here."

As I reached into my pocket, he stepped around the end of the grave toward me. He put Dana's phone in his pocket and took mine, moving back to the end of the gravesite. Meanwhile, Doe and Blair had moved another several inches in his direction, Blair sliding the baseball bat along the snow-covered grass. He turned my phone off. Almost immediately, it flicked back on and rang again. He glared at me. "What the hell game are you playing?" he screamed. "How are you doing that?"

"Doing what? You can see that I'm not doing anything." I held my hands up as evidence.

"The same message just showed up on *your* phone." His hand was shaking even more now.

"Oh, that. It's not me," I said, nonchalantly. "It's my mother."

"That's a crock. Your mother is dead."

"Yeah, that's the thing. She *is* dead."

Doe's phone rang. His head and gun jerked in her direction. She took a step back and raised her hands. "Careful! Do you want me to get it?" she asked with a nervous edge to her voice.

He was breathing hard now, his anger morphing into fear. "No. Maybe I'll just kill all of you right now."

"Better dig a deeper grave," Blair said, nodding at the hole.

Dana tried screaming through the duct tape at that.

"Get over there next to your friend," he ordered with a jerk of the gun. Doe and Blair looked at me and then back at him. "Go!" He jerked the gun again to indicate he wanted them to circle the other end of the grave. They carefully stepped around the hole, leaving the bat behind.

"What are you going to do?" I asked, stalling for time.

"I'll figure something out. I haven't come this far to let a bunch of old women stop me."

There was a loud click. The lamppost at the back of the property suddenly burst into life, bathing the area right in front of it in light.

Clay spun around. "Shit."

"The power is coming back on," I said. "Better think quickly."

We were still cast in deep shadow, but lights in houses on the far side of the cemetery had also come on.

"Yeah, Clay," Blair said. "Pretty soon the whole world will be able to see what you're doing."

"Shut up!" he snarled, turning back. "I need to think."

Clay glanced behind him. He was nervous. I wondered if it was the power company or my mother. The three of us now stood in a row on the north side of the grave. I was close enough to Doe to feel her reach into her left pocket. And then I felt something cold and hard being slipped into my hand. It was her cell phone. I wrapped my fingers around it and shot her a curious look. She nodded towards Clay.

She wanted me to throw it.

He was staring into the hole, concentrating on his predicament. So I wound up and threw the phone. Doe and I started forward, ready to rush him, but the phone flew right past his left ear, making him snap his head up. "That's it! I'll just kill you all and leave you here," he yelled, bringing up the gun.

Twang! The opening chords of Jimi Hendrix's iconic guitar reverberated out of the darkness around us, like something from a horror movie.

"What?" he cried, spinning towards the sound, the gun wavering.

A large rock whizzed out of a bank of bushes. He swerved to miss it, but it grazed his shoulder, knocking him off balance and dislodging his glasses. The gun went off, making us all flinch. Clay regained his composure.

"Come out, or I'll kill your friends!" he screamed, pointing the gun at the bushes.

A second rock came quickly on the heels of the first. I watched it emerge from the shadows as if in slow motion, praying that it would hit its mark. But it didn't come slow. It came so fast, Clay didn't have time to move. The fist-sized projectile smacked him right between the eyes with a sickening thud. His body stiffened. The gun dropped to the ground, and he toppled backwards into the grave.

"Whoohoo!" Blair shouted. She ran around and grabbed the gun and pointed it into the hole.

"Careful, Blair," Doe warned her.

"I'm not going to shoot him. Just watch him. You guys get Dana," she said.

Doe and I hurried around to the other side of the grave, just as Rudy climbed out of some bushes with a shit-faced grin plastered across her face. "Don't tell me I haven't got it anymore," she said, rotating her shoulder.

We all laughed. "You have it in spades," Doe said.

I had just taken the tape off Dana's mouth by the time Rudy got there to help.

"Are you kidding me?" Dana blasted, twisting her head up to glare at Rudy. "Your plan was to hit him with a rock? What if you'd missed? We could all be dead."

Dana rolled to one side, offering her hands to Rudy. "Here, get my hands first," she ordered.

Rudy crouched down to remove the bindings, but glanced up at me with a look of resignation.

"Rudy," I warned. "Don't…"

But as the forlorn sound of a siren sounded in the distance, Rudy put both hands under Dana's hips and rolled her face-first into the grave.

"Oops," she said with a sly grin.

Blair watched and then spit out a laugh. "Good shot, Rudy."

Doe and I stepped up to the grave. "Oh, dear," Doe said.

"Get me out of here!" Dana gave a muffled cry.

Blair and Rudy gave each other a high five, as Dana cried out again from where her face lay nestled in Clay's crotch.

"Just relax, Dana," Blair said with a laugh. "You're safe. I don't think that gun will be discharging anytime soon."

CHAPTER THIRTY-SIX

It was just a week after we'd hauled Dana out of her makeshift grave and helped to put her husband in jail. Roger had been found in a seedy motel in downtown Seattle and booked on conspiracy charges. And Goldie had offered to hold a kick-off party for Tony Morales' campaign for Mercer Island mayor.

The gnome home was all lit up for the festivities. We were gathered in her enormous rec room on the ground floor that looked out on Lake Washington. Little red and blue gnomes peeked out from behind picture frames, canisters and clocks, while an entire army of them lined a three inch shelf that ran the perimeter of the room, two feet from the ceiling.

Goldie and Ben had traveled the world, making their home a virtual museum of collectibles from other countries. Everywhere you looked was something that could spark a conversation, including a set of beer mugs from the pub in Boston that had served as the inspiration for the TV show, *Cheers*. And the furniture was an eclectic mix of leather and upholstery, plus some odd pieces brought home from faraway lands. This included an ottoman I was sitting on, that had been made to look like an elephant's foot.

Both Tony and his wife were there, along with their ten-year old daughter. Tony had purposely gone public with the news about his wife's college employment to avoid any campaign shenanigans. In the end, no one cared. We'd also learned that he'd asked Trudy to spy on Dana, only to find out if she was going to oppose the Mayor's proposal for an adaptive playground for both able-bodied and disabled children. Given her propensity to lavish her ill-will on Tony's physical limitations, he wanted to be prepared.

While Dana had decided not to attend the party, she *had* publicly endorsed Tony's candidacy. But besides that, she had gone underground. I suspected she would make good on her word and pull up stakes soon and move to another city, if not another country. I couldn't blame her.

Once everyone was assembled, Mayor Frum stood up and tapped his glass to get our attention. I was holding a small paper plate in my hands, filled with veggies and dip. The ottoman had been placed right next to the end of the sofa, where Blair sat, her long legs stretched out in front of her. Sitting next to her on the strange ottoman, I felt like her little sister, relegated to the kids' table at Thanksgiving.

I listened attentively while nibbling on a carrot, as Tony gave a short, scripted speech. Just as he was finishing, I decided to lean back and cross one leg over the other. Little did I know that the bottom of the elephant's foot wasn't flat *or* solid. It was slightly rounded. So, as applause rose to signal the end of Tony's speech, I slowly rolled backwards into a potted plant.

I took the plant down with a crash and ended upside down with my butt in the air. Thankfully, I was wearing pants. There were gasps and cries of alarm, but I righted myself, popped up and assured everyone I was fine.

"Really, Julia?" Blair whispered. "This isn't about you anymore. It's about Tony. Get a grip."

Doe and Rudy were on the other side of the room, and while Doe's expression was one of concern, Rudy just shook her head as a nice gentleman helped pull me to my feet.

"Sorry, I said, blushing. "Please continue, Tony."

"Well, Julia deserves a round of applause," Tony said. "If it wasn't for her, I wouldn't be here tonight announcing my candidacy for mayor. So, thank you, Julia."

Everyone joined in, making me blush even more. I leaned over to retrieve my plate and scattered veggies, when I noticed that David, Angela and Detective Abrams had just come downstairs. Thank God they'd missed my acrobatic stunt. I straightened my blouse and made my way over to them.

The girls followed me, and we took drinks and fresh plates of hors d'oeuvres upstairs to the living room.

"So Clay was the mastermind all along?" I asked.

We'd settled around a small table, ready to debrief. Detective Abrams had just grabbed a chicken skewer. "Looks that way. His collection agency was underwater, big time. Seems he overextended himself by opening two other offices – one in Renton and the one in Bellingham. Anyway, he needed an infusion of cash. But Dana controlled her own assets and refused to loan him any money."

"Maybe that's why she wanted a divorce," I said.

"That, and he was having an affair with his controller," David interjected.

Gasps all around.

"Anyway, he wasn't about to let her get away with all that money," Detective Abrams continued. "So he had to act fast. And…he knew about her first husband, the abuse, and the pictures."

"He knew about the nude pictures?" Blair said in surprise. "And he never said anything?"

"Apparently he figured he could use that information to his own advantage at some point. He even had copies made, just in case Dana got rid of them."

"Which she did," I said.

"Well, his opportunity came when he met Al Dente at the Emory Auto Shop. It turns out Dente served prison time with Dana's ex-husband."

"Huh? No way," Blair exclaimed. "What are the odds?"

"Prison is a small world," Detective Abrams said with a shrug. "That kind of thing happens more often than you'd think."

"Is that how Dente learned about the abuse?" Doe asked.

"I doubt it," Detective Abrams replied. "Believe it or not, child abusers aren't tolerated well in prison. They often end up dead. Remember that Vince Fragel went to prison for embezzlement *and* under a different name. So that's probably all that Al Dente knew about him, at least until Finkle came into the picture."

"But why would Clay Finkle ever become partners with Al Dente?" Rudy asked. "It's not like the two could have much in common."

"Actually, they had something very much in common," David said, speaking up. "Finkle isn't talking, but his girlfriend is. He and Dente knew each other in high school. They lost touch, but when Finkle took his car into the auto shop a few months ago, the two got reacquainted. It wasn't until Big Al saw Dana, though, that he made the connection to Vince Fragel, and he realized his old buddy Clay Finkle was married to his cell mate's ex-wife," Detective Abrams said. "It was probably Finkle who told Dente about the child abuse back in Vancouver."

"But how did they find out about Roger?" I asked.

"As it turns out, Roger was being honest," David said. "He *was* one of Vince's boys, and Clay figured it out from a picture on Roger's company website. When Roger was young, he had a recognizable birthmark on his cheek."

"The swoop!" I said.

"Right. But he was in a car accident a few years ago and after reconstructive surgery, the birthmark disappeared."

"And the picture on the website was before the accident?" Blair asked.

"Yes. But the birthmark matched a picture of one of the boys in Dana's possession. And when Clay realized it, he had Dente try to recruit him."

"So Big Al wasn't one of Dana's boys?" Doe asked.

"Nope. He only posed as one to gain Roger's trust. They needed Roger for a couple of reasons. First, he installed the alarm system at the library, where they planned the murder. They wanted to use it as a means of escape. That's why no one saw Dente leaving the property. He had dismantled the alarm and snuck inside, only to go out the backdoor. And secondly, they hoped to set Roger up for the murder itself. Remember the note we found at the library?"

We all nodded.

"It said, 'Ain't karma a bitch?'"

"Meaning the child abuse," I said.

"Right. They hoped to wrap this all around the fact that at one time Roger had been one of Vince Fragel's boys. But Roger resisted getting involved, so Dente threatened to expose him and eventually wore him down. By the way, we also found an employee at a hardware store in Renton that recognized Dente. That's where he bought the hammer that killed Trudy Bascom."

"And for what it's worth," Detective Abrams said. "We not only found Dente's fingerprints on one of those Smithwick's bottles you found, we found the place where he bought them." He suppressed a smile as he reported this.

"So we helped," Blair said, prodding him.

He turned his dreamy blue eyes in her direction. "Yes. I have to admit that you did."

Blair's grin lit up her face.

"So what about Vince Fragel? Did he have anything to do with any of this?" I asked.

David shook his head. "We don't think so. He's been living in Kent and saw Dana's picture on the news when Trudy was killed. It's the first time he even knew Dana lived in the area. But he hasn't been back to his house, so we still haven't found him. We learned all that we know about him from one of his neighbors."

"So Finkle recruited Dente, who recruited Roger, who never knew about Finkle?" Rudy said, trying to get it all clear.

"Right," David said. "Clay Finkle kept in the background and used Dente for everything."

"Where was Clay when Trudy was murdered?" I asked.

"He had an air-tight alibi for that one. He was in a restaurant with clients. But after that, he decided to be out of town," David said.

"So he went to Bellingham," I said.

David nodded. "Yes. And his controller went with him. She was prepared to be his alibi." David sat forward to continue the narrative. "He drove down after the failed attempt to kill Dana in your car. I guess by that time he figured Dente had become a liability, and so he killed him. Then he used his own cell phone to text Dana to get her out into the parking lot the night of your séance. She must have lost her phone in the scuffle, and he didn't have time to retrieve it in the dark. How did you find it, anyway?"

I laughed. "Mickey. He's little, but he has a nose like a bloodhound when it comes to food. Dana took a call from Clay earlier in the evening and she had a greasy chicken wing in her hand. Anyway, who was it who climbed the trellis to Dana's room at the Inn the other night?"

"We think it was Clay. There's a record of a phone call to Dana that night from his cell phone. It pinged off a local tower."

"I bet that's how he figured out what room she was in," Rudy said. "He just listened for the ringtone."

"Well, the Medical Examiner estimated Dente's death at some time earlier that evening, so Finkle probably figured that if he was successful in killing Dana, we would suspect Roger anyway, since Roger was the only person who knew the upstairs windows didn't have alarms. He had also installed the Finkle's alarm system, which would have pointed the finger at him for the theft of their guns."

"Remember, one of their guns killed Dente," Detective Abrams said.

"And since Roger knew nothing about Finkle's involvement, he'd be left holding the bag for both murders," David finished.

"Plus, if Dana had woken up and found Clay in her room that night," Doe said, "it's likely she would have been surprised, but not scared. He could easily have explained it away and gotten her into a position to strike her from behind and kill her. And then crawl out the window again and be gone."

My eyes grew wide. "I wonder if that's why Elizabeth appeared downstairs that night." I looked at Angela. "Remember the night the kids screamed because they saw a ghost? Typically, people see Elizabeth downstairs when she's randomly walking through rooms. But she appeared that night pointing at something. I thought it was the kids. But now that I think of it, her arm was raised. I think she was pointing to the upstairs bedrooms. She was warning us that Clay was there."

David and Detective Abrams shared a skeptical look.

"If you guys are going to date the Applegate women, you're going to have to accept the fact that the Inn is haunted," I said, bristling. "Why do you think Jason Spears was here last week to promote his book on ghosts?"

"You won't win this one," Angela said to both of them.

They both smiled, and Detective Abrams put his hands up in surrender. "Hey, someone grabbed my ass when I was in your study getting your computer, and there was no one around."

"I told you it was Chloe," I said.

"Humph," Blair smirked. "Woman after my own heart."

"Will Roger be convicted?" I asked.

Angela nodded. "Probably."

"But he was forced into it," I argued.

"I know, Mom. But it was his information that helped send Trudy to the library. And it was his information that allowed Dente to get away that night."

I sighed with disappointment. "So, Dana is safe, at least?"

"For now," David said.

"What do you mean?"

"Well, let's face it…she's made a lot of enemies in her life. This just may be the tip of the iceberg."

CHAPTER THIRTY-SEVEN

David and I were sitting on a love seat, sharing a piece of cheesecake after Angela and Detective Abrams left. The girls had gone back downstairs.

"I have to leave soon, Julia," he said. "Sean left the bulk of the paperwork for me. I'll need to finish it tonight if I expect to have any time off this weekend."

"Why does he get to do that?"

"He's the lead detective," David said with a shrug. "I don't mind. He's a good guy to work with. But I have big plans for Valentine's Day, so I want to get the work done."

My heart fell. "I see, well, then you should get going," I said without looking at him. I put the plate on a side table and stood up.

"Walk me out to the car?" he said.

"Um...sure," I replied without enthusiasm.

We went to a side bedroom and got our coats. He helped me on with mine and then we walked out to the street. The night was cold, but dry. The storms had moved on.

"I've been thinking a lot about us lately," he said, when we'd reached his car. "And I'm not sure it's going to work with me being a cop if you continue to get involved in my crime investigations."

I flinched as if someone had slapped me, and I felt tears begin to form. "Uh...but...I don't *try* to get involved," I said.

"I know," he said. "But it could happen again."

I felt my throat tighten. "I understand," I said, dropping my chin and taking a deep, shuddering breath. "Well, then...I guess I'll see you the next time someone tries to implicate me in a murder."

I started to turn to go back inside. He put a hand on my shoulder. "Whoa," he said. "Where are you going?"

I looked up into that handsome face and then looked away. "Back inside. You need to get going. You have a big weekend ahead."

"Julia, I'm hoping that big weekend includes you."

My head jerked up again. "What? But I thought you just said…"

"I said I didn't think this relationship would work if you kept getting involved in my murder investigations."

"But…"

"And that's why I'm going to put in for retirement." I inhaled deeply and held it. He watched me a moment and then began to laugh. "Breathe, Julia. You can't have dinner with me tomorrow night if you're in a coma."

I exhaled and laughed with him. "Dinner?"

"At my place. I make a mean pot roast. And afterwards I thought we'd go see that new play at the 5th Avenue." He took my head in his hands, leaned over and brushed his lips against mine, sending me into orbit. "Now, get inside before you catch cold. I'll give you a call tomorrow."

"Okay," I said. I smiled stupidly and then floated back to the house.

Doe, Rudy and Blair were standing to the right of the front door when I came in, pretending to put on their coats. But their smiles betrayed them.

"You were watching," I accused them. "Can't I have one minute of privacy?"

Blair whirled around as she buttoned her faux mink coat. "How could we miss it? You were standing right under a street lamp." She put an arm around my shoulders and began to guide me through the living room toward the stairs. "Now, Julia, if you need any advice regarding your…uh…new relationship, I'm here for you."

The four of us said goodnight to Goldie and Ben downstairs and headed back to the Inn via the forest path that ran along the lake. Rudy had a small flashlight and took the lead. Doe followed right behind her, while Blair moved in front of me, explaining how I should approach the first date at David's house.

"Play it cool," she was saying. "Don't jump the gun."

"Not *that* again," Doe said with a laugh.

We were stepping carefully around rocks and over tree roots.

"I just want Julia to take it slow," Blair said.

"Not like you, you mean," Rudy called out.

"This isn't my first rodeo," I said to Blair's back. "I think I know what to do. I'm not a complete klutz in the bedroom."

Just then, my foot caught on a tree root and threw me to the ground with an "oof!" Doe and Rudy kept walking. Blair kept walking and *talking*.

"You want to create ex-pec-ta-tion," she said, drawing the word out. "Leave him wanting more."

I lay face down on the ground spitting out sand, as they disappeared into the dark. Blair's voice drifted back to me. "So what do you plan on wearing tomorrow night, Julia? I'm thinking that nice velvet jacket."

Count to three.

"Julia? JULIA??"

THE END

Author's Notes

Child abuse is a devastating problem in this country, affecting thousands of children every year. According to the Children's Defense Fund's *Annual State of America's Children Report 2014*, almost 2,000 children are abused or neglected each day in the U.S.

How can we allow this to happen?

Many of those children die, or at the very least, grow up to face substance abuse, mental health issues, prostitution, incarceration, suicide, or becoming abusers themselves.

If you know of an agency in your area that supports the children and families facing the heartbreak of child abuse in *any* of its forms, please reach out to that agency and ask how you can help. A child's life may depend on it.

Thank you so very much for reading *A Candidate For Murder*. If you enjoyed this book, I would encourage you to go back to Amazon.com and leave an honest review. We "indie" authors survive on reviews and word-of-mouth advertising. So tell a friend. This will help position the book so that more people might also enjoy it. Thank you!

About the Author

Ms. Bohart holds a master's degree in theater, has published in Woman's World, and has a story in *Dead on Demand*, an anthology of ghost stories that remained on the Library Journals best seller list for six months. As a thirty-year nonprofit professional, she has spent a lifetime writing brochures, newsletters, business letters, website copy, and more. She did a short stint writing for *Patch.com*, teaches writing through the Continuing Education Program at Green River Community College, and writes a monthly column for the *Renton Reporter*. *A Candidate For Murder* is her fifth full-length novel and the second in the Old Maids of Mercer Island mysteries. She is hard at work on the third book in the series and the next Giorgio Salvatori mystery.

If you would like more information, please visit her website at: www.bohartink.com, where you can let the author know you'd like to be added to her email list to be notified of upcoming publications or events. You may also join her author page on Facebook.

Follow Ms. Bohart

Website: www.bohartink.com
Twitter: @lbohart
Facebook: Facebook @ L.Bohart/author